Moonburn

MOONBURN

A NOVEL

ANGUS TRUMBLE
AND
NICK TRUMBLE

NATIONAL
LIBRARY
OF AUSTRALIA

For Angus

6/10/1964 – 8/10/2022

"The Englishman foxtrots as he fox-hunts, with all his being, through thickets, through ditches, over hedges, through chiffons, through waiters, over saxophones, to the victorious finish."

Edna St. Vincent Millay
Distressing Dialogues
1924

"And hand in hand, on the edge of the sand,
They danced by the light of the moon."

Edward Lear
The Owl and the Pussycat
1871

CHAPTER 1

An Awkwardness at Government House

Mike and Sharon
2020

Fuck

What?

Just had txt from Brussels.
Nob in PMs office says
Macron threatening to walk
out of post Brexit round
trade negs

Shit

Says hes calling in from the
Embassy tardis in half. Must
be bloody big

You there?

No Im sunning topless in
Ibiza.

Whos the prat who takes

bookings for secure upstairs
conference room?

You mean Sarah?

Toff. Hot pink hair. Japanese
clothes that stick out in
weird places. About 85.
Lesbian. Up herself. Went
over there. Need urgent
access. Secure line from
Brussels. Need it now.
She goes have you made
a booking

Yes thats Sarah. Sounds a lot
like you too

She goes think we might be
able to squeeze you in. Please
fill out a fucking form.
So I go its only the PMs
office urgent from Brussels
Embassy. Then she asked for
photo ID. Cow

Yes Im seeing it clearly. Did
you try saying please?

*　　*　　*

1926

"Come in, Norman."

"Yes, Lady Sutherland."

"Sit down."

"Thank you, Lady Sutherland."

"I gather Foster has found something disagreeable in the motor car."

"Yes, Lady Sutherland."

"A torso, George said. Headless."

"Yes, Lady Sutherland."

"You're quite sure it is headless?"

"Quite, Lady Sutherland."

"Limbs?"

"I beg your pardon, Lady Sutherland?" Although dependable and thorough, Norman was at times slow on the uptake.

"Does it have *limbs*, Norman?"

"No, Lady Sutherland."

"How provoking."

"Lady Sutherland?"

"A headless torso is bad enough without being limbless as well. Four more stray parts drifting about. Four more *at least*."

"Indeed, Lady Sutherland."

"Sex?"

"Male, Lady Sutherland, as far as we call tell."

"Don't be silly, Norman. How can there be any doubt?"

"The Colonel felt we shouldn't unwrap it before Surgeon Commander Clark comes back from his golf."

"Unwrap it? What on earth is it wrapped up in?"

"A lady's foundation garment, Lady Sutherland."

Millicent Sutherland suppressed what might otherwise have been mistaken for a girlish giggle; Norman's phrasing was impeccable as always, but she formed a mental picture of the gentlemen of the Governor's household puzzling over a torso wrapped in smalls. She recovered her composure.

"Good Heavens! But you say Foster thinks it is, was, male—a *man*—never mind the foundation garment?"

"Yes, Lady Sutherland. He was very specific."

"Odd. Do we know him? I mean, is he, was he *known*?"

"I'm sure I cannot say, Lady Sutherland."

"No, I suppose not. Nothing much to go on, really, is there?"

"Quite, Lady Sutherland."

"What have you done with it—him?"

"The Colonel felt it best to leave—him—in the motor until Foster can find a suitable spot in the cool room."

"Out of the question, Norman. The motor is no place for a headless torso, wrapped or unwrapped."

"No, Lady Sutherland."

"Think of the germs, Norman."

"Yes, Lady Sutherland."

"The same applies to the cool room, apart from the obvious."

"Lady Sutherland?"

"Cook," said Lady Sutherland, "and to a lesser degree Mr Craddock."

"Ah," said Norman.

"In and out. The one constantly rummaging for comestibles; the other searching for drink."

"He is slightly short on imagination, Lady Sutherland."

"Which?"

"Cook."

"On the contrary, Norman. Cook has a vivid imagination. Lots of ideas, most of them dreadful. We don't want him grilling parts of it by mistake."

"I could speak to him."

"That's not a good idea, Norman. I doubt he's ever seen a foundation garment," Mr Craddock, on the other hand, she mused … "It's a recipe for disaster."

"I suppose so." Norman grasped the larger point, even if in this case, as in so many others, he found it difficult to trace the individual steps in Lady Sutherland's reasoning. "What about the tool shed?" he added doubtfully.

"Worse. Dear Sock would probably put it in the compost like everything else." Lady Sutherland sighed, and tapped the arm of her chair with a pencil. "Such a mania for compost … We had better persuade Solange to let Foster use the laundry."

"You don't think it might get mixed up with the washing?"

"I shall speak to Mrs Huntingfield."

"If you say so, Lady Sutherland."

"Right away, Norman. Chop, chop."

"Very good, Lady Sutherland."

"Oh, Norman?"

"Yes, Lady Sutherland?"

"I shouldn't say anything about this to Miss Davies. Rather overzealous and inquisitive just at present. Sleeping dogs, and all that."

"Quite, Lady Sutherland."

"That's all, Norman. Off you go."

Three months earlier

CONFIDENTIAL

THIS DESPATCH REMAINS THE PROPERTY OF
HIS BRITANNIC MAJESTY'S GOVERNMENT

The Right Honourable
Colonel The Earl of Axminster, KCMG, CB, DSO
etc. etc. etc.
Secretary of State for the Colonies
Colonial Office
Whitehall, SW1

Government House, St Edward
25th January 1926
No. 59

My Lord,

I have the honour to submit this, my last despatch upon preparing next Tuesday to relinquish the Government of St Edward, Gwern and the Thimble Isles (the Bailiwick of St Edward).

It is five years since my wife and I arrived in these beautiful islands. I am proud to submit that the progress of the Bailiwick under my administration of the Government has been prodigious. As Your Lordship is aware, deposits of guano were discovered in the Outer Thimbles in June 1911, which, when properly investigated, proved to be of colossal size. Efforts to extract unprecedented quantities of this valuable commodity redoubled after the Armistice, and continue to accelerate thanks to strong demand for nitrogenous fertilisers in South Africa, Australia, New Zealand, Argentina and many other places. The British and American Phosphate Company's mine on Great Thimble alone is now thought to be the largest in the world. The port, Exchange and Customs Houses, together with our railway and other facilities, have long served the plantations on the mostly arable north and eastern sides of St Edward, but the commerce in guano has generated much additional wealth and handsome royalties—as is made clear by my last three returns to H.M. Treasury.

As Your Lordship is aware, we have been fortunate in obtaining the services of Professor Gene Hodgkinson, the highly regarded banker, theoretical economist and creator of the "Hodgkinson Curve", formerly of the Chicago School. The Professor is now a resident of St Edward and chairman of the recently established Cincinnati Ohio & Delaware Banking Corporation. Professor Hodgkinson has been advisor to many of the large American businesses currently performing so spectacularly on the American equities market. Acting on Professor Hodgkinson's advice, the Bailiwick's economy has been reinvigorated, indeed supercharged, by the simple expedient of reducing income tax to 2.5 per cent, and by abolishing death duties, corporate and capital gains taxes. As a result, significant investment has already begun to flow into the islands, and such modest taxes and charges that are applied have furnished useful public works, proper defences and other improvements.

Despite the rapid influx of bankers, accountants, lawyers and guano miners from The Azores Islands and elsewhere, the last census shows that otherwise the population of St Edward retains its old proportions. The long-established French-speaking landowners retain a wholly unjustified sense of superiority with respect to everyone else, as if William the Conqueror had not brought the St Edward group with him to Britain in 1066, along with the Channel Islands and the whole of Normandy. Indeed the French government continues to take a keen interest in the affairs of the Bailiwick, and has always argued that while St Edward, Gwern and The Thimbles are technically grouped with the Channel Islands, the Bailiwick is much further away, well beyond the English Channel and many leagues out in the Atlantic, somewhat to the north of The Azores, and considerably closer to France than Great Britain. Thus the French position is that the islands are *not* Channel Islands, and should have been returned to France, along with the rest of Normandy, in 1450 after the Battle of Formigny.

Notwithstanding the French presence, the islands are robustly and loyally British. The British community more than maintains the social fabric in Port Charlotte, as well as sustaining most of the commerce and practicing such learned professions as exist here. Between them the old trading firms of Williams & Gosling and Burns, Philp & Co keep the islands supplied with most necessities. The Blue Moon Steam Packet Line carries passengers from Portsmouth to Port Charlotte via Guernsey and Jersey twice a week.

The mutiny, of which Your Lordship has been aware for

some time, consists of an unwieldy, loose-knit and, at times, quarrelsome alliance between the French landowners, farm labourers, fishing folk, trade unionists, communistic agitators, guano miners, and smugglers in the small villages and harbours towards the exposed western coast of St Edward. This fractiousness is, of course, an asset to my government. Fortunately the capacity of the mutineers to do serious damage is further restricted by their continuous consumption of a medicament extracted from the sap of a small but prolific native conifer (lately classified by Dr Godfrey at Kew as *Pinus hallucinagenii*). In its raw state, I am told, this sap or gum, known colloquially as "passamanana," is a narcotic that can be chewed, smoked, brewed as tea, stirred into soups and stews, or, in its pulverised form, used as a kind of snuff. The subsequent effects or symptoms range from the merely soporific to states of great excitement, depending upon the amounts so consumed, but among the agricultural workers and fisher folk, and of course the smuggling communities, the almost universal taste for passamanana is akin to the deep attachment to opium which proved such an outstanding resource in the Far East. As well, a strong cane liquor, known as "mastise," is produced from illicit stills in certain settlements on Gwern, and smuggled onto the main island in relatively large quantities. Combined with passamanana, this produces an ecstatic, trance-like state in which members of a local religious sect, linked to the mutineers and ludicrously named the Children of the Sun, undertake certain lascivious nocturnal rites, originally brought to the islands from rural France and dating from well before the birth of Christ.

These are accompanied by a primitive form of music, bereft of melody, harmony, etc., mainly consisting of the loud beating of drums, chanting, and discordant notes produced from primitive ram's horn trumpets, which can occasionally be heard emanating from the stone circle at Mount Raglan, particularly at the winter and summer solstices, where practitioners gather, I am reliably informed, to summon "the great beast", whomever that might be. Bishop Stanley continues to do his best to eradicate this ridiculous form of superstition but, while he is of course sound—Government House and Bishopscourt share a boundary, and Mrs Stanley has tirelessly supported Lady Strickland in connection with the St Edward Association of Girls' and Mixed Clubs—all such efforts to suppress this noisy occult nuisance have been fruitless. Nor have Monsignieur Lebecq and the Roman Catholic nuns managed to put a dent in it either; indeed, Bishop Stanley tells me that many of the religious trinkets they have worked so hard to distribute throughout the hills (rosaries and such-like) now adorn crude shrines to an obscene fertility spirit known as Cernunnos. Obviously one form of superstition far too easily adapts itself to another.

My own view is that while the mutineers are almost constantly quarrelling, or intoxicated, or diverted by chanting and drums, their ability to do substantial damage is thankfully diminished, so for the time being one turns a blind eye to passamanana and mastise; indeed, their consumption is to be encouraged. This is also the opinion of Special Branch who looked into the matter on their last six-monthly circuit from Jersey. However, as Your Lordship is aware, from time to time minor disturbances do continue to disrupt the public order, though rarely in town. Stretches of the railway have occasionally been damaged; semi-literate seditious slogans have been scrawled on cuttings, sidings and on some public buildings. Thefts of livestock are not uncommon.

With the aid of our colleague Commodore Bracegirdle of Naval Intelligence, currently posted to the St Edward station here in Port Charlotte, Special Branch have also ascertained that the mutineers are led by an apparently charismatic young black man, whose identity, despite their most energetic inquiries, is extremely well protected and unfortunately therefore remains unknown. Suspicions have been raised in connection with various persons, however, above all one Jacob Beck, a capable mathematician and engineer, currently employed by the firm of Rudyard Barton Riley, working on the construction of magnificent new premises for the Cincinnati Ohio & Delaware Banking Corporation over the ruins of the old Fort Henry.

The mutineers appear to maintain an avenue of communication with the Quai d'Orsay, probably through their consul in Port Charlotte, M. Orlando, a guano trader, speculator, money lender, and hideous voluptuary who is not on any account to be trusted. By that dubious conduit the Deuxième Bureau continues to find ways of supplying the mutineers with arms and treasure, probably landing these on the wild and sparsely populated western coast of St Edward, though none has yet been apprehended.

Despite all that has transpired since the Entente and indeed the War, it seems the traditional French posture in respect of St Edward—nakedly covetous, let us be frank—has been much inflamed by the lucrative trade in guano. It is widely understood that, when sober, the mutineers seriously entertain the impossible ambition of independence from the Crown; I strongly suspect M. Orlando (and such of his French agents who remain undetected) of encouraging them in that fruitless direction.

Meanwhile my government has made good use of the revenues generated by the trade in guano. Three new schools and a hospital (to replace the old infirmary) are under construction. A far more adequate post and telegraph office has been erected over the ruins of the old French barracks; the premises adjoining will be turned into a public library and mechanics' institute. Several branch lines have been added to the railway; a viaduct and two bridges have been built. The road has been extended. It is now paved for the most part and runs three-quarters of the way around the island. To mark this achievement the Executive Council lately acquired a Rolls Royce Silver Ghost motor car for the use of the Governor, which handsome gift allows Lady Strickland and myself to carry out our duties with greater dignity and despatch. I am glad to say that this has given much pride to the local people, whose enthusiastic expressions of pleasure have touched us both.

Having been for some decades a little neglected, Government House has also been repaired and extended. When I arrived, the kitchens were sadly archaic, but they are now even more advanced than those which, I gather, lately furnished comestibles to H.R.H. The Prince of Wales in

Nairobi. The mews have had to be enlarged to accommodate the Rolls Royce motor car. A tennis court is envisaged.

I have this week given royal assent to the Dog Act, the Fence Act, the Licensing and Excise Act, the Disorderly House Remediation (Amendment) Act, and two further Appropriation Bills. I have also by Proclamation extended the current State of Emergency for another year; hardly necessary but nonetheless in my view a prudent measure.

Five years is perhaps too long a post at St Edward, although the benign climate; the unique flora and fauna (above all the native birds—recently I shot an extremely rare blue-helmeted parakeet and have taken the liberty of sending it to South Kensington); the excellent fisheries, and the undisputed natural charm of the Bailiwick—all these have combined to ensure that Lady Strickland and I will miss it very much indeed.

I have the honour to be, Sir,
    Your Lordship's
        Humble and obedient servant,

                       H. Strickland
                          Governor

Enclosures

CONFIDENTIAL MEMORANDUM

Permanent Under-Secretary to Permanent Secretary, Colonial Office, Whitehall

It would be as well to remind the Secretary of State that as usual Sir Henry shows such a want of discretion as to be positively hazardous. Has His Excellency not heard of the cypher?

It did seem that Sir Henry would not be able to do much harm when he was sent to St Edward, after his disastrous tenure in Tasmania; it was understood that he would enjoy at St Edward a quiet sabbatical before retirement. Alas, we were wrong. The Chancellor of the Exchequer is apoplectic; the loss of revenue is already biting, and clearly will become worse in years to come. However there is nothing to be done. As you know, the Bailiwick of St Edward is a suzerain entity with considerable autonomy, a Crown dependency with fiscal sovereignty and accordingly can make its own tax laws, no matter how misguided.

Characteristic of Sir Henry, too, to imply that he has made a palpable difference, for—notwithstanding the reckless introduction of his so-called "tax reforms"—with such immense quantities of guano at present flowing out of St Edward a spotted gibbon could do just as well in Government House (with or without the unnecessary improvements), and might also make a better fist of putting down the insurgency, such as it is—"mutiny" and "mutineers," such absurd language. Still, this despatch confirms what we already knew vis-à-vis the Deuxième Bureau and their activities in the St Edward

Group. One suspects that Colonel Truffe has a hand in the mischief. May I have Musgrave at the Admiralty study the sample of passamanana? Could it perhaps be cultivated in Northern Ireland? P. M.-W.

CONFIDENTIAL MEMORANDUM

Permanent Secretary to Permanent Under-Secretary, Colonial Office, Whitehall

Agreed on all points. Such reckless behaviour. Who is this "Professor" Hodgkinson? And why has he taken refuge at St Edward? Another American snake oil salesman no doubt "on the run." Yet, as you say, there is nothing to be done.

Sir Henry is also good at spending large sums of money; no doubt retirement will come as a bit of a shock. Does that fool Jenkins still occupy the Channel Islands desk? Could be part of the problem. One trusts that Sir George Sutherland will plant a steadier hand on that particular tiller; according to Brydges in the India Office he has done wonders in Burma. I wonder if it was wise to persuade Sir George to take on Threlfall as ADC? Naturally I see your point—as far away as possible—but an indiscretion as unfortunate as his last would be most regrettable, even on St Edward. Meanwhile, what do we have on this Jacob Beck? A. C.

CHAPTER 2

Aux Armes, Citoyens!

Mike and Sharon
2020

Did you maybe try
saying please?

?

Didnt think so. Please and
thank you went out when you
joined Asst U-Sec didnt they?

Fuck off Sharon

Sarahs all right. Crazy hair
mad kabuki clothes (but
couture, not that youd know).
Definitely old school. And yes
posh too. Responds really well
to please and thank you

Tosser

Fuck

What?

Just took Nobs call from
Brussels. Macron still
threatening to piss off home
to Paris. But gets better

Has he promised to
stay there?

LOL. Last Tuesday badly
decomposed body parts
dug up in fucking shithole
middle of Atlantic near The
Azores. Allege these remains
of French military hero.
Vanished there 1926

So?

So, darling, veteran of
Mandingo Wars, whatever
they bloody were. Croix
de Guerre, posthumous
Legion of Honour + palm,
the works. Officially its
enquiry but nob reckons
PM says Macron says we
tortured him to death

Shit. Did we (meaning you)?

How would I fucking know?
Point is, Macron told PM
privately this morning, just
like that. Over a fag and a
coffee. Typical. Anyhow PM
having a meltdown

Sounds like youre having
one too

What?

Meltdown. Never mind

Plus Daily Mail put in FOI
request for St Edward file.
Cunts. Nob wants rubbish
briefing paper for PM, the
usual by COB

Dot points, little words,
big print?

LOL. Hang on. Sending
email. Need full CFO
denial. Just Googled St
Edward. Tax haven for
dictators gun runners drug
lords Russian gazzillionaires
sad old rock stars. They had
a hopeless island Mau Mau
thing going for years

So kick it to defence and save
me the bother

On 29 Jan 2020, at 10:44 am, Mike Carter <<u>dcarter@fcoff.gov.uk</u>> wrote:

Dear Ms Julius,

In relation to the multilateral post-Brexit trade negotiations currently taking place in Brussels, the Secretary of State has asked me to supply an urgent briefing paper to assist the Prime Minister in the next stage of their formal discussions with the President of France.

He would appreciate any light that can be shed on the discovery of the remains of an alleged highly-decorated French national in an unmarked grave in the Bailiwick of St Edward, Gwern and the Thimble Isles. A further allegation is that that individual was last seen on St Edward in 1926.

Ideally, he would appreciate receiving confirmation that he is able categorically to deny these and other detailed allegations to which I referred in private. However, the draft briefing paper should be worded so as to enable the Prime Minister and/or the Secretary of State to describe any further discussions and/or developments as "helpful" and/or "constructive."

Yours sincerely,

Dr Mike Carter
First Assistant Under-Secretary, Political Affairs
Foreign and Commonwealth Office
Whitehall

The FCO is an equal opportunity employer. The FCO supports gender equity, ethnic diversity, disability awareness and LGBTQIA+ affirmative action programs. As part of our commitment to improve the health and well-being of the multicultural community we serve, the FCO believes that we have a responsibility to take a leadership role by prohibiting the use of tobacco products on FCO premises and in all UK missions, chanceries and residences abroad. This includes all porticos, verandas, drives, gardens, gazebos, swimming pool areas and adjacent areas, garages, pavements and cul-de-sacs within 50 metres of the point of entry, security access and/or metal detector: The FCO is smoke free. Please consider the environment before printing this email message.

This email (including any attachments) may contain information that is intended solely for the named addressee. It is confidential and may be subject to legislative and/or national security restriction. Any confidentiality or privilege is not waived or lost because this email has been sent to you by mistake. If you have received it in error, please let us know by reply email, delete it from your system and destroy any copies. This email is also subject to crown copyright. No part of it should be reproduced, adapted or communicated without the written consent of HM government. Failure to comply with this advice may result in prosecution, a fine of up to £50,000 and/or a sentence of up to five years' imprisonment. If you have any doubts about the authenticity of an email purportedly sent by us, please contact us immediately.

Got it? Like my naff new
signature box?

                                        Gender equity? Piss off Mike.

New broom in legal. OTFT.
Wanker

                                        And I promise you Im not
                                        going an extra 50 m for a fag.
                                        Its already about 500 from my
                                        office to the FCO skip

*　　*　　*

1926

Government House, St Edward, looked its best in the early morning, when the monkey-puzzle trees in the home park cast long shadows over the formal garden in front of the portico. The east wing, the sandstone tower and flagstaff were still bathed in the pink light of dawn. Surrounded on three sides by a wide veranda, the house commanded extensive views over the ocean, glittering in the morning light, framed by stands of native conifers and other exotic trees planted by previous governors: China firs, swamp oaks, camphor trees with tangled roots, mahogany trees, Chinese pines, almonds, talipot palms and cannon-ball trees. The harbour could also be seen on the other side of the observatory bluff, alive with the clanging of cranes, tenders and barges just in from the quarry on the Thimbles. The old French quarter of Port Charlotte lay at the bottom of the hill, a gay profusion of brightly painted terraces, many with wrought-iron balconies overhanging the shops. The long gravel drive, lined with oak and ironwood, island cherry and toyon, wound its way up from a little stone gatehouse by the quay. Behind the house, a handful of outbuildings concealed from public view extended in the direction of Bishopscourt, a squat Gothick villa of red brick, below which was a small sheltered beach. A little orchard lay on a gentle slope on the sheltered side of the mews, together with a large kitchen garden which had long supplied the vice-regal kitchen.

On this mild March morning a lone figure could be seen, as usual, wheeling his barrow along the garden path. Amid much fanfare and bunting the last Governor had departed the colony six weeks earlier, so Government House still dozed peacefully, her blue and white striped canvas awnings flapping in the breeze, pending the arrival of Sir George and Lady Sutherland from Rangoon by way of Colombo and Mauritius. Old Sock remained *en poste*. He had been there for as long as many people could remember. He came from Aberdeen, they said. No-one could recall when; no-one knew why. Tall and lean of frame with a long white beard, dressed in baggy overalls, ancient boots and a wide-brimmed hat, Old Sock seemed as permanent as Government House itself, his familiar figure pacing the garden path as predictably as an old timepiece. He lived in two small rooms adjoining the laundry. Most evenings he sat on a bentwood chair by the door, smoking his pipe and gazing into the distance. So much did he belong to the establishment that it felt, at times, as if the establishment belonged to him—especially as, to those few souls who knew him well enough to gauge it, his mood only ever shifted restively between almost imperceptible grades of taciturn. Everyone called him Old Sock, or Sock for short.

Old Sock set down his wheelbarrow beside the bed of peas, stood up straight and inspected the sky. A moderate breeze, no rain. For decades, Old Sock had struggled against a marine climate hostile to the cultivation of vegetables, yet by dogged persistence and in the teeth of, by turns, squalls and the beating sun, he succeeded in harvesting peas, broad beans, cabbage, Brussels sprouts, carrots, parsnips and swedes for the vice-regal table. He continued to wage war against those pests that thrived in the often challenging *terroir* of St Edward: grey mould, cectria canker, black scale, leaf gall, the clearwing borer, false wireworm and the cryptic mealybug. Each and all faced a daunting adversary in Old Sock, and he derived quiet satisfaction from successive tactical victories in what proved to be a Sisyphean campaign, for, facing just as many minor defeats, he simply shook his head and reached for his hoe.

"Sufficient unto the day is the evil thereof," he muttered.

The brief interregnum permitted Government House to doze peacefully between incumbents, but Old Sock was not alone. Mrs Huntingfield the housekeeper took advantage of the temporary lull to sit a little longer after breakfast each day in her cosy attic sitting-room. She was a tall, slender but strong woman of fifty-eight, and wore her long wiry grey hair in a defiantly unfashionable bun. That morning Mrs Huntingfield was reading a long and fascinating article in the latest issue of the *Theosophist*, about the Order of the Star in the East, a society in India whose members anticipated the imminent arrival of a messianic entity, a great teacher and Brahmin who, they believed, would soon reveal himself in Madras. Before the poor wee pet contracted diphtheria and died suddenly, Mrs Huntingfield's husband had for several years been clerk to the Magistrates' Court in Madras. How curious. She took off her reading glasses, folded the *Theosophist*, adjusted the hairpin behind her ear, consulted her fob watch and then, with a sigh, glanced at the chest of drawers in which she kept her Ouija board. Just then she heard sharp military footsteps on the gravel drive.

In his quarters in the East Wing, meanwhile, which looked over the mews, Surgeon Commander Clark was already hard at work with his tape measure and magnifying glass. He was cataloguing a new addition to his collection of medical and other curiosities, which occupied shelves and cabinets in an otherwise sparsely furnished room. A large steel engraving hung over the mantelpiece. Mottled in places, it represented the Charge of the 21st Lancers at Omdurman—Surgeon Commander Clark had been present. There were bottles and jars, specimen boxes, and a large steamer trunk—all kept some distance away from his medical things, and his locked brown bag. This lived on a small table next to the door, in readiness for any sort of emergency. He sat at his desk, facing the window, jotting some notes in his day book. The ink that was just then drying on his newest label read, "Primitive human skull, female, distinctly French."

In the kitchen pantry Cook and Mr Craddock the butler were discussing arrangements for the arrival of Sir George and Lady Sutherland. Colonel Pole had indicated the previous afternoon that a household dinner would be held following the swearing-in. Cook was proposing Mock turtle soup, fried sole, pigeon pie, saddle of mutton with celery sauce and garden vegetables, followed by jam pudding à la reine and Welsh rarebit—best foot forward. Naturally the menu would have to be approved by Lady Sutherland, but it was as well to be prepared with suitable suggestions. Cook's repertoire was respectable, if ponderous, but always safe. With all this in mind, Mr Craddock, whose speech exhibited a slight but discernible sibilance, shifted his thoughts to the distinguished contents of the cellar—the wines and spirits for which Government House, St Edward, was justly celebrated.

"The *vin de constance*, I think, to go with the pudding," said Mr Craddock. "Five small bottles in the ice-box when the time comes."

"Perfect," said Cook, with ill-concealed enthusiasm.

"And the 1899 Château-Margaux with the mutton. Yes."

"*Yes*," said Cook.

Down in the mews, Foster in his shirtsleeves was busily polishing the enormous Rolls Royce, the motions of his chamois cloth brisk and circular. The black carriage-work, the radiator and the head-lamps positively gleamed in the morning sun. Foster was strong and good-looking. His glossy black hair was neatly trimmed, and he wore a military moustache. He had served with distinction in the Coldstream Guards. Foster was immoderately proud of the Rolls Royce. After all, the Austin had been completely inadequate, so small and cramped that, when driving Sir Henry and Lady Strickland to the ceremonial ribbon-cutting at the Cool-Stores, for example, or to divine service in the Cathedral, or to the Treasury Building for the King's Birthday levee, Foster felt instead as if he was taking them fishing, and he felt it deeply.

When the Rolls Royce had first laboured up the drive, the Governor's standard fluttering over the front mudguard, Old Sock was horrified. Where on earth would they keep this damned gyre? The mews were hardly big enough; he sensed a possible incursion onto ground currently occupied by his vegetable garden, the orchard, or, worse, his carefully tended compost patch. Not long afterwards Old Sock protested to Mrs Huntingfield that the dependable Austin had been superseded of with unseemly haste. Foster's new bottle-green uniform with jodhpurs and peaked cap, meanwhile, made him look like something from the music hall, or a French farce. Old Sock glanced up from his row of carrot seedlings, removed his hat, mopped his brow, and frowned in the direction of Foster, who was once more energetically worrying over the head-lamps.

"Turn away mine eyes from beholding vanity," Sock muttered, before turning back to his seedlings.

Farther up, in the laundry, Solange was taking advantage of the temporary lull by teaching her new girl Aimée how to clean a rusty iron. Like Sock, with whom she enjoyed cordial relations, Solange had for years formed an indispensable part of the household. Her enormous aprons and bulky white headscarves were always spotless. Her capacious copper boiler was emptied and scoured daily, and her mangle invariably adjusted after use so as to take the weight off the rollers, thus extending their working life by several years. Above all, her irons were all in gleaming state, but Solange knew perfectly well how to redeem a neglected one, in the unlikely event that this ever became necessary.

"Tie a lump of beeswax in a piece of muslin," she explained to Aimée, in her patient, wide-eyed contralto singsong. "Heat the iron, and rub it first very hard with the piece of wax, and then with a dry cloth sprinkled with plenty of salt, just so."

Aimée was in awe.

"Sea salt at first, because it is rough!"

"Oui, Madame."

"After a bit you can change to Cerebos salt, 'like driven snow in its crystalline purity,'" she said, reading from the box. "Do it again, back and forth, wax and salt, wax and salt, for as long as it takes to make the flat of your iron as smooth as silk. You see?"

"Oui, Madame."

"But it is much better not to let it get into this sorry state in the first place."

"Mais oui, Madame."

"Now see how you get on with this one."

Solange was huge, and her physical strength was prodigious. She was proud of her vocation. She had learned the art of the *blanchisseuse*, together with much else, from her wise old mother whom she visited in Baie du Diable on her monthly day off. Solange had come to the laundry as a girl of fifteen. She thought nothing of the heat, and the heavy work. Indeed, she worked so hard and well that soon after Hortense had her stroke, Mrs Huntingfield put Solange in charge. Solange was, if anything, even prouder of the laundry than she had been when she first assumed command. It was clean, efficient and, above all, fast. No collar, however grimy, could not be laundered, starched, ironed, shaped to perfection and returned to its wearer, spotless and shining, long before tea. No careless, unnoticed peach or raspberry stain down a pale silk blouse was beyond her power of removal—by using droplets of warm water and many careful applications of powdered starch.

"Brown stockings should never be ironed," said Solange. "The heat of the iron will spoil the colour. It produces an ugly yellow tint. Remember this, Aimée."

"Oui, Madame."

"Shantung silk should be washed in bran water and allowed to get perfectly dry before you iron it. Otherwise it will be patchy."

"Oui, Madame."

Solange enjoyed instructing Aimée in the art of *blanchisserie*. She was good at it. However, it was not yet time to instruct Aimée in certain far more important matters, private matters; matters Solange saw it as her responsibility to disclose to any young island girl who fell under her direct supervision. Aimée was not ready, but soon she would be. On her neat work table, next to the linen book, wax pencils, and balls of string, Solange kept only one ornament, a small silver bowl or chalice with the embossed figure of a man, crude certainly, but distinctly recognisable, with the antlers of a stag, holding a torque in one hand and a cornucopia in the other. If you had looked closely you would have seen that he was accompanied by a smaller female figure in a flowing garment, also horned. But nobody ever did look closely. Only Solange knew them to be the Horned Man and his consort the Lady Hecate, and that her strange cup held herbs too sacred to be named, a ritual offering to Cernunnos, lord of the great forest— that terrible sphere of darkness in which, having beforehand carried out the sacred leaf-gathering ceremony, having made the necessary *vévé*, having danced in a circle around the *moto-pitan* in the centre of the stone circle, the supplicant may, with luck, in her wild ecstasy, regain a virgin state of being. Solange left Aimée to labour away at the rusty iron with beeswax and sea salt, and went across to stand in the open doorway. She placed her hands on her hips, stretched her back, gazed out towards the orchard, and emitted a low and sonorous chuckle. Soon, very soon. He is coming.

Norman Threlfall had arrived in St Edward ten days earlier. He was the harbinger of a new dispensation. He had sailed to Port Charlotte aboard HMS *Terrible*, having been hurriedly gazetted at Colombo. There, Sir George and Lady Sutherland, persuaded to do so by a number of different but apparently synchronised appeals from radically different quarters, had had the opportunity to inspect this neat, certainly; bright, unquestionably; likeable without doubt, but nevertheless slightly melancholy naval lieutenant with clear blue eyes, straight dark hair, handsome eyebrows and, above all, impressive height on the positive side of the ledger. At the time, Sir George had half thought to make further inquiries as to the particular reason or reasons why Norman had sought leave to vacate a perfectly creditable, actually hush-hush spot in Room 9 of the Admiralty and, instead, embark (sight unseen) upon a far more conventional tour of duty in as unlikely an outpost as St Edward, Gwern and the Thimble Isles, the Bailiwick of St Edward. However, being a man of the world, Sir George decided against this course of action, having already satisfied himself that Norman was obviously not mad, and almost certainly not bad. Perhaps the thing that swayed him more than any other was the surprising discovery that Norman was passionate about dancing. There had been a time, prior to the advent of Millicent Sutherland, when Sir George had shared this enthusiasm. Any ambitious young officer did, for was it not Admiral of the Fleet Sir John Fisher who did more than anyone else successfully to ignite in the breast of such officers of the Royal Navy who could be coaxed into kindling it, the flame of ardour for dances and dancing? Long before the Fashoda Incident this proved to be highly contagious, even in the Corps of Royal Engineers. In those days, it was the old-fashioned Viennese waltz, the sultry tango and the Boston two-step. Sir George had missed out on Ragtime— that occurred since Millicent—but Norman had mentioned a new-ish thing called the foxtrot. Still, dancing was healthy and creditable, *ubique*. No, Sir George was sentimentally moved by this point, but finally persuaded by a direct personal appeal from the Brigadier, writing from Cheltenham. It was years since Sir George had seen or heard from Wringer Threlfall, but he was a very distant cousin of Millicent's and, for that reason, Millicent herself took up Norman's case. It wouldn't have been necessary; Sir George had carefully noted the unanimity with which various references furnished by Norman's various superior officers (up to and including the Vice Admiral) were slightly shrill in their superlatives. It had obviously been decided at the highest levels that Norman should go to St Edward. Curious.

Norman had been in Paris for the Peace Conference. He loved Paris, and had sought leave to stay on at the Embassy, but leave was not granted. The Brigadier took it badly when, inevitably, he found out that Norman had ever put himself in the position of requesting something so frivolous and, worse, of being turned down—officially. Such paternal irritation would have been violent had violence been known to the Threlfall family. As it was, displeasure was quite enough, sealed as it had been by Mrs Threlfall's tacit concurrence. Norman remembered re-reading his mother's letter: brisk and full of dull news; firm in its underlying message, and made wholly dispiriting by the cheerfulness with which she urged Norman, her eldest, to buck up and think instead about what exciting things lay in store for him in the Admiralty.

Much as it vexed Norman to admit it, his mother had been right. He did enjoy the Admiralty and, having mastered *The Times* crossword puzzle, it was not long before he was given hush-hush work in Room 9. At first, this concerned the unfortunate incident in the Jallianwala Bagh and other atrocities that soon followed in India, but there was much other absorbing intelligence work as well, much of it involving political matters in the Irish Free State and on the Continent. He excelled at it and for a while, quite a long while, he prospered. His confidential report "On the Political and Military Consequences of the Assassination of Giacomo Matteotti" even reached the desk of the Foreign Secretary. Norman was being noticed, and not only because of his superb dancing.

By what inconceivable series of misfortunes had his orderly world been at length turned upside down? Each was, in itself, fairly trivial. Gradually, however, over a period of only a few months, they snowballed. At first, Norman merely sensed a certain frostiness among certain colleagues that had definitely not existed before. Reasons were found to postpone or defer meetings that he would usually have attended. He became aware of hushed confidential discussions in twos and threes (figures seen through panes of frosted glass), from which he was excluded. On a brief visit from Paris, where he was Head of Station, Fitzroy Bancroft had made some oracular but pointed remark to the effect that Norman had better consider his position. Finally, there had been a strangely formal, disturbingly brief appointment with the Vice Admiral, among others, including a senior civil servant from the Foreign Office who did not speak. Norman never knew the exact nature of the complaint that had been made against him, nor the specific grounds upon which it was decided that he should be redeployed. His fresh orders were bluntly worded. Proceed to Colombo and await further instructions. Now he was well and truly banished to St Edward. Why?

Norman brightened up. He was by nature resilient, not to say cheerful, and not prone to extended periods of mawkish self-pity. He had liked Sir George and Lady Sutherland when he had first met them, and was quietly pleased that H.E. had decided to send him ahead to prepare for their arrival. It could have been worse. And his first impressions of the islands had been overwhelmingly positive. How could anyone not be lifted into a thoroughly good mood when confronted with something so delightfully batty as the cannonball tree? Batty, yes, but sensual too. There was something about its shapely fruit that brought back memories of Paris. He made a mental note: could there, perhaps, be a distinctive variant on the foxtrot—the cannonball rag? He smiled to himself, and just then heard the crunch of footsteps, military footsteps, on the gravel drive below his window.

Few members of the household knew that once or twice a week Colonel Pole, the governor's Private Secretary, liked to spend a few pleasant nocturnal hours at leisure in Madame Beck's establishment above the Café des Artistes in the French Quarter. Those who did not know merely presumed that he was returning from a brisk early morning walk to the observatory bluff. Those few who did regarded the fact that the Colonel had been out all night as the unquestionable province of a much-decorated retired artillery officer whose behaviour was in every circumstance beyond reproach. The tastes of an English gentleman were a mystery, to be sure, but, no matter how raffish, one presumed that by definition they were correct. Of course, Mrs Huntingfield knew. Housekeepers far less able than Mrs Huntingfield knew everything, but she did wonder how the puir man managed with nae but one arm.

That morning, however, Colonel Pole, whom she and Norman glimpsed from their respective windows, was striding up the drive with uncharacteristic urgency, even anger. He looked agitated, his arm swinging violently. His face was red, but not from his exertions in Madame Beck's establishment. Old Sock looked up from his parsley. He too noticed Colonel Pole striding towards the portico. He heard the front door slam—most unusual. The Colonel re-emerged a minute or two later with Norman and Mr Craddock, their voices raised but indistinct. Together they hurried back down the drive.

"A fule may gie a wise man counsel," muttered Old Sock, for he was devoted to Colonel Pole—indeed the Colonel was the only person in the household of which this could be said except for Mrs Huntingfield. Something was definitely afoot.

Sure enough, once they reached the bottom of the drive, Colonel Pole, Norman, Surgeon Commander Clark and Mr Craddock stood staring in disbelief at the mellow stone wall of the gatehouse. For on it were daubed in fresh red paint and foot-high letters, crude but perfectly legible, the words

AGIR!

DÉSOBÉIR!

CHAPTER 3

MV Dormouse

Mike and Sharon
2020

Its already about 500 from my
office to the FCO skip

Smelly spot to smoke

Tell me about it.

Give up then

Piss off Mike. Did Macron
people say why they think
its that particular war hero.
At this early stage couldnt it
be anybody?

NFI

Must have a reason

Shit. Basic details already on
al Jazeera website. Click on
link to <u>body parts found in
unmarked grave</u>. Blah blah
grim discovery made on
grounds of old Government

House blah now gated
casino resort with 9 hole golf
course and timeshare units

Sounds crap

Building new wellness
centre. Dug hole for eco spa
plunge pool when excavator
hit object six feet down.
Locked trunk marked
NOT WANTED ON
VOYAGE LIEUTENANT
NORMAN THRELFALL
RN allo allo allo contains
body parts. Investigation
ongoing. Matter before
coroner blah mystery blah

?

Wait

???

I said wait

*   *   *

1926

The Blue Moon Steam Packet Line's *Dormouse* was neither the newest nor the fastest steamer making the run between Portsmouth and St Edward via Guernsey and Jersey, but it was the most comfortable. It was also the sleekest and most attractive. Her first-class cabins were large and well-ventilated. Regular passengers such as Bishop and Mrs Stanley, who were returning from the synod in Canterbury, delighted in the breadth of her lower deck aft (for quoits), the fading elegance of her old-fashioned saloon, the assiduousness of her ageing stewards and the absence of riff-raff—except for that frightful M. Orlando, the French consul, who had been doing business in London, something to do with guano. And, of course, money.

This voyage, however, had additional cachet because Sir George Sutherland was proceeding aboard the *Dormouse* to assume the government of St Edward, Gwern and The Thimble Isles (the Bailiwick of St Edward). Indeed, this was for the other passengers a thrilling opportunity to observe at close quarters the new Governor and Lady Sutherland, their daughters Lettice and Harriet and their personal staff, for upon arriving in Port Charlotte the social advantage of having made their acquaintance, however tenuous, however much the vice-regal party did their best to avoid it, could not be overstated or too often mentioned in passing. The weather was fair.

"She is larger than her photographs suggest," remarked Mrs Stanley, thoughtfully placing a red jack over the black queen. She was seated at a small table under the porthole in their cabin. Bishop Stanley was seated opposite, reading a slim volume of occasional sermons lately published in Cape Town. He looked up and blinked.

"I said she's stout, John."

"Who?"

"Lady Sutherland." Mrs Stanley adopted that sharpness of tone with which the Bishop was depressingly familiar. "Lovely clothes, though," she added wistfully, smoothing her skirt.

"Yes dear, lovely."

"Still, she's a *huge* improvement on Lady Strickland. Such a ghastly snob. Will you ever forget that extraordinary Regatta Day when she made a point of saying to the footman, 'Young man, please move that table. I wish to curtsey to His Excellency'?"

"No, I suppose I shan't," said the Bishop.

"I gather she did it first thing in the morning and last thing at night," said Mrs Stanley, confidentially.

"What's that dear?"

"Curtsey, to *him*," said Mrs Stanley, approaching exasperation. The Bishop could be quite obtuse.

"How could one possibly know?" The Bishop looked up.

"Smith heard it from a housemaid who *saw* her, John." A lengthy silence supervened. "Lady Sutherland has none of those airs. She's very interested in birds, too. I don't think I've seen her without those huge binoculars."

"Who?"

"Lady *Sutherland*, dear. She knows all about *birds*." Sometimes Mrs Stanley wondered how her husband ever managed to reign over a diocese, even one as small and unimportant as St Edward. "*He* seems better too," she added, willing herself back into something that resembled cheerfulness; she placed a red seven on the eight of spades.

"Far better, dear, and I daresay brighter."

"Oh?"

"He reads the *Church Times*."

"Hardly a reliable indication, John, but I suppose he can read, which is a step up."

"Charity, my dear," muttered the Bishop. He was trying to return to his book.

"Unfortunate about the daughters. So plain," Mrs Stanley ignored the Bishop. "I do like poor Captain Campbell. Where did he lose his eye?"

"Passchendaele, I think."

"All their staff seem nice," continued Mrs Stanley, for whether it was Passchendaele or Fromelles hardly mattered— an eye was an eye. Still, the black patch was frightfully gallant. "Mrs Hodgkinson seems to think he might be roped into the Cathedral choir."

"Jolly good." The Bishop glanced over the table. "Three of diamonds."

"Yes, I know dear, thank you." Mrs Stanley suppressed her irritation, for it was true that the Bishop did occasionally notice things. She looked up. "You know how hard it is to find a really decent manly baritone."

"Yes dear." The Bishop reached for his pipe.

"The other ADC is a Lieutenant Threlfall. Navy. He's gone ahead. Lady Sutherland mentioned he too is musical."

"Embarrassment of riches."

"Tenor, John."

"I really don't see how the Governor's military gentlemen can be in attendance upon H.E., which I gather is what they are here to do, *and* rehearse twice a week, let alone be relied upon to do justice to Stanford's evening service in C. I doubt it."

"Well, you could at least explore the possibility, John." Mrs Stanley looked closely once more, frowned, and then shuffled her cards.

That same evening Norman took only the second opportunity since his arrival to wander down into Port Charlotte. He sauntered along the quai, he explored a little the deserted principal streets with no particular purpose, instead musing upon the full moon, and, it must be admitted, upon the relatively reduced character of this tour of duty, charming though the island seemed to him at first. He decided to explore a little farther afield the curious, twisting streets and lanes of the old French quarter, the *Vieux Carré* as it was still known, with its charming little shops and a few cosy pubs. He turned up the lane beside an airy large ground-floor establishment, the Café des Artistes. It was nearly closing time, and Norman was gladdened to observe that although they had almost finished packing up, there was an orchestra and a little dance floor. Brought to a standstill by this welcome discovery, but remaining outside, Norman was intrigued to see, through the open door and windows, the remnants of a lively mixed gathering of which no doubt the Brigadier and Mrs Threlfall, he mused, would look askance, but not half as much as they would thoroughly disapprove of "Madame." She was almost the first person that Norman noticed from that distance, a most exotic looking small woman dressed in spangly blue and fuchsia who was circulating from table to table after the manner of a *maître d'hotel*, but, more like a proprietor, exchanging words with regular patrons, whom she obviously knew. The woman was laughing musically and gesturing, such that her heavy freight of costume jewellery caught the lights, which, because they were just then turned up, sparkled the more brightly. Customers were beginning to leave; others were getting to their feet and putting on their hats and coats. Norman's eyes alighted upon the sign above the door:

Café des Artistes
Propriétaire: G. Beck
Est. 1912

He strolled on and, turning the next corner, heard faint music drifting through an open upstairs window towards the rear of the same building. He stopped again beneath it. Music, yes, he knew it. This was the music of Paris, the cafés, the nightclubs, the apache dancers; music that touched his heart and raised the little hairs on the back of his neck.

> *Sur cette terre, ma seule joie, mon seul bonheur*
> *C'est mon homme.*
> *J'ai donné tout c'que j'ai, mon amour et tout mon cœur*
> *À mon homme.*

And in the window, he saw a girl, swaying to the song. So far as Norman could tell, she was alone. She was tall and somehow angular and most unconventional looking, a slim girl with a narrow waist, slender arms, sloping shoulders and short dark hair. She did not strike him as especially pretty, nevertheless he found himself watching her languid movements to this strange music with real fascination. They were fluid movements, unselfconscious and confident and sinuous. He was quite sure she would be an excellent dancing partner. If she were a shy girl—something about her suggested this to him—then the privacy afforded by her room and her gramophone was all the more sacrosanct. With this thought, Norman suddenly felt as guilty as he would have done had he opened the door of her room without knocking, and sauntered in. At the same time, the girl abruptly turned and stopped, having somehow sensed Norman's presence. She made to draw her shabby curtain—once a Spanish shawl with long fringes—but their eyes met, and Norman, regretting that he had given her a start and that he had interrupted her dance, raised his hand and shook his head slightly, as if to say, please do not stop. The girl remained still, one hand clasping the curtain, the other resting on her collar bone to which the surprise had brought it as a first reaction. There they remained for a few moments, caught in each other's benign but cautious gaze. Norman could see that she was not frightened of him; perhaps she was unperturbed by the sight of well-dressed Englishmen coming and going down that little lane. It would be some days before Norman learned that this was true, and that the girl was also intrigued by his looks; relatively few of the well-dressed Englishmen who came and went down that lane below her window were as good-looking as Norman. As if to break some sort of impasse, maybe because the haunting music was still playing and he wanted to encourage her to carry on, Norman did a few graceful dance steps out over the cobblestone, dancing with his shadow under the brilliant full moon. He looked up and she smiled. The song ended. Norman bowed to her, just like Ivor Novello in *The Bohemian Girl*, then went on his way, but the music and the girl: both were fixed in his mind. And, who knows? Perhaps he too was fixed in hers.

Miss Davies lay down on her bunk. She wondered about Colin, such a good-looking young man. And so charming. Such a pity about the eye. St Edward promised to be a delightful tour, cooler and hopefully more civilised than Rangoon, although ... Miss Davies frowned. Yet again there were the most peculiar noises emanating from the next stateroom. Mrs Hodgkinson, did she never sleep? Professor Hodgkinson spent so much time in her stateroom that one would never guess he had one of his own. Lively conversation one minute. Shrieks of laughter ... silence ... more laughter ... silence again, and a loud sort of bumping— such an odd time for physical jerks—silence ... murmuring, then more conversation. Always curious, Miss Davies could stand it no longer. She fetched her toothglass and gingerly placed it against the dividing wall.

"... my glorious, wicked Magnolia ... simply must give you a great big smack on your bottom ..." Peals of laughter.

Miss Davies hovered between curiosity and discretion. Curiosity won.

"... you are a perfect *beast*, Gene! ... Wait, there ...No, *there* ..." Silence, then something that sounded like groaning. Was she being sick? Was *he* being sick? Possibly both?

Good God.

Miss Davies's experience of sexual intercourse was regrettably sparse, and did not extend to anything remotely like this, which was beginning partly to resemble certain scandalous passages in *Seraglio Governess* ...

"... you frightful, *heavenly* man ... don't stop ... harder ... Oh, daddy!" More laughter, and a kind of high-pitched whinnying noise.

"... play the hunting game ..."

"Stop it, Gene."

"... such excellent camouflage ... but I'll bag my precious cheetah yet ..." Shrieks of laughter, then ... loud clatter, and— surely not—growling?

"... swear I shall take a leaf out of Gwladys Baring ..."

Miss Davies's heart missed a beat, and came close to missing a second. Gwladys Baring? What an astounding coincidence. Mr Hodgkinson *appeared* to be respectable, but she was quite obviously a tart. There was a pause.

"... Do it again ... Yes, yes ... My Caesar!"

Miss Davies glanced guiltily at the hat box in which she kept hidden her copy of *Seraglio Governess*. Though her ear was getting tired she maintained her vigil. There was another, longer silence.

"... knowing your wife writes salacious novels? ..."

".... tease and fascinate ... you've been bad haven't you? ..." Giggles, and then a sort of paddy-whack sound, "... naughty girl ... shameful harlot ..."

"... never fail to arouse me, you utter, *utter* darling ..." More extended bumping. "Oh, Gene...Gene!"

A high-pitched squeal, followed by further prolonged silence.

"... know you're far naughtier even than my worst, most hateful sheikh ..."

"... this time I shall call you Gwladys, ravish ..." renewed shrieks of laughter, hoots of it, "... deserve another great big smack on your wicked behind ..." Indistinctness, and then more bumping.

Miss Davies blinked with incredulity, and removed the tooth glass but it slipped out of her hand, fell to the floor and broke with deafening reverberation.

There was silence, silence as of the tomb, on both sides of the wall.

Miss Davies held her breath, blushed deep crimson, and crept stealthily back to her bunk. What possible calculus of improbability could result in that tart Mrs Hodgkinson being one and the same as the notorious romantic novelist Gwladys Baring? And that she should occupy the cabin next to Miss Davies' aboard the *Dormouse*? And that Miss Davies herself should be in illegal possession of Gwladys Baring's latest novel, the shocking *Seraglio Governess*? Inconceivable! But more importantly did they hear the tooth glass break? Of course they did. The Hodgkinsons seemed in total possession of all the usual sensory faculties—and obviously some very unusual ones in addition. Miss Davies was gloomily certain that neither of them remotely suffered from deafness. Not for the first time Miss Davies felt utter mortification. She could not sleep.

M. Orlando was one of those large middle-aged gentlemen who seem not especially bothered by the sheen of liverish perspiration over the brow with which they present themselves to the world. His reputation as a bon vivant and boulevardier fitted him just as well as his elegant but capacious white suits, and the little black cigarillos he had sent from San Sebastian, but there hovered about him more than a suggestion of the rogue. He was known, above all, to frequent Madame Beck's establishment above the Café des Artistes in the French Quarter, which was a short and easy stroll from his office in Port Charlotte—*Orlando et Cie., commissaires en guano*. Although, or perhaps because, he had lived his whole life in the Bailiwick, his manners were theatrically Gallic, so that when seated on a divan, for example, M. Orlando lent to an ordinary piece of furniture a hint of salaciousness that lingered a good while after he vacated it. The same was true when he handled a butter knife, or stooped to kiss the hand of a young English lady—usually plump, his favourite sort. His other gestures were expansive, his speech flowery, and his general demeanour almost always cheerful. Among the new community of guano traders, bankers, financiers and business advisors he was the most conspicuous, for he was very rich.

The following afternoon, M. Orlando was taking a turn on the aft deck, smoking one of his little black cigarillos. When he swung into view, Colin Campbell, who was strolling in the opposite direction, was not in a position to avoid him.

"Good afternoon, consul."

"Ah, Lieutenant Campbell—am I pronouncing it correctly?" Orlando did not wait for confirmation. "I hope you are enjoying this serene voyage as much as I am."

"Yes, splendid thank you."

"This will be your first visit to St Édouard, yes?" Orlando took Colin's arm, so they strolled together. "An island group of rare *beauté*, not sufficiently appreciated in Whitehall I think?"

"I'm sure I cannot say," said Colin doubtfully. "But, yes, this is my first visit."

"Tell me, Captain, what marks of distinction, which of your many talents persuaded Sir George to appoint you and Lieutenant Threfall as his aides-de-camp, in readiness for our *champ de bataille*?" M. Orlando tightened his grip. "No false modesty, I insist."

"Lieutenant Threlfall and I were both gazetted at Colombo," said Norman. "It's usually a matter of which officers can be spared. Sir George was kind enough to …"

"Come, come," said M. Orlando. "I am told you sing exquisitely." Colin blushed, for this had not occurred to him as any sort of qualification. And how did the consul know?

"I trust you will find the society of St Édouard amusing and gay," M. Orlando ground on, patting Colin's lapel. "There are many young ladies who are already anxious to make your acquaintance. They have told me so."

"I'm sure they are very kind," said Colin, experiencing a twinge of seasickness.

"Madame Beck arranges the most delightful *thés dansants* at the Café des Artistes, a charming établissement. You must be my guest."

Colin thought this most unlikely, actually inconceivable. "Too kind, consul. But I rather suspect Lieutenant Threlfall and I will be in attendance most days."

"Lady Sutherland is a devotee of rare birds, I see. I am sure you know the British Ornithologists' Union maintains a lively interest in St Édouard."

"Yes, quite." Colin tried as subtly as possible to loosen the consul's grip on his arm. "Lady Sutherland has been corresponding with the Royal Society of St Edward. Their committee is anxious to secure her patronage. They wrote ahead to Rangoon. I'm sure Miss Davies will look into the matter after we reach Port Charlotte."

"It is fervently to be hoped," said M. Orlando. "The famous red-collared loverbird urgently requires vice-regal protection, as do so many others. And now I must beg to be excused, for *des choses consulaires* oppress me, even on board ship."

He released Colin, and made an absurd little bow.

"Of course. Good day, consul."

The following day Norman continued to explore the old French quarter of Port Charlotte. It reminded him of Paris. Behind the guano traders, the banks, and the dealers in fish and livestock was a network of narrow streets, shops, small businesses, boot makers, potteries, hardware retailers, an apothecary, a carpenter, a painless dentist, and a small establishment with a sign that read *À l'étourderie. Propriétaire*. M. Réné Aziz. It was a lazy day, Norman had time on his hands, and so, drawn by curiosity, he entered. At once he realised that M. Aziz was a tobacconist, for the atmosphere in the place was heavy with the smell of a particularly fragrant tobacco.

M. Azis stood behind his counter, a small stooped man, wearing a fez, his face brown and polished, almost the colour of the tobacco in jars on the counter. On shelves behind the tobacconist, rising to the ceiling, to Norman's astonishment, were neatly arranged shellac discs, and gramophones on which to play them.

"Bonjour monsieur."

"Bonjour."

"You would like to buy some tobacco perhaps?"

"No, monsieur, I do not smoke."

M. Aziz looked astonished. "You should try my friend."

"Maybe, but not today I think. However I see you sell gramophone records."

"I do. They are very popular with the young."

"Perhaps you can help me."

"I hope so."

"I heard music from a gramophone record recently. It went something like this ... *Sur cette terre*," Norman sang in a surprisingly confident tenor. "*Ma seule joie, something something something c'est mon homme ...*"

"Sir, I know that tune." Monsieur Aziz reached behind the counter and brought forth a record in its paper sleeve. "And may I say you sing it very well. It is a recording of a local artiste, Claudette Moreau, *l'oiseau chanteur de Saint Edouard*, singing her version of the well-known song, 'Mon Homme,' very popular at the moment sir."

"Thank you Monsieur Aziz, I will take it."

"Thank *you*, sir. And please, will you not also try a little tobacco, the restorative leaf, if I may say, to augment your enjoyment of the music?"

"Maybe another time. Thank you."

"Certainly sir. But think on this." He lit his pipe, and drew deeply. Fragrant smoke filled the small shop. "'Thou, matur'd by glad Hesperian suns, Tobacco, fountain pure of limpid truth, That looks the very soul; whence pouring thought Swarms all the mind; absorpt is yellow care, And at each puff imagination burns.' Do come again sir," as Norman closed the door gently.

CHAPTER 4

Modern Romance

Mike and Sharon
2020

I said wait

DTF, what are you
doing later

This you horny pillock.
Ever tried locating a 96yo
closed file on St Edward? No
you havent

Temper

According to wiki Mandingo
Wars were Ivory Coast. For
once had nothing to do with
us (you).

Here we go. Ms Chippy
back on the fucking war
path again

Mike nobody in my family
ever colonised anything.
Too busy cutting cane in

Belize then being exploited
in Brixton

While hard work self
discipline and your Dad's
successful small mixed
business contributed with
hundreds of thousands of
other Caribbean migrants to
economic boom of the 60s.
Get over it

Jesus Mike. Im not taking
the bait

Love you too GF

Just focus for once. Mandingo
Wars had nothing to do with
us although they were near us
(you). Ghana, Sierra Leone,
Gambia. But nothing to do
with bailiwick st edward
either. Theyre still member
state Commonwealth

Which?

All of them

LOL

Seriously, BP will care and
when BP cares PM cares

Why BP? Is there gas oil £££

Buckingham Palace
you moron

GR8

* * *

1926

With much hearty thudding and laughter and clapping of hands, half a dozen other English first-class passengers were playing quoits on the broad lower deck aft. Mrs Hodgkinson reclined in her deck chair, smoking one of her slender black Sobranie cigarettes, pointedly ignoring the fun. She was reading Mrs Woolf's new novel. Though positioned some distance away, and facing the opposite direction, at the same time Mrs Hodgkinson deftly made sure that she was conspicuous. She was a very tall, handsome woman, fashionably dressed—her filbert nails brightly varnished in the Parisian mode. The light breeze played among her long floaty scarves, one of which was casually wrapped around her brow and knotted at the side. Mrs Hodgkinson was troubled. Gene was a perfect gem, a model husband, and the bank and his consulting work with the government of St Edward kept him fully occupied. Granted, he was a foot shorter than she might have preferred, yet Gene acquitted himself admirably in the intercourse department. No, she couldn't fault him in that regard—possibly a little less often? She sighed. True, Mrs Hodgkinson enjoyed her charitable work in connection with the

St Edward Association of Girls' and Mixed Clubs, the Cathedral choir and Chapter auxiliary. Mrs Stanley really was such a saint, and not at all starchy—not like that awful snob Lady Strickland. And when Mrs Stanley asked for aid who could possibly refuse?

The Hodgkinsons' secluded villa, *Les Humeurs*, and their jungly garden high above the beach on the northern fringe of Port Charlotte, was the ideal spot in which to compose works of romantic fiction. Thanks to her own considerable astuteness, Mrs Hodgkinson had attained much commercial success which the recent obscene libel action in the High Court of Justice had done little to dampen. Thank goodness that unpleasant affair was finally over—although in retrospect the remark of her barrister that had stung the most, and still rankled very much indeed, was that, even if it could be established in the eyes of the law, "which was doubtful," literary merit could never be any sort of defence. What rubbish! Dear Lord Justice Gannet had seemed sympathetic throughout; for long stretches of the trial His Lordship had been thoroughly absorbed by her books—which was gratifying, as was His Lordship's lengthy judgment when at last it came. Thank goodness for legal technicalities. Mrs Hodgkinson could now concentrate once more on her brooding sheikhs and pirate captains, the arrogant lairds and dissolute younger sons, the vicious eastern princelings, the magnificent Cossacks and Ch'ing emperors whom, with her rapid pen, she bade rend, gash, tear, rip, slash, cleave, untether—it varied but the formula was reliable—those gauzy bodices, the thin muslin, the tapes, the delicate lace that clung to the heaving bosoms of sloe-eyed virgins. *My Captive Heart*, published under the agreeable nom-de-plume of Gwladys Baring, had done moderately well.

However, *The Marquis of Hazard*, *Handmaid to the Pasha* and *Forbidden City*, which followed in rapid succession, had been enormously profitable. It didn't really matter that the shocking *Seraglio Governess* had been banned throughout the Empire; according to her publishers' last post office telegram, sales in America were accelerating if that were possible, and the French translation had been reprinted twice. And yet, and yet ... Mrs Woolf was far more artistically ambitious, if less entertaining. Still, the Modern novel was *interesting*. Mrs Hodgkinson could see that, but how could one gussy it up a bit? She lit another cigarette and gazed out to sea, loftily continuing to ignore the quoit players. Who could have imagined that one might garner critical acclaim with a title as dull as *Mrs Dalloway*? Never mind. *Do What Thou Wilt* was coming along nicely. The sexual intercourse would no doubt cause another sensation. It generally did. No doubt Gwladys Baring would have to sift through yet another mountain of letters of protest, which would be nearly as numerous as all the cards, notes and cables she received expressing warm appreciation. She smiled at the thought.

Still, Mrs Hodgkinson could not quite account for the restlessness that had overtaken her on this voyage. Could she be in danger of straying into a literary rut? Was there not plenty of room for artistic growth? Might not one or two of Mrs Woolf's less subtle techniques—even a few of Mr Joyce's, only a very few—might not these be harnessed somehow, borrowed let us say, gently to enlarge, to extend, to deepen her own work, without losing any of the romantic tension, the swooning and the delicate sheen of perspiration with which her heroines were now synonymous among so many loyal readers? Might not there exist an as yet undetected thirst for the "Modern romance," a thirst that her daring *Do What Thou Wilt* might reveal, and then slake? Mrs Hodgkinson felt a little shiver of excitement at the thought. Following the *succès de scandale* of *Seraglio Governess*, Venus & Crabb had already paid a handsome advance against royalties, and her editor Miss Lamb was such a pet. Those carping critics who sneered at her earlier novels, above all *Fie! Your Eminence* and *Homeless Vestal* (or, admittedly, ignored them altogether) would have no choice but at last to acknowledge the existence of Gwladys Baring.

"Come, Fang," she purred. "Tea time." The stately white Afghan rose from his spot beside Mrs Hodgkinson's deck chair, and followed his mistress with an elegance of gait that perfectly complemented her own, natural poise.

"Commodore Bracegirdle says he's odious," said Miss Davies. She and Colin were having tea in a distant corner of the saloon. "And not to be trusted. On any account."

"Yes, I know," said Colin. "He's certainly a poseur, and rather oily. I can't imagine why they ever made him consul, although they are French, and, I should imagine, hardly spoiled for choice on St Edward." He reached for another currant bun.

"Colin, listen to this," said Miss Davies. She had *Muirhead's Guide to St Edward, Gwern and the Thimble Isles* open in her lap. "'The avifauna of the St Edward Group is among the richest and undisturbed in the mid-Atlantic Islands, surpassing in diversity and number even those of The Azores, St Helena, Ascension or Tristan da Cunha.' Lady S. will be in heaven."

"That's the other thing. He knew about the Royal Society's invitation," said Colin.

"Did he just? Pushy swine. It won't make a jot of difference. Lady S. considers all such invitations on their merits, and she trusts one to make proper inquiries in the appropriate way, and in due time." She poured another cup, and reflected for a moment. "Thank goodness for dear Mr Jenkins in the C.O. His guidance is invaluable, such a help with learned societies and so forth. Colin dear, do have a cup of tea."

Commodore Bracegirdle joined Colin and Miss Davies. He sank into the other armchair.

"Here he is."

"Thank you, Miss Davies. Campbell," said Commodore Bracegirdle, crossing his legs.

"Bracegirdle," returned Colin affably. Richard Bracegirdle was stocky but athletic. His complexion was ruddier than Colin's, and his neatly brushed hair was fair.

"Now Richard, it's high time you called me Maud, at least in private. Colin does," said Miss Davies. "Colombo and Mauritius is one thing, but I think St Edward will call for informality." Commodore Bracegirdle touched his other cuff, and cleared his throat.

"If you say so ... Maud," he said. Colin shifted, vaguely embarrassed that Miss Davies had not urged this adjustment upon Bracegirdle sooner.

"*Much* better," said Miss Davies in her slightly irritating sing-song. She was one of those imperial spinster ladies whom the marcel wave did not suit.

"I just saw that wind bag Orlando," remarked Commodore Bracegirdle. "He's certainly taken a shine to you Campbell. Somehow sniffed out your semi-professional baritone. Made a point of mentioning it."

"The impertinence," said Miss Davies, wondering if M. Orlando were also capable of discovering certain facts about herself, above all certain of her reading habits. "I'm sure it's not especially audible unless you deliberately plant your ear …" She changed the subject. "I was just saying to Colin that you think he's odious and not to be trusted, not on any account. I profoundly agree."

"That much is obvious just from looking at him," said Colin.

"The stickier part will be dinner tonight," said Richard. "Full mess kit."

"Obligatory, I'm afraid," said Colin. "Nice old chap though, the Captain."

"He hasn't asked M. *Orlando*?" asked Miss Davies with distaste.

"Afraid so," said Colin. "And the Stanleys."

"I should have thought it strictly vice-regals only," said Miss Davies.

"I gather that's all though," said Richard.

"Thank God," said Miss Davies. "I thought you were going to say he'd invited that tart Mrs Hodgkinson."

On the last evening of the voyage the Sutherlands, their staff, and the Captain's other guests, including Bishop and Mrs Stanley, M. Orlando, and Professor and Mrs Hodgkinson, foregathered for cocktails under the awning on the upper deck aft, adjacent to the saloon.

"Ah, Sir George," effused M. Orlando in his vulgar way, "alas I have not yet had the pleasure of meeting your delightful daughters." Lady Sutherland gave her husband no time in which to frame a cool response, for she presumed Sir George would spectacularly fail to be cool.

"Lettice, Harriet, this is Monsieur Orlando, the consul of France," said Lady Sutherland.

"How do you do?" said Lettice and Harriet in weak unison.

"Charmed," said M. Orlando, advancing upon Lettice much as a blue-footed booby displays himself before the female of the species. He executed an over-elaborate kissing of hands, moist in his sincerity. "Charmed," he repeated, before turning upon Harriet with even greater assiduousness.

"M. Orlando also trades in guano," said Lady Sutherland. "I'm sure it keeps you terribly busy."

"I am a simple man of affairs, Madame," said M. Orlando, spreading his arms, his eyes hovering over Harriet's ample bosom for a fraction longer than was necessary, "but I always make time for my friends." He smiled his most ingratiating smile. Lettice and Harriet were exactly the sort of healthy, curvaceous English girls that he liked.

"Jolly good," said Sir George, obliviously. "I'm quite sure we shall see you often at Government House." Lady Sutherland discreetly drove the blunt end of her fan into the small of her husband's back, and turned to Mrs Stanley.

"Good evening, dear Mrs Stanley," she said. "Such a lovely sunset."

"Oh yes, Lady Sutherland, our sunsets are always beautiful," said Mrs Stanley, rather breathlessly. "The Bishop often mentions them in his sermons, don't you dear?"

"Yes, indeed. Only last Sunday my text was, 'The heavens declare the glory of God; and the firmament sheweth his handywork,'" said the Bishop. "Psalm 19." There was an awkward pause.

"What fun, you must lend it me," said Lady Sutherland.

"... Dear Miss Davies, I don't believe you have met Mrs Hodgkinson," said Mrs Stanley with a cautious gesture.

Miss Davies felt physically ill. Her copy in plain wrappers of the shocking *Seraglio Governess* by Gwladys Baring had been difficult to obtain. Dear Cousin Cynthia was something hush-hush in the Embassy in Paris, and had bought it from an artistic bookseller on the Left Bank several months earlier. Having devoured it with great excitement, Cynthia wrapped the novel carefully in several layers of wax paper, and concealed it inside a tin of biscuits, which dear Aitken in Chancery tossed in the Diplomatic Bag, a thoughtful Christmas present destined for Rangoon. Such a dear.

"We haven't met," said Miss Davies drily. She felt the dreadful stirrings, the upward creep, of what would soon erupt into a crimson blush.

"Such a pleasure, Miss Davies. Cigarette?" offered Mrs Hodgkinson in her slightly unusual contralto.

"No thank you. I don't smoke."

Mrs Hodgkinson laughed. "But you must let me teach you!"

Something in her manner suggested that Mrs Hodgkinson could gaze with her perceptive author's eye—especially an eye as dangerous as Gwladys Baring's—into the deepest recesses of Miss Davies's soul.

"You're blushing, how delightful," said Mrs Hodgkinson, a sinuous plume of smoke rising from her parted lips.

"The heat, I expect," said Miss Davies.

"It is a little ... steamy," Mrs Hodgkinson paused. "So few people blush nowadays. What have we become?" She laughed again.

Quite, thought Miss Davies. She swallowed hard.

"All my heroines blush," continued Mrs Hodgkinson. "So useful in romantic fiction, don't you agree? Are you feeling all right, Miss Davies? ..."

Colin had rescued Harriet, and Richard Lettice, each from the ministrations of M. Orlando—in a superb tactical manoeuvre worthy of the Royal Marines.

"Thank you, Colin," said Harriet. "Who is the lady in that toxic shade of green?"

"Mrs Hodgkinson," said Colin. "Rather modern sort of fish. Her husband is Professor Hodgkinson, some sort of banker. I gather she writes romantic novels."

"Really?" said Harriet, who very much liked romantic novels. "She has bright yellow paint on her fingernails, perfectly bilious. Lettice, don't look now ..."

"I've seen them, Hat," said Lettice. "Richard says she's very fast."

"I think we're going in," said Colin ...

"... And you must be Mrs Hodgkinson," said Lady Sutherland brightly. "Dear Mrs Stanley has told me so much about you."

"How do you do, Lady Sutherland," drawled Mrs Hodgkinson. "Cigarette?" Lady Sutherland ignored the gesture.

"I do look forward to learning more about your charitable work. So useful," she said. "You must be so proud, Professor Hodgkinson," turning on him with alarming suddenness.

"Immensely proud, Lady Sutherland," said Gene, tilting on the balls of his feet. "My wife's energy is prodigious." Mrs Hodgkinson cast her eyes down, she fancied, in the manner of Jane Austen.

"Yes, I'm sure it is," said Lady Sutherland, with a brisk smile. "And such an asset to the local laird of the Cincinnati Ohio & Delaware Banking Corporation," she added wittily, before swinging back towards Sir George and the Captain, extending her hand. "I must congratulate you, Captain. This is the first voyage I can recall when Sir George has not fallen horribly seasick. How do you do it?"

Sir George chuckled affably.

"These are fair waters Your Ladyship, and a fine stable vessel, though I say so myself," said the Captain. "Shall we go in?"

"Rather," said Lady Sutherland. "I'm sure I could eat a horse." In fact, she was about to.

The dinner was, in the old-fashioned phrase, a great success—largely buoyed by eager anticipation, for the *Dormouse* was due to approach the northern coast of St Edward early the following morning, and drop anchor in Port Charlotte by mid-afternoon.

"Tell me, Richard, how long have you been posted to St Edward?" asked Miss Davies.

"Four years," said Bracegirdle. Though a good and dependable officer of the Royal Navy, Maud was beginning to sense that he lacked social fluency.

"Four? A good spell," said Miss Davies. "And before that?"

"Trincomalee," said Bracegirdle, "ADC to the C.-in-C., North Atlantic."

"Splendid," said Miss Davies, feigning delight. "I'm told Scapa Flow is *such* fun to live in, not merely to visit. Not at all like Rangoon."

"No," said Bracegirdle. Miss Davies was beginning to feel a little desperate.

"No," she said …

"… Sir George was telling me that your bank is one of the biggest in the world. Can that possibly be true Professor Hodgkinson?" said Lady Sutherland.

"Well, hardly, Lady Sutherland," said Gene. "Although it's a mighty big operation, and worth every penny."

"Oh?" Lady Sutherland knew the banks earned the Bailiwick a fortune, but it hadn't occurred to her that they might cost anything to operate.

"The Company had to bring in all the capital, recruit and train staff. Then build or otherwise acquire premises. The costs are very high," said Gene.

"But you make a handsome profit even so?" Lady Sutherland sought clarification.

"Correct," said Gene. If she only knew.

"Excellent," said Lady Sutherland. They, too, seemed to have reached a conversational cul-de-sac …

"… Miss Davies tells me you are an authoress, Mrs Hodgkinson," said Commodore Bracegirdle.

"I dabble in romantic fiction, yes," drawled Mrs Hodgkinson, "and not without success. Are you perhaps a passionate but covert reader, Commodore?"

"Detective stories, mostly," said Bracegirdle, blanching slightly at the word *covert*, "and, of course, anything to do with the sea."

"Ah crime. Far too clever for me," said Mrs Hodgkinson. "I am mainly interested in sex." Miss Davies was seized by a fit of coughing. There was a brief hiatus, punctuated only by the clinking of knives. An ancient steward topped up the Commodore's glass.

"Which?" asked Bracegirdle, recovering himself.

"*Both*, dear Commodore," said Mrs Hodgkinson, with relish. "Each in its separate sphere; the eternal dance of love that binds male to female." She glanced meaningfully across the table and caught Gene's eye. "You are a bachelor, Commodore, I think?"

"Yes," said Bracegirdle.

"Oh, but we must do something about that," said Mrs Hodgkinson ...

"... What may your loyal subjects expect from this new and enlightened administration, Excellency?" Orlando dripped with insincerity. "Sir Henry Strickland interested himself in the roads and the railway, and of course taxation. What, pray, will be your sphere of influence?"

"Business as usual, Monsieur," said Sir George. "Long experience has taught one that the Empire quietly prospers on that basis—and so do your French possessions I think, M. Orlando?" He raised a finger and twinkled mischievously.

"But business is hardly *comme d'habitude* on St. Édouard, Sir George," said Orlando. "The banks and the mine are bringing much change to our beautiful island home, is it not so Professeur Gene?"

"True," said Gene, "much change."

"*Plus ça change*," said Sir George. "Crown dependencies may grow, even transform themselves in the white heat of economic novelty, but it is the rule of law that binds the whole thing together. This is the genius of Britain's gift to the world, don't you agree?"

"Ah, Excellency! Such wisdom." The twin worms of anger and hate, never wholly inactive, suddenly reawakened in his breast. "We simple island folk are fortunate indeed, are we not Madame Stanley?" said M. Orlando.

"Very fortunate, I'm sure," said Mrs Stanley, thoroughly irritated by having been tarred with the brush of simplicity, and, worse, by someone as revolting as M. Orlando. Miss Harriet, she noticed, seemed strangely attentive, if plain. The young were so difficult to understand.

"Ladies, shall we?" said Lady Sutherland, rising. It was not an invitation.

At a distance of some 150 nautical miles south southwest of the sleek *Dormouse*, a radically different sort of vessel was approaching the St Edward Group by way of channels far less frequently plied. For, comparatively shallow, the Gwern Banks were known to be treacherous. The rusty tramp steamer *Marianne*, registered under a tattered flag of convenience, that of Liberia, laboured through a sluggish swell. Shirtless Lascar stokers toiled in the boiler room under the harsh supervision of an engineer who was, like the rest of them, covered in sweat and coal-dust grime. The engine wheezed and groaned. The fat boatswain in his filthy sweat-stained string singlet complacently stood sentinel in the wheelhouse, from time to time taking a swig from a battered pewter flask. Below decks, the captain amused himself on his narrow bunk with a pliant cabin boy, several empty absinthe bottles occasionally clinking in the corner of his cabin as the vessel gently rolled towards her destination.

Alone on deck Serge Di Bartolo, veteran of the Mandingo Wars, leant on the rail, smoking a dirty French cigarette, gazing out at the shifting reflection of the moon which followed them over the swell rolling in from the north Atlantic. He coughed and spat, stretched and yawned, then flicked his cigarette over the rail. He adjusted the thin shoulder-strap of the delicate silk foundation garment he habitually wore next to the skin, concealed beneath layers of well-worn military fatigues. Serge Di Bartolo took up his hurricane lamp, and hastened towards the pitching bow of the vessel. He lifted the hatch and peered down into the hold. There lay his precious cargo of antique firearms, and his boxes of dynamite—sweating nitroglycerine, but otherwise undisturbed. Serge Di Bertolo didn't trust the crew. He certainly didn't trust the Captain. He didn't trust anybody; he could rely only upon himself to deliver this shipment to the brave freedom fighters of *Les Îles de Saint-Édouard*. Very gently he lowered the hatch, and extinguished his hurricane lamp.

CHAPTER 5

Landfall

Mike and Sharon
2020

GR8

Database has quite a bit on St
Edward, plus contact name
and number in MI6 but no
further deets. Apparently
features in Panama *and*
Paradise Papers

You might want to ask
Julian Assange

No need wanker.
panamanana.com
and Beckcorp GmbH
"correspond" with Appleby.
Tax. Dodgy as fuck

Nice one. Post Brexit trade
negs. French fucking body
parts, alleged torture and
now money laundering.
Anything else?

Consular doesnt go back to 1926, besides St Edward was suzerain entity. Ever heard of them? You know, eg Hong Kong. So didnt come under old FO. High Commissioner Pretoria covers St Edward. Want me to email?

Heard shes a tosser. Used to shag Derek Urquhart B4 he was posted to Kinshasa poor bastard. Waste of bloody time

BTW heres another weird thing. Wiki footnote refers one of those old 60s National Geographic articles about quaint trad folk religion in St Edward Islands.

Midnight knees up round roaring bonfire? Fire water? Black magic? Saggy tits?

Saggy tits? You can fucking talk you sexist racist prick. Old people in hills revere small headless armless legless effigies made of hemp.

Worship with offerings of lacy
French knickers. Not joking

Why?

No idea

*　　*　　*

1926

The following morning a number of passengers aboard the *Dormouse* rose very early to catch their first glimpse of St Edward off the starboard bow. Harriet borrowed Lady Sutherland's binoculars, and hastened with Lettice to the upper foredeck, just below the bridge. At first only the sugarloaf silhouette of Mount Raglan, the dormant volcano that was the island's highest peak, was visible above the horizon. Then by degrees the north-eastern coast, at first a thin line of emerald green, gradually lengthened, and soon turned into a fine prospect, consisting of headlands and inlets, forests, small villages and prosperous looking farms—an essentially benign landscape with hints of lushness, and a wooded hinterland. The *Dormouse* altered course, and followed the coast.

"It looks just like Dorset," said Harriet.

"What nonsense, Hat," said Lettice. "When have you ever seen palm trees in Swanage?"

"I meant the shapes," said Harriet wistfully, "soft and rounded..." Her thoughts strayed.

"Rubbish," said Lettice. "Give me the binoculars." Lettice

squinted carefully. "Parts of Cornwall, possibly, though exaggerated. But Dorset? Never."

"Can you see any people?" asked Harriet.

"I can't see anything much," said Lettice, "just ... island, really." Bishop Stanley approached.

"Good morning, Bishop," said Lettice. "Here at last!"

"Indeed, yes. Good morning, Miss Sutherland," said the Bishop, "and Miss Sutherland, good morning."

"Good morning, Bishop," said Harriet, rather redundantly.

"The parish of St. George les Bains," said the Bishop, "begins about here, and goes all the way down to ... there." He gestured with economy. "A good sound man, Archdeacon Pearson." Lettice and Harriet had no reason to doubt it, but the Bishop could be pretty hard work. There was a long pause, while the Bishop filled his pipe.

"Mama says we are to be neighbours, Bishop. What fun," boomed Lettice.

"Indeed we are," said the Bishop. "Alas, Bishopscourt cannot compare with Government House for charm or convenience, except there is a flight of steps at the bottom of our garden that leads down to a secluded beach, very good for bathing. Mrs Stanley would be delighted to show you the way. Thenceforth you and Lady Sutherland must feel free to come and go as you please."

"Thank you so much, Bishop," said Harriet. "I'm sure we shall."

"Do you bathe, Bishop?" said Lettice.

"There is, I think, no absolute prohibition upon clerical bathing," said the Bishop, striking a match, "but," he puffed, "I find it is best avoided, unless the heat becomes unbearable."

"Is it unbearable very often, Bishop?" said Harriet, thinking of Rangoon.

"Fortunately not," he said with a kindly look. "Only between May and October."

Just then Mrs Hodgkinson approached, wearing a sort of shift-like burnouse of russet slub silk and a head-scarf.

"Good morning, Bishop," she said, by way of warm greeting.

"Good morning, Mrs Hodgkinson," said the Bishop, disguising some uneasiness with a gallant little bow.

"Good morning, Miss Sutherland," continued Mrs Hodgkinson, "and Miss Sutherland, good morning to you. *Sit*, Fang."

"Good morning," said Lettice, somewhat startled by Mrs Hodgkinson's appearance, to say nothing of Fang—with its big brown hungry eyes, dirty creature.

"Home," breathed Mrs Hodgkinson, with a hint of drama.

"Have you been away for long, Mrs Hodgkinson?" asked Harriet.

"Alas, far too long," Mrs Hodgkinson smiled faintly. "An extended sojourn in London, unavoidable I'm afraid."

"How I envy you. Mama seems to think London *is* best avoided," said Lettice. "We hardly ever go."

Mrs Hodgkinson fixed her gaze on the horizon. "There," she said, with elevated tone, pointing with the yellow forefinger of her right hand. "Cap Madeleine! They say it reminded Admiral Dubois of the breast of one of his many mistresses."

"Where?" asked Harriet with real interest. "Give me the binoculars, Let."

"Do please excuse me," said the Bishop, sensing danger. "I

must read the office." Mrs Hodgkinson smiled sweetly, as he turned and hurried away.

"It is the … formation … just to the left of Mount Raglan," she said, retracting her finger and touching her cheek. "Under certain conditions the rock resembles warm flesh. Yes, I quite see it," she turned to Harriet, "don't you?"

"I think so," said Harriet, doubtfully.

"Looks more like a loaf of bread to me," said Lettice loudly. "Are you sure we're looking at the same thing?"

"Quite sure," drawled Mrs Hodgkinson, lighting a cigarette.

"She must have been a bit flat-chested," Lettice added, uncooperatively.

"Recumbent," said Mrs Hodgkinson, patiently. "Merely recumbent. It is a place with many strong associations."

"Is that a village to the right of it?" said Harriet. "It looks tatty."

"Baie du Diable," said Mrs Hodgkinson. "An old French settlement. I am told each year on the Summer solstice, many islanders converge there from all corners of the Bailiwick and practice some of their charming local customs. Alas we Englishwomen are not welcome … Cigarette?"

"No thank you, Mrs Hodgkinson, we don't smoke," said Lettice, speaking as usual for Harriet.

"So kind of you to offer, though," said Harriet, who was simply longing to try.

"Local customs," reverted Lettice. "You mean no clothes? How shocking."

"Quite," said Mrs Hodgkinson, with a look. "You *are* well-informed." Lettice blushed.

"Commodore Bracegirdle has told us all about the locals, hasn't he Hat?"

"Yes, but he didn't say anything about the Summer solstice," said Harriet. "It sounds exciting. Perhaps we could dress up as men and make an expedition."

Mrs Hodgkinson reached down and touched Harriet's cheek.

"Dear child," she said, amused by the thought that not even the most voluminous French farmer's smock would conceal that huge bust.

"What an absurd idea, Hat," said Lettice, also thinking through the contents of the dressing-up box. "Besides, St. Francis of Assisi is not C. of E.," said Lettice. "Strictly out of bounds."

Sometimes Harriet found Lettice's firmness a little oppressive.

Miss Davies closed *Seraglio Governess* and carefully concealed it in one of her hat boxes. She then made sure that that particular hat box was concealed behind and beneath several others, and a large suitcase placed in front of these. She lifted the blind a fraction, ascertained that the coast was clear, then raised it all the way up and peered through her porthole. Miss Davies had been so absorbed by reading since breakfast, and so pleasantly distracted, that the sight of the island, not unexpected, nevertheless gave her a start. What a lurid, Oasis of Shalimar sort of green, she thought. Those poplars and whatnot must almost resemble the lush date groves that surround the Palace of Huffuf in which the Sultan detains those of his wives who are inclined to be rebellious, as well as his slaves and eunuchs ... On the other hand, no doubt there were masses of birds, which would keep Lady S. happy. Such an extraordinary predilection, bird-watching, in which one was naturally obliged to share with equal if not even greater enthusiasm. The forested hinterland certainly looked suitable for brisk walks, possibly even riding, picnics, and shooting. The coast was a different matter. The beaches looked mercifully hemmed in by ugly brown cliffs, *that* one in particular—not unlike the one from which the Sultan's bodyguard hurls to her certain death the lately ravished younger daughter of his sworn enemy, the Caliph—so thank goodness there could be no question of bathing. Unfortunately, Lady Sutherland was very fond of bathing, which of course meant that, officially, Miss Davies liked nothing better than to bathe too. In point of fact she loathed it. Her least unflattering bathing costume was made from a thick dark blue woollen material, which, following immersion, persisted in clinging to her body, very heavily, and not in any of the ways that Gwladys Baring described in such astonishing detail. Yet the same was true of Lady Sutherland's costume—it clung and clung—but *she* didn't seem to mind that it made her look exactly like the Michelin man. Nor, come to think of it, did Lettice and Harriet. Miss Davies thought of an article in one of the illustrated weeklies that she had been reading a few days earlier—where could it be?—which dealt with the new fad for beauty patches worn on the back of the neck or the shoulder, to draw attention to the milky whiteness of the skin. She might have tried it, except the authoress went on to say that this was a fancy … where was it?—*here*! "a fancy only for the really young and plump, and not for women who have what a well-known artist describes as 'corrugations at the nape.'" Miss Davies threw the paper aside with disgust. Lettice and Harriet were young and definitely plump—actually fat. Miss Davies peered into her mirror and sighed. Her marcel wave was terribly smart, if hard to maintain, but there could be no doubt that her nape was what that well-known artist would almost certainly describe as corrugated. And if he was so very well-known, why not name the swine?

Commodore Bracegirdle and Sir George Sutherland strolled to a private spot, universally eschewed by all the other passengers, on the windward side, facing away from the island.

"No fresh signals, I'm afraid Sir George," said Bracegirdle. Sir George pondered over his pipe.

"I suppose the knack with Orlando is not to give him the slightest reason to suspect."

"Exactly."

"Lady Sutherland is transparently hostile, which is inconvenient."

"Not at all, Sir George," said Bracegirdle. "It would be far more suspicious, ludicrous even, if Lady Sutherland welcomed the blighter with open arms. Even polite neutrality would be most implausible. I think you have struck the perfect balance, if I may say so."

"How does Whitehall think he communicates with these blasted rebels?"

"Uncertain. As you know, the strongest suspicions relate to Beck, but we daren't give him any reason to think they exist."

"But he'd be severely touched if he thought they didn't." Sir George paused. "Or perhaps whoever is running the show genuinely thinks we are the greater fools."

"One does one's best to encourage it."

"And Strickland certainly succeeded. Damned fool will have convinced them."

"I'm sure I can't say."

"And meanwhile this Beck is a positive asset to Runyard Barton Riley?"

"Quite," said Bracegirdle. "He's working on the headquarters of the new bank, and according to Hodgkinson they can't function without him. Of course he *may* be loyal. His railway viaduct even won a prize."

"Did it, by God?"

"Thought to be something of an innovation."

Sir George pondered this. "Yes, I do see the problem. You have confidence in Pole?"

"Absolute confidence, Sir."

"So does Whitehall. It is true, however, that extended tours can cause even the best men to wobble."

"Not in the Colonel's case, I'm quite sure of it Sir."

"Glad to hear it."

Bracegirdle cleared his throat.

"If I might venture to suggest ..."

"It would be criminal if you didn't, Bracegirdle." The Governor-designate twinkled. The brilliance of Sir George was that the sharpest tactical mind was deftly concealed beneath cuddly layers of good nature, and the appearance of something that veered dangerously towards half-wittedness. Bracegirdle had at first been surprised, then impressed, but now he was lost in admiration. After all, with Strickland it had been the opposite, a genuine half-wit masquerading as a self-declared genius of strategy.

"... If Lady Sutherland were to accept the invitation of the Royal Society," ventured Bracegirdle.

"Ah yes, I see," said Sir George. "Engage him in that way? Watch him in less formal situations too, is that it?"

"Precisely." They looked thoughtfully out to sea. A mist was in the offing.

"One might say, Bracegirdle, that not since the Glory Days of Rome has the flight of birds assumed such economic and strategic importance. And you should know that Her Ladyship is easily capable of reading the entrails," Sir George puffed affably. "*Not* to be underestimated." He laid particular emphasis with the stem of his pipe.

"I don't doubt it, Sir."

"Just keep it in the back of your mind. And now I suppose I must go and put on those absurd clothes."

"Ah, Madame," said M. Orlando. "What feelings of joy arise in the bosom?" He gave Mrs Stanley a fright. "At last, St Edward, our island home."

"Good morning, M. Orlando," returned Mrs Stanley, adopting a brisk tone, for she made a point of avoiding the subject of bosoms. "Not long now."

"She is like a beautiful maiden, caressed in the morning sun, yes?" He gestured with unctuous rapture.

"Always charming." Mrs Stanley wondered at the impertinence of the man.

"A *sirène* ... what is the English word, Madame?"

"Mermaid," said Mrs Stanley, through reluctantly unpursed

lips. Of *course* he knew the word for mermaid, what did he take her for?

"A *mermaid*, yes, calling us back with sweet songs of love!" M. Orlando sighed.

"So vivid," said Mrs Stanley, "but you know perfectly well the Bishop's call is a higher one." She took a deep breath, and adjusted her head-scarf. "'Lead Kindly Light', M. Orlando. For us it is the call of *duty*." M. Orlando ignored this gentle reproach.

"The Bishop is quite well today?"

"Quite well, thank you."

"We are fortunate indeed that relations between His Lordship and Monsignieur Lebecq are so cordial. Gone are the *désagréments* of recent years ..."

"Too kind," said Mrs Stanley, who disliked the nuns and regarded Monsignieur Lebecq with scarcely conceivable distaste. "I'm sure the Bishop merely reflects the current view at Lambeth."

"So enlightened," purred Orlando, noticing that Mrs Stanley made no effort to agree with him.

"Good morning, Colin," said Lady Sutherland.

"Good morning, Lady Sutherland." Colin was in uniform.

"What a splendid sight," she went back to her binoculars. "An Ashy Stormpetrel, how marvellous. We've already spotted the Wedge-tailed Shearwater, and a Sooty Tern—quite a long way farther out than one might expect. Plucky little thing."

Colin noticed Lady Sutherland's use of the first person plural. He made a satisfactory little "ah" sound. "The Captain says we are two and a half hours out."

"Excellent." Lady Sutherland lowered her binoculars. "Colin, dear, you will keep an eye on Harriet, won't you? Oh, I'm so sorry …"

"That's quite all right, Lady Sutherland." Colin was used to it.

"So thoughtless, I'm sure …" She reverted: "I am thinking in particular of that grotesque M. Orlando."

"Quite."

"You noticed too?"

"Yes."

"Impressionable girl. And *very* young."

"I shall watch closely." Colin tapped the cheekbone adjacent to his good eye, and smiled a smile of reassurance.

"Thank you, Colin." Lady Sutherland, suppressing all doubt. "I'm quite sure you will. And now I suppose I must dress."

The pilot went aboard at half past two. The *Dormouse* reached the outer harbour at half past three. The Commanding Officer, St Edward Station, the Chief Justice, the Chief Secretary, and Colonel Pole went aboard a little later. The Governor had spent some considerable time clambering into his Colonial Office uniform, with sword and cocked hat and white ostrich feathers, from the ancient firm of Ede, Son & Ravenscroft of Chancery Lane. Accompanied by Lady Sutherland and their suite, Sir George transferred to the tender, and approached Queen Victoria Quay. There, amid bunting and cheering crowds, Sir George took the salute of the 2nd (Duchess of York's Own) St Edward Rifles; carried out a lengthy inspection, before he and Lady Sutherland entered the rear compartment of the Rolls Royce. Foster gingerly guided it the short distance to Treasury, where, on a dais, Judge

Box, the Chief Justice, who had followed in the cramped little Austin, administered the oath of office. There was more cheering; the presentation of Executive Councillors, and many officials in descending order of importance, whereupon His newly-sworn Excellency and Lady Sutherland re-entered the Rolls Royce, which made its lumbering way back through the narrow streets of Port Charlotte, along the quay, where by then the *Dormouse* was docking. Foster turned past the gate-house of Government House, and laboured up the drive. For the first time in more than a month, the Governor's standard was broken out, and fluttered from the flagstaff. The customary seventeen-gun salute rang out from the observatory bluff. Thus Sir George Sutherland assumed the government of St Edward, Gwern and the Thimble Isles, the Bailiwick of St Edward.

In the midst of general excitement, and with the seventeen-gun salute booming in the background, general disembarkation was about to commence. Gene appeared at the door of Mrs Hodgkinson's state room. She was arranging a few filmy things into the last of her trunks.

"Gene, darling. Ready?" she said.

"Not quite, my dear," said Gene. He hovered, exhibiting that tense, slightly feverish expression Mrs Hodgkinson knew well, but preferred to think of as his method of "smouldering." Gene entered, and abruptly closed and locked the door behind him.

"Oh darling, really. They're coming for the trunks in a minute," said Mrs Hodgkinson, and then, with an indulgent smile, "You are *naughty*."

Gene advanced, looking shifty, his complexion slightly orange.

"Kiss me, Magnolia," he panted, not enfolding Mrs Hodgkinson in the warmth of his embrace so much as executing a brilliantly effective mid-field diving tackle.

"Oh, Gene ..."

A few minutes later, surprisingly few, Mrs Hodgkinson reclined in some disarray, smoking one of her black Sobranie cigarettes. Such passion on a Thursday afternoon! She began to think about getting dressed. From time to time Gene reminded her of the rooster which had ruled over the hen house at Little Mainwaring, Mrs Hodgkinson's childhood home near Lewes in Sussex—the sidling motion, almost furtive, with which he approached; the sudden pounce; the vigorous but brief coupling; above all, the flamboyant preening afterwards. All quite similar. She adjusted her stays. Mrs Hodgkinson had been an only child, the neglected daughter of minor gentry. They would have been landed gentry except there was no longer any land. Of course, Sir Carrick, her father, had maintained appearances, setting himself the task of polishing off such contents of the ancestral cellar as had rapidly dwindled through the previous two generations. Shoes, where? There.

Then, during the Panic of 1893, Daddy sold Julius, her pony, for which Mrs Hodgkinson never could forgive him. Or did they eat the poor creature? She couldn't be sure they hadn't. Powder compact. She shuddered, looked in the mirror once more, adjusted her toque, smiled faintly, and took up her reticule.

"Come, Fang," said Mrs Hodgkinson. They swept out.

High on the eastern slopes of Mount Raglan, where the old, disused bridle path widened into a small clearing overhung with vines, tangled but lush, Jacob Beck watched the arrival and disembarkation through his new field binoculars. With him was a lanky youth, not much more than a boy with a knapsack. They had come from opposite directions, carefully signalling at first with an exchange of low whistles.

"So, Mimo, this is the great Sir George Sutherland," said Jacob. They lay side-by-side on their tummies at the edge of a little escarpment from which there was a clear view over Port Charlotte.

"Yes boss."

"He looks just as ridiculous as Sir Henry Strickland. Take a look."

Mimo laughed. "They love their ostrich feathers, boss."

"Don't be fooled, Mimo my friend, this Sir George is a very dangerous man." M. Orlando had warned Jacob.

"Yes boss." Mimo squinted for a bit. "But see? They are fat. We can run much faster," he said with a grin.

"Not when you're full of passa, Mimo," said Jacob, shaking his finger. "Pole can do more with his one arm than the rest of you can do with both of yours when you are full to the brim with passa. Never forget that!"

"Yes boss." Mimo looked down sheepishly.

"And that's without a cask of maman mastise," scolded Jacob. He paused for a moment, then, smiling, reached for his flask. "Here."

"Thanks boss." Mimo grinned once more, and took a swig. "Cripes boss, whew," he said with a grimace.

"This new batch is *good*," Jacob chuckled. "But that's all you're getting today."

"Yes boss."

Jacob took back his binoculars. "We shall see, my friend, we shall see," he said.

"Yes boss." Mimo was not quite sure what they would see, but like all young rebels, proud fighters for freedom, he earnestly hoped that, whatever it was, they would see it very soon.

"You delivered my messages?"

"Yes boss."

"And we're all ready?"

"Yes boss."

"And no passa till after we take delivery?" Jacob frowned.

"No boss."

"Easy on the mastise too." Jacob wagged his finger again.

"Yes boss."

"He is a great hero, this man from Paris. You must show him you are worthy."

"Yes boss."

"And follow his instructions to the letter, is that understood?"

"Yes boss."

"Tell the others I said so."

"Yes boss."

"What did I say, Mimo?"

"That you said so boss."

Jacob breathed a silent prayer for patience.

"No, Mimo. What did I tell you to say *before* I told you to say it?"

Mimo thought hard for a moment. "To follow his instructions to the letter, boss?"

"Yes Mimo. That's right."

"Boss?"

"Yes, Mimo."

"What does this man from Paris look like? How will we know it is him?"

"You will know. He will be in charge. It will be obvious, Mimo. He is a great soldier, a hero of the Mandingo Wars."

"Yes boss." Mimo had no idea what the Mandingo Wars were, but they sounded fierce. And Mimo was not sure how obvious it would be. For Jacob alone was his hero. There was no other.

"Any questions?"

"When can we get the new mastise boss?"

"Forget about the mastise, Mimo," Jacob raised his voice. "Afterwards. *Not* now."

"Yes boss."

"You know the signal?"

"Yes boss."

"What is it?"

"One long flash, two short, one long. Then wait a minute. Then the same."

"That's right Mimo. And the proper response?"

"Boss?"

"So you know it's them, and not the pilot or a fishing boat. Concentrate Mimo."

"Oh, yes boss. Two...no...Three short flashes, one long, then three short."

"Correct. Very good Mimo."

"Thanks boss." Mimo was inclined to preen.

"All right. Now go."

"Yes boss," said Mimo.

"And *be careful*," Jacob cried as Mimo darted off along the mountain path, back the way he came.

Merde, thought Jacob.

His field binoculars were a gift to Jacob from the Royal Society of St Edward, of which he had recently become a member. It was a fine optical instrument, supplied by the firm of Kershaw & Sons of Leeds. Jacob was very proud of his binoculars, prouder of them, in fact, than Foster was proud of the Governor's Rolls Royce. Jacob could see how well his binoculars were made, how ingenious was the mechanism, and how fine the quality of the lenses. Zeiss, he thought to himself; precision German lenses, what an irony!

In the beginning M. Orlando had suggested Jacob might begin to correspond with the British Ornithologists' Union about the rare birds of the St Edward Group. Jacob was patient. He looked into the matter very carefully. He visited the public library. He knew what he was doing. Carefully he wrote and posted his first letter concerning the southern-most recorded sighting of Baer's Pochard, at a spot farther south by a thousand miles than anywhere it had ever before been spotted. Just think of that! In due course this was greeted with much enthusiasm in London. Inquiries had been made, and a request for more information addressed to Jacob with lively interest. In his methodical way Jacob responded to each and all subsequent letters from the British Ornithologists' Union. And, at length, this was the happy result: full membership of the Royal Society of St Edward, despite raised eyebrows, and a fine new pair of

Kershaw field binoculars. Jacob took another swig from his flask. It was all part of M. Orlando's plan but, somewhat to his surprise, Jacob had become genuinely interested in birds. He took up his binoculars once more. Aha, Xantus's Murrelet, he thought. Now that is unusual. He put his binoculars back in their leather case, jotted in his little notebook. He got up, brushed his hands on his jacket, adjusted his satchel, then strode back down the mountain path towards Port Charlotte, a satisfied bird-watcher merely taking full advantage of the public holiday.

Closer to home, having skirted the bosky perimeter of the secluded Villa Les Humeurs, Jacob took the roundabout route that would take him past the new viaduct. Without stopping, he needed discreetly to check the exact position of the transom seats.

CHAPTER 6

A Hero of the Mandingo Wars

Mike and Sharon
2020

Why

> No idea. What about
> Norman Threlfall, name on
> trunk. Nothing in database,
> Google, wiki.

Who cares? Just get research
to locate file then fucking
deal with it normal way. But
make sure you do it yourself.
End of story G2G

> ILY2 wanker

On 29 Jan 2020, at 6:43 pm, Sharon Julius <u>sharonj@fcoff.gov.</u><u>uk</u> wrote:

Dear Dr Carter

All Foreign and Commonwealth Office records relating to the
suzerain entity and Crown Protectorate of St Edward, Gwern and

the Thimble Isles (the Bailiwick of St Edward) were unfortunately destroyed during the Blitz.

Obviously, moving forward, all police, forensic and coronial issues relating to the discovery of which the Prime Minister has confidentially been made aware are in the hands of the relevant authorities in the Bailiwick.

HM government is not in a position to make any further comment, other than that (should it become necessary) any suggestion that British authorities have ever engaged in, sanctioned or condoned the use of torture—in this or any other case falling under the jurisdiction of the St Edward Group (or merely relating to it)—is preposterous and unfounded.

Yours sincerely,

Ms Sharon Julius
Second Assistant Under-Secretary, Political Affairs
Foreign and Commonwealth Office
Whitehall

Please consider the environment before printing this email message.

Fuck

What?

Nob in PMs office seeking
more detail

*　*　*

1926

That evening there was an informal household dinner at Government House. Lady Sutherland had made certain revisions to the menu upon conferring for the first time with Cook and Mr Craddock. Clear Gravy Soup, Stewed Eels, Fried Soles, Curried Lobster with Rice, Croquettes of Fowl with Piquant Sauce, Saddle of Mutton, Conservative Pudding, Stilton and Celery. Start as you mean to continue, she thought, and Cook's initial proposals had seemed a little mendicant. Mr Craddock's sibilance, meanwhile, was slightly surprising, but harmless enough.

"Your Excellency, dinner is served."

Issuing from Mr Craddock's lips that familiar phrase, heard throughout the Empire, sounded slightly ridiculous, a line from a music hall review. Never mind. All in all, the domestic arrangements seemed first rate, and the housekeeper, Mrs Huntingfield, a model of efficiency. None of the arcane complexities attaching to the habits of dear, obtuse Mrs Jhunjhunwallah and her vast army of difficult house-servants in Rangoon—so many of whom were prevented from carrying out certain perfectly simple tasks by virtue of caste. Such a relief to be able to leave all that behind. Lady Sutherland could tell that she and Mrs Huntingfield would see eye to eye.

After dinner the ladies retired to the large drawing-room, and, over port and cigars, the gentlemen discussed the most recent and alarming display of civil unrest.

"Agir! Désobéir! Indeed," said Sir George. "We'll see about that."

"Obviously the offending graffito was removed immediately," said Pole.

"In red?"

"Sir George?"

"It was written in red?"

"Yes, Sir George."

"Capitals?"

"Yes, Sir George," said the Colonel, doubtfully.

"Emphatic. Hints at Bolshevism. It simply won't do."

"Dangerous," said Norman.

"Outrageous," said Colin.

"I doubt if the locals have the foggiest notion of what a Bolshevist is," said Surgeon Commander Clark in his balanced way. There was a pause. "Reassuring?" he added hopefully.

"If I may, Sir George," said Bracegirdle. "Nothing in the past has been so bold as this."

"That is certainly true," said Clark.

"Bold it may be, but still rather childish. I mean there was no other damage?" asked Sir George.

"Nothing physical," said Pole. "though one's concern is that it was so plainly visible. The whole town saw it."

"Indeed. Can't have that. I suppose we shall have to telegraph Whitehall. How secure is the cipher?" Sir George's eye narrowed.

"Quite secure," said Pole.

"Yes, but assuming it *isn't*—nobody's fault, you understand, a bright spark in the Post Office, a spy (God forbid), or some other exposure, even in Whitehall ..." Sir George lit his pipe.

"Sir George?"

"I mean the contents must be factual, and obviously true,

but the tone, Pole … the tone must be supremely complacent, even oblivious. Steady as she goes. We don't want to frighten the horses. Not at least until we have successfully engaged with Beck."

"Yes, I see." Colonel Pole enjoyed schemes. Bracegirdle nodded.

"One should assume that, for whatever reason, by whatever means, my despatches and telegrams are reaching the French, possibly even through Orlando, but without giving them cause to suspect we know they are. Of course, they may not be reaching the French, but we cannot rule it out. You follow?" Sir George twinkled in his rotund, enigmatic way.

"The constabulary are rather excited," said Bracegirdle.

"So they should be," said Sir George. "But are they any good?"

"Hopeless."

"Running around in circles," proffered Clark.

"So there is no possibility that they will make an inconvenient arrest, however remote?"

"None, Sir George," said Bracegirdle with firmness, vaguely suggesting—had one chosen to notice this—that Naval Intelligence was on top of that particular problem.

"Do make sure of it," Sir George gestured with the stem of his pipe. "That would complicate matters fearfully. This passamanana," he continued brightly, apparently changing the subject.

"Sir George?"

"Have you tried it, Pole?"

"Once or twice, Sir. Seems harmless enough. There can be difficulties when it is taken to excess."

"Grave difficulties," said Clark.

"Jolly good," said Sir George thoughtfully. "Shall we join the ladies? I fancy a rubber of bridge …"

As the gentlemen were deeply preoccupied by this discussion and with passing the port to the left, M. Orlando was panting slightly as he started to climb the stairs above the Café des Artistes in the French Quarter, unable to restrain himself from indulging in a little diversion following upon such a prolonged absence in London. But there was another reason.

Madame Beck was a handsome, middle-aged woman, fully accustomed to moving effortlessly between her two establishments, the one downstairs—where she was spry, affable and public—the other, upstairs, necessarily private, occasionally requiring a much firmer disposition. She was dressed suitably for both businesses, except that she wore on most of her available fingers many unusual rings; on her breast a curious brooch of luminous blue-green opal—intricately carved with the head of the Medusa—and around her neck a long sautoir. The untrained eye presumed that, in combination, all these improbably flashy stones were mere paste, cheap and gaudy—congruent, let us say, with the slightly theatrical toilette with which the hard-working proprietress of the Café des Artistes presented herself to her guests. Mrs Huntingfield, however, had long since concluded that they were the real thing, magnificent jewels in the moribund Edwardian taste given to Madame Beck in her youth by a succession of wealthy lovers, and, in one far more recent instance, by Sir Henry Strickland himself—such a reckless act of indiscretion. Aquamarines, peridots, fancy pink and yellow diamonds of impressive size, toxic-looking jades, astringent square citrines, flashing amethysts, cabochon emeralds.

To the extent that it was knowable, the history of Madame Beck was far more colourful even than her personal appearance suggested. Her late husband was said to be the younger son of a large old French family in the north of the island, who was peremptorily disowned after contracting a scandalous, prodigal *mésalliance* with the racy and much older Madame Beck. In fact, there was no Monsieur Beck, and never had been. He was a carefully concocted fiction, one of those vital assets with which Madame Beck surrounded herself as a form of insurance. She had learned, correctly, that money is the most effective protection against the uncertainties of fate, so she was, with her overladen fingers, deft in the rapid but invariably accurate counting of sheaves of crisp St Edward pound notes. That is what she was doing while M. Orlando slowly climbed the stairs. Seated at a charming little bureau in the style of Napoleon III, she checked her tally of cash-in-hand against the relevant column in her account book.

Madame Beck grieved the loss of her two eldest sons, for whose violent deaths in France, one at Vimy, the other at Fromelles, she bitterly blamed the British. She was fiercely protective of her daughter and surviving son. She had no intention of allowing Nathalie to work in her establishment in any capacity other than that of laundry maid. Even that gave her some anxiety; she worried more generally about the future of her children. Jacob, with his crazy ideas of independence, ran the risk, it seemed to her, of losing his good job with the engineering firm, Nathalie with her romantic dreams, forever wanting to go dancing at the Dreamland Ballroom. Madame Beck sighed. She had had dreams of her own, so it was hardly surprising. Still, she would have liked to see them both respectably married, just as her own poor maman had nurtured the same ambition in the disgraceful nineties. How they had quarrelled.

Madame Beck looked about her anteroom. It was decorated with fading portrait engravings of illustrious French courtesans: Madame du Barry, Rosalie Duthé, Claudine de Tencin, La Païva ... Through an amusing bead curtain was the big parlour, dimly lit, in which most of her other girls reclined, in various states of déshabillé, on hard divans with dusty velvet cushions. The desultory motions of a ceiling fan stirred the perfumed air, but failed to relieve the atmosphere of its cloying stuffiness. The Siamese cat stretched on the mantelpiece. One of the girls was filling an exotic-looking pipe. Soft murmurs, as well as more suggestive noises, drifted from the direction of the narrow dark corridor farther distant.

M. Orlando reached the landing, paused, mopped his brow, wiped his hands, and knocked at the door, the customary knock.

"Entrez, s'il vous plaît," sang Madame Beck, after closing her account book, locking it with the cash in her drawer, and concealing the key deep within her proud embonpoint. The outer door opened.

"Ah, M. Orlando, we have missed you," cried Madame Beck, rising to her feet and extending her hand in a crisply professional way.

"Dear Madame, ravishing as always," replied M. Orlando, stooping sweatily to kiss her hand.

"And how are our dear friends in London?"

"Prospering as always, Madame. They particularly asked me to send you their warm greetings."

"But monsieur," she laughed, "one's bankers always do!"

"Madame will not be disappointed."

Madame Beck sincerely hoped not. She continued to smile as brightly as possible, but could see that such matters were best left for the hours of daylight. "And which of my girls is to be favoured by Monsieur this evening? You cause me a great deal of trouble, Monsieur! They fight over you. I hear whispers of your prowess."

"Madame is too kind."

"And not only whispers, *mon vieux*!" chuckled Madame, who was not being kind at all. Madame was at the highest level of alertness, laced with fear—for in her mind Orlando's power knew no bounds. And in a very real sense she was right. The consul of France had the means to ruin her; but so did Colonel Pole. It was, in both cases, a *mariage de convenance*, impossible but necessary—financially necessary, legally necessary, vital every way one looked at it. Flattery was essential, but not too much. Never once abandoning her bright tone of welcome, Madame Beck went on to ask M. Orlando whether this evening—such a fine evening!—it was to be the exotically tattooed Angeline? Yvette, the Venus Butterfly? Ingenious Agmaya, mistress of the tantric arts? The lovely, compliant sisters Lulu and Valérie? Mademoiselle Ch'ang, lately arrived from Shanghai, renowned for her unusual skill with lengths of twine? Madame Beck lowered her voice.

"René, there was a time when..." She picked a spec of lint off M. Orlando's lapel.

"Dear Madame," said M. Orlando, coldly ignoring the gesture, "will you not relent, and permit me this evening to love Nathalie, your beautiful laundry maid?"

"Mais non, you *rascal*," said Madame Beck, with a ripple of finely calibrated laughter. "You know perfectly well she is my only daughter. What kind of mother do you take me for?"

M. Orlando, a man of the world, understood the true nature of a mother's affection, and therefore offered Madame double the normal rate. Madame Beck considered the offer for a moment, then slapped him playfully on the wrist.

"Perhaps *mon vieux*, we shall see. *Mais une autre tard peut-être*." He really means it, *ce cochon-là*, she thought with dread.

M. Orlando made a great show of disappointment, then agreed to settle for Lulu and Valérie. However, he begged first to have a quiet word with Nathalie. He had a message for her brother Jacob.

"Nathalie!" called Madame Beck.

At Government House the party had broken up. Sir George and Lady Sutherland had retired. Mr Craddock had cleared the table, and, having shared the last of the port with Cook and Foster in the butler's pantry, all had gone to their beds—Mr Craddock, as usual, after a discreet interval, silently slipping into Foster's room.

Colonel Pole, Captain Campbell, and Surgeon Commander Clark slept restlessly, troubled by indigestion.

Lettice Sutherland snored peacefully, but, in the next room, under the bedclothes with a strong torch her sister Harriet was reading *Seraglio Governess* by Gwladys Baring, from time to time wiping the fog from her spectacles.

... while Cynthia shrank beneath the Sultan's volcanic gaze. She desperately sought some route of escape, some path to safety. There was none. The rope ladder had been removed. The caravan had long since departed. The Begum's mysterious elixir of love, tasting of cloves and hashish, had gone to her head.

"You must know how completely you belong to me," rasped the Sultan, looming closer, the hilt of his bejewelled dagger glinting in the moonlight.

"Vile beast!" spat Cynthia, "You shall never possess me. I should rather die!"

The Sultan laughed his cruel laugh, fixed her with his flashing coal-black eyes, then seized Cynthia to his manly breast. "Ah, you English—such defiance," he breathed, touching her cheek. "You would do well to learn the ancient customs of the desert, for there can be no escape from the Palace of Huffuf."

"Take your hands off me, or I swear I shall scream," gasped Cynthia, beating with her clenched fists His Highness's superbly muscular chest, but struggling in vain—beginning, alas, to waver in her resolve. There was something in his voice. What was it? What was the strange power that lurked beneath his superb, dreadful countenance, behind that diabolical beard? Cynthia swooned.

"You *dare* to resist me? You are mine, wholly mine, I tell you," he barked suddenly.

A blond tress fell across her heaving, milk-white bosom.

"Monster! Blackguard!" Cynthia's heart beat faster. She felt his hot breath on her cheek as the Sultan tore the thin veil of silk from …

In his tiny room next to the laundry Old Sock had been dreaming of gloomy, windswept moors; the lowering Highland mists, the frigid damp, to which, in waking moments, he knew he would never return. Instead he sighed, turned over, and fixed his mind on the prudent layering of compost.

And in his quarters Norman quietly wound his gramophone, and, placing a pillow in the amplifying trumpet to muffle the sound, put his recently purchased record on the turntable. As the moonlight flooded through the window, he swayed slowly, and thought of the girl from the Café des Artistes.

Much later that night, while with impressive vigour above the Café des Artistes M. Orlando disported himself with Lulu and Valérie; while in Government House Colonel Pole sat in his office writing diligently; while, unable to sleep, Mrs Huntingfield once again laid out a *most* unpromising arrangement of Tarot cards; far away, atop the high cliffs that line the rugged west coast of St Edward—daunting ramparts that plunge sheer into the Atlantic Ocean, unusually calm under a brilliant full moon—there were flashes of light. From his vantage point above the sandy inlet, the only break in the western cliffs, Mimo struggled with his lantern. One long flash, two short, one long—followed by a long pause. He had been doing this for several hours, but just when he was about to give up, there was an answering flash from out to sea. Mimo's heart started pounding. They're here! Faintly he made out the dark silhouette of a vessel which carried no running lights. He thought with envy of Jacob's binoculars. He stared hard for a minute, and realized the vessel was riding at anchor. Three short flashes, one long, three short. The proper signal in return. It's them! Scarcely able to contain his excitement, Mimo checked and adjusted his wick to increase the flame, and hung his hurricane lamp from the nearest thorny branch of a stunted ox tree. Then he half-ran, half-stumbled back to join the others.

"Gabriel! Patrice! Léo! Wake up! They're here!"

Huddled bodies stirred around the embers of a neglected camp fire. Groans and giggles mingled with yawns and sceptical noises of protest.

"Come on!"

"Take it easy Mimo."

"You know what the boss said. Léo! Help me with the mules. They'll be landing any minute."

"What's the rush? They can land, but where will they go?" There was general laughter.

"We must show them we are worthy!"

"Worthy of a bit more passa before we go, Mimo," There were one or two unruly hoots.

As rebels went, this was a sorry assortment, but after a few more minutes of catarrhal laughter, unsuitable badinage, and other disorderly conduct, Mimo managed to lead the undisciplined little party—not more than a dozen slouching men and three mules—down the steep narrow path to the beach. There they lolled waiting, chewing and smoking their passamanana and gulping mastise from battered flasks, from time to time giggling.

Once or twice even Mimo took a guilty puff from Léo's pipe. "You will thank me, Léo, after this is done," he said.

"Oh will I?"

"Jacob will reward us."

"Maybe he will reward himself."

"Léo, that's a terrible thing to say."

"You think with a few boxes of old rifles we will get rid of the English?"

"Enough of that."

"Just saying." Léo puffed on his pipe.

"We shall gain our independence, Léo! And France will help us!"

"If you say so, Mimo. *Republique du Passamanana...*" laughed Léo.

"Be quiet, sssh!" Mimo heard the creaking of rowlocks, and the gentle plash of oars.

"*...Royaume de Mastise!*"

"Léo, shut up!"

They saw a dark shape against the moonlit wash of surf. The longboat scraped gently onto the little sandy beach. Three Lascar crewmen jumped out and carefully heaved it farther up. Urged to action by Mimo, the men, each taking a last, generous slug of mastise, rose somewhat unwillingly to help. A big man, more powerful than the other newcomers, leapt out of the longboat into the shallows and waded onto the beach. Serge Di Bartolo, veteran of the Mandingo Wars, had arrived with his load of antiquated ordnance.

"Welcome to Saint-Édouard, Monsieur. I am Mimo."

Di Bartolo sniffed, and looked around.

"Commandant Jacob sends his warm greetings," continued Mimo. "We are at your service. *Vive la France*!" He stood to attention and saluted.

But this is a boy, thought Di Bartolo, a child! He sniffed again. "Bring the mules closer," he snapped.

"Yes boss," said Mimo.

Mimo ran up the beach, and returned with the men and the mules. Bunch of scrawny no-hopers, thought Di Bartolo. They'd have lasted five minutes on the Côte d'Ivoire! Not even. He gave a sign. The unloading began.

Léo, Gabriel and Patrice struggled at first with a heavy crate full of rusting Franco-Prussian War rifles, huffing and puffing and making heavy weather of it. But they managed to lift the crate out of the longboat and onto the back of the first mule. The animal whimpered under this unaccustomed burden, but Mimo led it, wobbling, up the beach and onto the steep path that led up the gully.

This was his own mule, and he loved the poor beast.

Di Bartolo tugged at the back of his trousers, adjusting his unruly foundation garment, and bent down to lift the second crate, unassisted. Like most veteran *légionnaires étrangères*, Serge Di Bartolo was very strong and could never resist an opportunity to demonstrate his physical prowess—despite, in this case, or perhaps because of, the laughably poor quality of his audience. As Di Bartolo heaved the massive box to his chest, Gabriel and Léo, who both had clearly consumed far too much passamanana, together with a lot of mastise, each carelessly picked up a box of dynamite. Di Bartolo was alarmed. He froze. Peering over the top of the box of rifles, he just managed to hiss, "*Mais non!*" before Gabriel stumbled on a cleat and fell, landing heavily on the other boxes of dynamite, which were well past their prime, and very unstable.

ST EDWARD CLARION

"Society Notes," by Sylvia.

All Port Charlotte flocked to Queen Victoria Quay yesterday to greet the new Governor, His Excellency Sir George Sutherland, his family and their suite. Among other notables aboard the *Dormouse* were the Bishop and Mrs Stanley, Mr Orlando, and Professor and Mrs Gene Hodgkinson, returning to us at last from their extended stay in London. The ceremonies evinced the most enthusiastic interest among the ladies of St Edward. Sir George, utterly resplendent in his court uniform and cocked hat with ostrich feathers, was escorted by the gentlemen of the household, led by gallant Colonel Pole and our own dear Commodore Bracegirdle. But the new aides-de-camp, handsome Lieutenant Threlfall, R.N. (who, it will be recalled, preceded the official party by several days and is therefore by now familiar to us all) and dashing Captain Campbell won the hearts of the debutantes, between whom we gather the lines of battle are now being drawn.

Their mothers, meanwhile, who greeted the new Governor's lady with particular warmth, looked at her cool beige frock of georgette with panels of silver tissue, her handsome Burmese emerald brooch, her broad-brimmed hat of moss-green crinoline adorned with bird-of-paradise feathers, and sighed enviously, for Lady Sutherland and her daughters possess that ravishing English complexion which novelists and poets have made famous. Miss Lettice wore Jade marocain with an enchanting fawn threaded hat, and Miss Harriet pale powder-pink moirette, and a sweet little cloche hat of matching hue. Smart envelope purses, we noted, in winning contrast to brightly-coloured shoes and gloves to match, the latter carried, not worn—too clever. Miss Maud Davies, who was in attendance, wore an interesting frock of plain grey velour and a brown hat of straw. With Lady Sutherland as châtelaine, we feel certain, Government House will sparkle as it rarely has in recent years. We are told the Visitors' Book is quite mobbed, for many ladies are already vying for their invitation to the first Sutherland garden party, soirée, or, dare we hope, a dinner-dance?

"Who is Sylvia?" asked Lady Sutherland, looking up from that morning's *Clarion*. She and Miss Davies were conferring after breakfast in the small upstairs sitting-room.

"What is she?" replied Miss Davies, wittily, touching one of her corrugations. "I am making inquiries, Lady S."

"She must have been carrying a telescope, although I would hardly describe Lettice's hat as 'fawn.' 'Oyster-gold,' isn't that how the nancy milliner in Jermyn Street described it? Still, she could be *very* useful."

"Yes, Lady S.," although Miss Davies doubted it: *Not* plain. *Not* grey. Definitely *not* velour. And straw? She had been assured that the finest "sisal capeline" was intricately woven by delicate Chinese fingers under ice-cold water for optimal suppleness and density. The shade was cinnamon, *not* brown. Inaccuracy and distortion—what could one expect from the provincial press? Miss Davies returned to business. "Have you any thoughts about the invitation to attend the ornithological meeting?"

"Oh, yes, thank you, Maud," said Lady Sutherland. "George thinks it sounds a splendid idea, and a useful way to get started. But perhaps we could ask Mrs Stanley to tea beforehand so she can tell us all about it?"

"It seems almost certain they will seek your patronage," said Miss Davies cautiously.

"Quite right, too. It will be a singular pleasure." Lady Sutherland glanced at her binoculars.

"Very good."

"A common noddy, this morning Maud. The first I've seen."

CHAPTER 7

The Rolls Royce

Mike and Sharon
2020

Nob in PMs office seeking
lots more detail. Reckons
PM, when briefed, said
quote Bullshit why do we
have FCO if FCO cant
dig up a single thing on
suspicious death in Brit
crown dependency unquote.
Not prepared to go back
to Macron empty handed.
Reckons smooth post Brexit
deal rides on this

                    Bollocks

Whose fucking side are
you on

                    We can spin it

How

                    Ive checked. There wasnt
                    much anyway, mainly

potatoes and fish. And guano
of course. Princess Margaret
made official visit opening of
new States Assembly House
1962. Remaining records
some sort of official gift?

Serious?

Of course not you half wit
but whos going to fly to Port
Charlotte *in light plane* and
fill out a fucking call slip

Shit

Dangerously short runway.
We (you) built it

Please focus

Look Mike its post Brexit. All
PM needs is some dot points
and a spine. Keep your hair on
(whats left)

Piss off Sharon

*   *   *

1926

Early the following morning Old Sock made his way as usual to the kitchen garden. He stood motionless, experiencing deep within something akin to choleric rage. Someone had trampled through his lettuces. He followed the trail of heavy footprints past the carrot seedlings, the broad bean patch and out the other side of the garden. Muddy footprints, several pairs, led him across the gravel and into the mews, directly towards the Rolls Royce. Old Sock stopped short. He approached the Rolls much as Job, instructed out of the whirlwind, might have beheld the Behemoth, now in a state not of anger so much as of trepidation. Old Sock warily peered through the window of the rear compartment, blinked, let out a long, guttural sigh, and shook his head, as if unsurprised by what something as dubious and inexplicable as the rear compartment of a Rolls Royce motor car might contain.

"Look on every one that is proud, and bring him low; and tread down the wicked in their place," he muttered.

Old Sock quietly returned to his hoeing.

Maud Davies was one of those imperial spinster ladies who, despite much evidence to the contrary—largely because there were so many servants whose purpose in life was to do almost everything for her—nevertheless managed to convince herself daily that she was run off her feet, especially in the mornings. This particular morning was no different. Maud had so much to do. First, she needed to confer with Mrs Huntingfield about a new pair of curtains for her room, because the existing ones were so wan. Such an oracular, strange old thing, Mrs Huntingfield, but pleasingly cooperative, even if she didn't seem to embrace Maud's project with quite the enthusiasm that inspired real trust. Were better chintzes even available on St Edward? And would Mrs Huntingfield know the difference? There was the usual debrief with Cook and Mr Craddock in the butler's pantry, the previous evening's dinner having been satisfactory but slightly parsimonious in the sauce and savoury departments. Maud also needed to find Colin in the ADCs' room and let him know that Mrs Stanley was expected for a morning tea with Lady Sutherland. Strictly informal, so not one to include in the vice-regal notes. She also needed to seek out Colonel Pole and clarify a point—briskly and briefly—arising from a potential clash next week between the diaries of Sir George and Her Ladyship, the latter being fully determined to mount a bird-watching expedition with Mr Beck, on a date and at a time with which Miss Davies was not at all confident. And there was an especially unsatisfactory piece of correspondence, a letter from the editor of the *St Edward Clarion*, that she needed to discuss with Lady Sutherland herself, and it was for that and related purposes that Miss Davies reached the landing, turned the corner and, in her slightly stentorian way, approached the small upstairs sitting-room just as Norman disappeared inside.

"... Come in, Norman," she heard.

"Yes, Lady Sutherland ..."

Norman closed the door firmly behind him.

"... Sit down."

"Thank you, Lady Sutherland ..." The phrases were duly muffled, but quite distinct.

Maud Davies was naturally curious about the world around

her, at least those bits of it she found it useful or expedient to see. She was, as we know, amply endowed with skills of observation. She was particular, too, about certain points of detail. But even Miss Davies did not often attempt to eavesdrop on private conversations, especially when there was between her and them a firmly closed vice-regal door. However, something in Lady Sutherland's bright but business-like tone, and the fact that she and Norman were engaged in an upstairs private discussion, and alone—most unusual—suggested to Miss Davies that the substance must be "significant." Hovering there, she looked somewhat furtively back down the corridor in the direction of the staircase. No heavy footfall, no suggestive hearty thudding, alerted her to the approach of Lettice or Harriet. She looked the other way, past Sir George and Lady Sutherland's bedrooms and the Governor's dressing-room towards the servants' stairs, and that coast looked reassuringly clear as well. Maud felt entirely justified in pausing there to collect her thoughts, and if any stray snippet passed through the door then so much the better. It was obviously her duty to be fully informed of household matters, even if (for perfectly good reasons, she had no doubt) Lady Sutherland had chosen not to broach them with her before broaching them with Norman; that would have been the correct, the preferable, course of action but, again, there would surely in due course be a perfectly logical explanation. Without a tooth glass, from her interstitial spot, hovering in the upstairs corridor, and being made to feel vaguely guilty by the close proximity of a foxed and particularly forbidding print of Queen Victoria, Maud was at a considerable disadvantage. Try as she might, straining hard, she could hear only indistinct fragments, only parts of phrases, and while she began to experience some vexation arising from this, she was also struck with considerable force that Lady Sutherland's tone was unusually piano, as was Norman's. This was even more "significant," so Maud's inability to catch far more than a phrase here, a word there, lifted vexation to an altogether higher plane of annoyance. Her vague feelings of guilt therefore evaporated. She edged closer, and listened harder.

"… Limbs?"

"I beg your pardon, Lady Sutherland?"

"… two arms, nether regions …"

So it was bodily; Maud was pretty quick on the uptake. In her relatively limited experience, Maud knew that hushed tones generally indicated matters of the body. "Nether regions," on the other hand, left her in absolutely no doubt about it. She couldn't imagine what on earth could possibly pass between Lady Sutherland and Norman that concerned nether regions.

"… Sex?"

"Male, Lady Sutherland, as far as we call tell."

"Don't be silly, Norman. How can there be any doubt? …"

Of course! They were obviously discussing Mr Craddock. First, there was the sibilance. Hardly conclusive evidence, but circumstantially very persuasive. No, from the very outset Maud Davies had strongly suspected that there was a loose connection somewhere in that particular fuse box; an "unmentionable party line at the bachelor exchange," as Cousin Cynthia used to put it. Maud was amused at the recollection, and uttered a strangled little mew that students of the English Upper Middle Classes would no doubt correctly identify as laughter. On the other hand, the crossing of such wires was not exactly unknown in the servants' hall. But what possible occasion or indiscretion could have lifted Mr Craddock's private arrangements out of the normal, appropriate sphere of Mrs Huntingfield's sitting-room and into higher realm of Lady Sutherland's?

"... A lady's foundation garment, Lady Sutherland ..."

Dropping into the very path of her thoughts, bringing sharp focus to what was previously vaporous suspicion—just as the mango tree outside her bedroom window in Rangoon so noisily used to shed its revolting fruit—this pungent phrase, "a lady's foundation garment," slotted perfectly into that portion of the jigsaw puzzle over which, in her mind's eye, she had just been musing. Scandalous! Mr Craddock discovered with ladies' smalls. It was so obvious, so sickeningly obvious.

"... never mind the foundation garment ..."

Never mind? Lady Sutherland was not usually so forgiving. Was there more? Strain as she might Maud Davies was well aware that she was missing far more relevant detail than she was gleaning. She looked again, both ways, and moved a little closer to the door.

"... Think of the germs, Norman."

"Yes, Lady Sutherland ..."

Germs! What germs? It seemed to Maud that the issue was not only centred upon germs; there was the dignity of the office to consider. Miss Davies was genuinely perplexed. She wondered how, tactfully, she could alert or brief the Colonel without revealing the precious source of this potentially explosive information. And how (by whom?) had this startling discovery been made? Not Norman, surely?

"Dear Sock would probably put it in the compost like

everything else ... I shouldn't say anything about this to Miss Davies. Rather overzealous and inquisitive just at present. Sleeping dogs, and all that."

In the hours of disturbed cogitation that soon followed, Maud had plenty of time to puzzle over the part played by Sock in this rapidly evolving but still critically incomplete narrative, and the fact that for whatever strange reason it had been decided to dispose of the offending, germ-laden smalls in Sock's compost. How could she make an adequate inspection without being detected? However, for the time being, that closing phrase, which, because it concerned herself and was couched in such deeply unflattering terms, made Maud feel even sicker. She felt a deep blush of mortification rise from the corrugations at her nape, and travel northwards. However, Maud was also suddenly made aware that Norman had got up, and was about to leave Lady Sutherland's sitting-room. Mid-blush, and with surprising speed and stealth, Miss Davies darted along the corridor and descended the first few steps of the servants' staircase, which hiding place merely added to already oppressive feelings of mortification. She waited while Norman hurried in the opposite direction and, carefully noting the most uncharacteristic urgency of his stride, counted to thirty, counted to thirty again (by which time her blush was beginning to subside), smoothed her hair, altered her plans and made her slightly irritated way back to her room, and by the shortest possible route.

It was often said that calm motions were essential for the smooth running of a vice-regal establishment, and in this respect Norman was a model aide-de-camp, self-contained, efficient, and mostly unflappable. Even so, the events of the morning that culminated thus far in his memorable interview with Lady Sutherland gave to Norman a sharp burst of forward propulsion.

Had one of the footmen seen Norman emerge from Lady Sutherland's upstairs sitting room on the east front of Government House, descend the stairs, cross the hall, dart through the pantry door, trot down the back stairs, and head out along the path towards the mews, he might have paused to take note. However, that morning all three were distracted by preparations for a luncheon, so Norman's swift passage was observed only by Miss Davies, always alert, and Old Sock, who was, as usual, working in the kitchen garden.

When Norman returned to the mews Foster and Craddock were still craning through the opened door of the rear compartment of the Governor's Rolls Royce.

"The Colonel, Bracegirdle and Captain Campbell are briefing H.E.," said Norman, somewhat breathless. "Has Surgeon Commander Clark returned from his golf?"

"Any minute I should think, Sir," said Foster.

"So grotesque," muttered Craddock, carefully unfolding a freshly laundered white handkerchief, preparing gingerly to mop his brow, "such unsightly stains."

"We'd better see about moving it somewhere less conspicuous," said Norman.

"At this stage, Sir, I wonder if moving it, moving it anywhere, would be more conspicuous than leaving it here." Foster had a point.

"I daresay," said Norman. "Perhaps you could move the car closer to the laundry? I gather Mrs Huntingfield will ask Solange to make room for it." Norman craned farther. "Are you quite sure it is a lady's foundation garment?" Norman found himself thinking of a succession of more modest undergarments, playfully discarded, depressingly long ago, in the corner of a smart Parisian hotel room.

"Absolutely certain," said Craddock. "Silk, lace, slender straps—beautifully sewn, and without question costly."

Norman knew better than to challenge the butler's close observations.

"Quite a solid chappie," said Foster. "Foreign Legion."

"How on earth can you tell?" Norman glanced up at Foster, realizing that he was straying into territory that ought perhaps to remain unknown.

"See the tattoo on the left shoulder, Sir?"

Norman squinted.

"Crudely inscribed," said Craddock with distaste.

"Singed and badly damaged, but still quite legible no doubt about it," Foster went on, with precision acquired through the experience of a former Coldstream Guardsman. "It's part of the— what do you call it?—emblem of the Foreign Legion; there's the motto: *Honneur et Fidélité.*" Foster's French pronunciation was defiantly poor.

"Well done, Foster." Norman was impressed but not surprised.

"What on earth would a Foreign Legionnaire want with a silky ..." wondered Craddock, realizing almost immediately that he was, in a very real sense, answering his own question.

Just then Surgeon-Commander Clark appeared at the gates to the mews, wearing plus-fours and an incongruous tweed hat; he was carrying his golf clubs.

"Ah, Clark," said Norman. "Not a moment too soon."

"So I gather," said Clark gruffly. "It had better be good; Solange's new girl disturbed me on the fourth tee—terrible slice. Lost my ball, damn it." Surgeon-Commander Clark strode across the mews and joined the others, who stood back. He peered into the rear compartment of the Rolls Royce.

"Foster has discovered something unsavoury," said Norman, lowering his voice. Craddock's sibilance was not only conspicuous but also, at times, infectious.

"Good God," said Clark.

"Quite," said Norman. "The Colonel, Bracegirdle and Campbell are briefing H.E. Lady S. feels it might be wise to put it in the laundry."

"Some sort of ... *torso*," said Clark, his analytical medical eye at once grasping the essentials.

"Yes," said Craddock. "Headless, and almost completely limbless also."

"So I see," said Clark, ignoring the butler's blinding glimpse of the obvious. "Male, Caucasian. What the devil is that ..."

"A lady's foundation garment," said Norman.

"Of exceptional quality," said Craddock. "Quite possibly Parisian." He cleared his throat. "Only a guess, you understand."

"Good God," repeated Clark. "Well, we'd better get it up to my room."

"Lady S. mentioned the laundry in the first instance," said Norman. "Just for now."

"Yes, I do see. Can't be seen hauling a headless torso upstairs in broad daylight." Surgeon Commander Clark generally brought upstairs certain additions to his collection of medical and other curiosities at less busy times of day; though most were far less bulky.

"Quite," said Norman. "Foster, can you possibly drive the motor up as close to the laundry as you can? Surgeon Commander, will you and Craddock crouch on the floor of the compartment? And help Foster to shift the damned thing indoors? I shall go ahead on foot, and come up with something to distract Old Sock. Give me five minutes."

Upstairs in her ascetic little room, having at once successfully conducted a thorough audit of her smalls—all present and accounted for, thank goodness—Miss Davies re-read the most unsatisfactory reply to her private letter to the editor of the *St Edward Clarion*, in which she had sought, please, the full name and address of the columnist known as "Sylvia." She merely indicated that it was Lady Sutherland's particular wish to extend to Sylvia the usual courtesy of an invitation to tea. Miss Davies trusted that the editor would oblige her with a swift response. Though invariably correct, Miss Davies's official correspondence tended to adopt a tone as stentorian as her gait, as if to suggest that immediate compliance with any such vice-regal request, no matter how inconvenient, was expected, indeed required. Miss Davies had therefore been unprepared for the unctuous reply. While it went without saying that the editor could not hold Lady Sutherland in higher esteem, and indeed craved an early opportunity to extend to her Ladyship in person, and on behalf of all his readers, the warmest possible welcome to these beautiful islands, no doubt Miss Davies realized that, to insure the independence of the gentlemen of the press, a principle long upheld by Fleet Street, and universally respected by governments of all persuasions, and also to protect the confidentiality of their sources of information, which were many, varied, and, of course, not always accustomed (as individuals) to receiving the high honour of an invitation to tea at Government House, it was to be sincerely regretted that the editor of the *Clarion* was not in a position to accede to Miss Davies's request, even if, as was entirely understood, the inquiry was made merely so as to enable Lady Sutherland to extend the usual courtesies—for which the editor begged leave to thank Lady Sutherland most sincerely, remaining, as ever, Miss Davies's humble and obedient servant …

What rubbish; and what an outrageous impertinence to advert, almost in the same breath, to humility and obedience! Miss Davies tossed the letter to one side, and reflected. The editor of the *Rangoon Herald* had without hesitation offered up "Doreen" when Miss Davies had besought him to do so, much as the King of Thera rendered a hecatomb unto the Great Sybil in the Sacred Precinct of Delphi—with even greater ceremony, she recalled, if that were possible. And that particular burned offering had in due course proven extremely useful. What was so special about Sylvia? Tart.

There was a crunch of rubber tyres on the gravel below her window. Miss Davies looked up, and shifted her position so as partly to conceal herself behind the limp net curtain. From that vantage point she observed the Governor's Rolls Royce drawing up at a spot roughly adjacent to the pantry and the laundry, a most unusual position, so far as she could tell, at which that splendid vehicle might be expected to halt, especially at this still comparatively early hour in the morning. She heard Foster rather forcefully engage the handbrake—despite the difficulties she had experienced outside Lady Sutherland's sitting-room a little earlier, Miss Davies was heartened by the quality of her hearing. She then watched Foster step out briskly, in his shirtsleeves, and hurry around to the Governor's side, the left, and—even more curious—open the door of the rear compartment, lean inside, and struggle for a few moments with what appeared to be a large, cumbersome object. This duly emerged, rather fitfully, looking very much like a large mottled pink sack of potatoes. Lifting a finger to one of her corrugations, Miss Davies was surprised to observe that the sack of potatoes was gingerly supported on its other end by none other than Mr Craddock and Surgeon Commander Clark, both looking rather crumpled; she hadn't noticed that they were riding in the rear compartment. She was far from sure that this was entirely proper. Commander Clark, possibly—but Mr Craddock, of whom she had so lately formed such potentially, no *actually*, sordid conclusions? The three of them then hurried the sack of potatoes around the corner and into what Miss Davies surmised must be the pantry, there being no other doors on that side of the house except for the laundry and Old Sock's quarters, which were adjacent. She could not imagine Old Sock needing quite so many potatoes. And if he did, there were far less distinguished, even extravagant ways in which to convey them to his room. Miss Davies had no intention of inspecting Old Sock's room, other than in an emergency or, by and by, in pursuit of such inquiries as might become necessary, however distasteful. There was also the matter of an unavoidable inspection of Sock's compost to consider. Until that dirty, smelly exercise had been successfully undertaken she had better give Sock a wide berth. No, it was quite obviously the pantry; that theatre of germs to which Maud's attention had been so lately directed. Was there, perhaps, playing out here before her very eyes, some extended consequence of what she had so far been able to piece together? Indeed, did this mean that, either unwittingly or even by design, Mr Craddock was introducing harmful germs into this unusually large supply of potatoes? She shuddered at the thought, noting also that that evening's dinner menu made a bit of fuss over *dauphiné* potatoes; a distinct change of direction for Cook—was he complicit after all? But wait: Norman suddenly appeared from around the same corner, an unexpected but entirely germane addition to this little cast of characters. He promptly closed the door of the rear compartment, and hurried back the way he came. Too fascinating. Some thirty seconds later, perhaps a little longer, Foster returned. He climbed back into the Rolls, started the motor, changed the gears, and backed it cautiously down the way it came, and out of sight. Miss Davies uttered a faint mew, this time of exasperation. There was something altogether furtive about what she had just witnessed; a shiftiness she recognized in the method, for example, with which she herself had spirited her illicit copy of *Seraglio Governess* out of the hat box and onto the top shelf of the capacious wardrobe in her bedroom, concealed there under a neatly folded knee rug; a shiftiness, moreover, which she herself had earlier exhibited while hovering in the corridor outside Lady Sutherland's sitting-room. Miss Davies sat down and thought hard. In the circumstances, she made a mental note to confer with Cook as soon and as casually as possible.

In a small clearing on the far side of Mount Raglan Jacob was berating his rebels.

"Fools! What were you thinking?"

"It happened so suddenly, boss," said Mimo.

"Shut up! I'm trying to think."

"Yes boss." Mimo and the other rebels shifted uneasily, avoiding Jacob's eye, like naughty schoolboys.

"A joke? You thought it was *funny*?" Jacob paced impatiently.

"Boss." Mimo's assent was scarcely audible.

"What did you do with everything else?"

"Boss?"

Jacob took a deep breath. "You say you salvaged most of the guns?"

"Yes boss."

"But the boat was completely destroyed?"

"Not much left of it, boss."

"What about the other bodies?"

"Not much left of them either boss."

"*Merde.*"

"The big ship vanished; they must have sailed away. That bomb was loud boss."

"It wasn't a bomb, Mimo. It was dynamite. And now, thanks to you, we don't have any dynamite."

"Sorry boss; yes boss."

"Go on."

"Well, boss, we collected anything metal that we could find, and buried it. There wasn't much. Oh, and I got the hurricane lamp from the ox tree." Mimo was inclined to preen. "High tide did the rest."

"*Jésus Maria*, so you put to sea any number of human remains and all the bits of a boat that was destroyed by explosives?"

"Yes boss."

"And Di Bartolo?"

"That was the strange part boss."

"What was strange?"

"Well, boss, I don't like to say ..."

"*Mimo*," Jacob raised a fist.

"When we found all that was left of him ..."

"What do you mean, *all that was left*?!"

"There wasn't much boss of him either, only the bomb ... the dynamite ... tore off most of his clothes as well as the rest of him ... It was horrible," Mimo's voice quavered.

"Keep going Mimo."

"Well boss, when we found him, all that was left of him, he was wearing something strange."

"What?"

"He was wearing something very strange."

Jacob took a deep breath. "Mimo, *what* was he wearing?"

"It was silky and had lace and looked a bit like what girls wear underneath ..."

Jacob blinked.

"You're sure it was Di Bartolo?"

"Yes boss. He was *big*. And the Lascars weren't wearing shirts. Neither were Gabriel and Léo ... Poor Gabriel ..." Mimo bowed his head. "Poor Léo!"

Jacob sighed, bowed his head, and placed his hand on Mimo's shoulder.

"I know it is difficult Mimo. We have lost our comrades. But I need to know ..."

"Yes boss."

"You said Di Bartolo had on ..."

"It was *pink*...the bits that weren't burned or covered with blood ..." Mimo spoke with emotion.

"Pink?"

"*Yes* boss. With tiny little straps, and some lace ... You said he was a great warrior!"

"That he was, Mimo." Yet Jacob permitted himself a tiny smile, acknowledging that, yes, this did have its amusing aspect. "Serge Di Bartolo, hero of the Mandingo Wars ..." He said this more to himself than to his rebels; Jacob was thinking with some perplexity about what he would be obliged to report to M. Orlando, and what, in turn, M. Orlando would perforce convey to their masters in the Quay d'Orsay.

"Yes boss," said Mimo rather redundantly, but feeling, on the other hand, that Jacob was beginning to take his point.

"So you clowns decided to put him in the Governor's car?"

"Yes boss."

"Wearing this pink thing?"

"Yes boss."

"You couldn't bury him, or set fire to him, or put him down one of the old wells above the Rochers Sainte-Beuve?" Mimo and the rest shifted once more. "No, no. You decided instead to carry him all the way across the island, break into Government House, and put him in the Governor's motor car?"

"We used Francesca."

"Francesca?"

"My mule, boss. And we didn't break in. We went through Bishopscourt. They never lock the gate. We tethered Francesca to it." Mimo seemed to think that this measure warranted praise.

"Shut up!" Jacob couldn't believe it, although with these idiots anything was possible. "What time was that?"

"About an hour and a half before dawn."

"Did anyone see you?"

"No boss."

"How do you know?" Jacob shook his head. "Remember what I told you? Not seeing anyone at night is not the same thing as nobody seeing *you*. Use your *head*!" He let out a long breath. "You realize what you have done? You have stepped up the campaign. You have opened a hornet's nest. You have ... you have ..." Jacob was by then speechless. Yet after a long pause, he chuckled some more. "I don't know how or why you did it, but you did it. And you *might* just get away with it, if you are very very lucky—*merde*." There were a few sniggers among the rebels; someone reached for his passamanana. Someone else began passing around a battered flask of mastise.

Norman hurried back to the Governor's study, where Sir George was seated behind his enormous desk in front of the bow window. A copy of the *Church Times* lay open in front of him. Colonel Pole, Captain Campbell and Commodore Bracegirdle were all standing in perplexed silence.

"Come in, Norman."

"Thank you, Your Excellency."

"You've removed the offending article?"

"Yes, Sir George."

"I shall not ask you what you have done with it."

"No, Sir George."

"Damned odd business. Need to get to the bottom of it." The Governor reached for his pipe.

"Foster recognized a tattoo …"

"Steady on, old chap," said Sir George. "The less we know about the detailed aspects of this strange business, so much the better." In fact, after he had been made aware of its existence in the rear compartment of the Rolls Royce, Sir George was far more reluctant to learn anything more about the headless torso than Norman was to reveal to Lady Sutherland any more particulars than were strictly necessary; yet, unaided, Lady S. had formed an impressively complete picture.

"As far as I can see, Your Excellency, we have contained this curious discovery inside the grounds of Government House," proffered Colonel Pole, ever logical. "The constabulary cannot become involved; I agree with Bracegirdle that down that path lies disaster."

"I suppose there is no need for any fuss," said Sir George, further pondering the matter. "Yet we have to face the fact that whoever is responsible for putting the damned thing in my car must know by now that we have found it, and that this places Government House in the invidious position of having to get rid of the blighter. Point one."

"Quite so, Sir George," said Pole.

"The Colonial Office List makes no mention of headless torsos." Though Sir George was a stickler for regulations, he was also nimble in seizing to himself areas of considerable latitude.

"You, Bracegirdle, I think, can, in this instance, stand in for Special Branch, should that in due course become necessary."

"Yes, Sir," said Bracegirdle doubtfully.

"Which means Surgeon Commander Clark shall conduct a post-mortem examination in his rooms," continued Sir George. "To the best of his ability. Meanwhile, Norman, Colin, you will both assist Clark, and afterwards conduct whatever inquiries you can to ascertain its ... identity, the cause of death and so on and so forth, and, above all, to account for these ... exceptionally unusual circumstances. There may be some use to which one might put a headless torso, but I am afraid for the moment I cannot think of one. I do *not*, at this stage, propose to telegraph Whitehall. Is that clear?"

"If I might, Sir George," said Bracegirdle. "Supposing whoever placed the object in the Rolls—and for whatever reason—contrives to put it about the town that he has, or they have, in fact, done so?"

"Hardly likely?" Sir George turned in his chair. "You mean put their hands up to murder, possibly manslaughter; dismemberment; disposal of a corpse with intent to obstruct or prevent a coroner's inquest; prevention of the lawful and decent burial of a dead body; indecently interfering with a corpse, or misconduct regarding a corpse; above all *trespass* and interfering with *the property of H.M. Government*? Need I continue, man?"

"I don't think it's a serious possibility, Sir George, but ..."

"... but we have a handful of seditious but incompetent rebels up in the hills who think—to the extent that they *do* think—that it may be in their interest to own up to these outrageous offences, or at least to advert to their existence? That's your point?"

"Yes, Sir."

"That is a risk that we shall simply have to run." Sir George pondered further. "I suppose it's all completely deniable?" The gentlemen of the household looked at each other rather uneasily. "Damn it, who knows about this … thing? Foster, Craddock—what was *he* doing in the mews at that hour? Never mind," Sir George continued counting on the rest of his available fingers. "You Pole, self, Bracegirdle, Threlfall, Campbell, and now Clark. Lady Sutherland, of course, Mrs Huntingfield, and Solange. What about Old Sock? Doesn't matter. Wouldn't mention it, would he?"

"No," said Pole with utter certainty.

"I suppose there is always the compost," muttered Sir George.

"Sir?"

"Oh nothing, just a stray thought."

"Sir."

"That leaves Miss Davies. Keep her busy, will you Bracegirdle?"

"Certainly Sir."

"Damned rum business. I do *not* like surprises!" Sir George resumed scanning the list of clerical appointments. "Bubbles Henderson has been translated from Lichfield to Gambia and the Rio Pongas; *extraordinary* appointment!" There was an awkward silence, before "That will be all."

CHAPTER 8

The Joys of the Pipe

Mike and Sharon
2020

Piss off Sharon

Any better ideas

?

???

Didnt think so

Just flick me an email. Best
you can do.

On 29 Jan 2020, at 6:47 pm, Sharon Julius <u>sharonj@fcoff.gov.</u><u>uk</u>> wrote:

Dear Dr Carter

Further to my previous message, I can confirm that the vast majority of Foreign and Commonwealth Office records (to 1940) pertaining to the Crown dependencies of St Edward, Gwern and the Thimble Isles (the Bailiwick of St Edward) were destroyed by enemy bombs during the Blitz.

However, we have since ascertained that a small cache of additional documents (all generated after 1940) were in 1962, on behalf of Her Majesty The Queen, formally presented to Sir Jacob Beck, Chief Executive of the Bailiwick, by H.R.H. The Princess Margaret, Countess of Snowdon, on the occasion of opening of the new States Assembly Building at Port Charlotte.

We understand that these documents, mostly relating to agriculture, tourism, fisheries and the further relaxation of rules governing the keeping of financial records, were intended to form the core of a new St Edward National Archives (StENA) to which H.M. government also committed to providing a new, fit for purpose building to house the national archive, but that both the completed building and its contents were destroyed in 1968 during the student riots.

Yours sincerely,

Ms Sharon Julius
Second Assistant Under-Secretary, Political Affairs
Foreign and Commonwealth Office
Whitehall

Please consider the environment before printing this email message.

Get it?

Jesus Sharon

Youre so fucking welcome.
I reckon it ticks off a couple
of KPIs

Shag?

Better be good

*   *   *

1926

Sir George Sutherland smoked his pipe for two reasons, apart from satisfying a mild addiction to nicotine. His Excellency's soothing after-dinner pipe was a ritual with which he would never dream of dispensing. Were he to do so, his whisky and soda would be sadly diminished, just as his pipe would suffer from the absence of that complementary whisky and soda. Sir George was never in his lifetime made aware of the ancient Chinese twin concepts of yin and yang, but if he had been, he would have grasped their universal significance, their superabundant importance, based alone on his pipe 盒 and his whisky and soda 陽. However, there were other times, and this was one of them, when he thought going for a short walk and smoking his pipe in the open air was a perfect indeed necessary adjunct to creative thought, even powerfully promoting of calm and objective consideration, especially when he was faced with a particularly daunting problem. It is well known that pipe-smoking and depth of thought are synonymous. So it was following upon the curious events of that morning.

The fact was that he had a headless torso on his hands, a male one. A person or, more probably, persons had under cover of darkness illegally entered the grounds of Government House and illegally deposited this offensive thing in the rear compartment of his Rolls Royce. Inasmuch as the headless torso was temporarily housed with minimal reverence—this troubled him—in the *chapelle ardente* of Solange's laundry; and inasmuch as Colonel Pole had insisted that His Excellency could not hope for more reliable servants than Old Sock, Mrs Huntingfield and Solange herself to stand sentinel, but without in any way appearing to do so, the fact remained that, the torso apparently being still reasonably fresh, a heinous crime must have been committed recently somewhere on St Edward, and he was in possession of material evidence the existence and necessary concealment of which might at length prove embarrassing. A person or persons unknown obviously knew this; had clearly observed that the local constabulary were disbarred from any involvement, and were evidently awaiting a reaction either from Sir George himself or from Government House more generally. To what use did they hope to put this knowledge? What investment did they have in any such reaction, or none at all? And who *was* the blighter? Sir George was not thinking of the culprit or conspirators in this awful affront upon the dignity of his office so much as the man of whom until recently the torso formed the central portion. And where were the other bits?

Just then Sir George spotted Bishop Stanley standing on a small grassy eminence only a short distance uphill, beyond Old Sock's compost heap. The bishop was gazing out to sea and he too was smoking his pipe. The Governor hastened to join him.

"Good morning, My Lord."

"Good morning, Your Excellency."

"Here we are: Church and State." Sir George regarded the ocean, and for a few moments he joined the bishop in serene and silent contemplation. The early promise of brightness, freshness and clarity early that morning had blossomed into glorious but temperate sunshine as noon approached, yet there was a gently softening sea breeze. "I see you are thinking about something, bishop."

"Yes, Sir George. I like to smoke my pipe in this spot. It helps me to frame a difficult sermon."

"In due course, I am sure I will thank you for drawing my attention to it—the spot—although of course I look forward to hearing your sermon."

"I find gazing at the sea here," the bishop continued, "while I smoke my pipe, helps to untangle my thoughts. Such a beautiful colour in this light."

"What?"

"The colour of the sea."

"Oh yes, the sea. And there is no doubt the spiritual dimension, I daresay." Sir George quoted from the hymn:

And may there be no moaning of the bar
When I put out to sea

There was a rather long pause.

"I gather one of the more recent Guinnesses chose those very lines for his epitaph," said Bishop Stanley, at length. "The late Lord Iveagh, I think. A wall monument in Christ Church Cathedral, Dublin. Half-wit dean never grasped it was their idea of a joke until after the stone was cut and set in the wall of the chancel—Farrelly and Son of Glasnevin, do you know them?"

"I'm afraid not."

"Marvellous job of stonecutting. At any rate, it was too late." The bishop turned to Sir George and smiled faintly. There was something a little glassy to the bishop's eye and a certain vagueness in his speech, neither of which Sir George had ever noticed before.

"Good Lord," said Sir George, adopting a suitably disapproving tone.

"I think it's rather good one, myself."

"The monument?"

"The joke."

So, in all honesty, did Sir George. He was growing fonder of the bishop. "Tell me, bishop, what sort of tobacco do you smoke? It has a particularly good aroma."

"Ah, yes. Well, the base, one might say, is Bells' Three Nuns. Bit of irony there. Imperial. Glasgow."

"The base?"

"Yes, the base. However, I get mine from a little tobacconist in town who does his own blend, *building* on Bells', a chap called M. Réné Aziz. His shop is *À l'étourderie*. It's in the rue Cardigan, just around the corner from my Cathedral. Both the dean and the precentor independently urged me to visit him. Strength in numbers, I suppose."

"Incidentally, Millicent and I are very much looking forward to our first Divine Service next Sunday."

"Are you? Nothing special. The dean is vulgar and mendacious, and the precentor is a nancy. I inherited both, and it has proven impossible to dislodge either one. I thought I might make progress several years ago when the dean fell gravely ill with the Spanish flu. At first, they didn't tell me he was sick. Then I chaired a meeting he was supposed to attend, and the precentor had to tell me that the dean was sorry he was indisposed owing to ill health. I said, 'Nothing trivial, I trust?' and I'm afraid it wasn't."

"I'm sorry."

"No need to apologise. Unfortunately, he recovered."

"I see."

"And, alas next Sunday I will be on my annual visitation to Gwern. Confirmations: notching up a few more numbers for the Lambeth Imperial and Dominion Faith Commission."

"I'm sure we need every last one."

"What?"

"The numbers."

"Oh, yes, of course, although in the farther flung bits of St Edward one is made to feel one is competing a bit too directly with Cernunnos and his sordid consort the horned serpent woman, the Lady Hecate; the more so on Gwern."

"Superstition?"

"Yes. Monsignieur Lebecq wastes an awful lot of energy chasing after his damned rosaries because as soon as the poor well-meaning nuns hand them out, the villagers drape them over something either inappropriate or, more often than not, extremely inappropriate and put whatever it is in a jerry-built shrine under a sheet of rusting corrugated iron. Ideally, one would prefer Christ Crucified, our Saviour, not to hang at the end of a string of beads anyway, far less from a string that is, in turn, dangling from a large phallus placed between a human skull on one side and a bottle decorated with sequins and turkey feathers sticking out. I mean, really!"

The bishop turned again. His was a countenance in that moment that evinced high serenity, but with a little pain.

"Yes, I do see your point."

"We can at least safely say that that is hardly a problem for the Church of England in St Edward. One generally bolts one's crosses and crucifixes to the wall. At a certain point one had to issue instructions."

"Of course."

The bishop took in a deep breath, and changed course. "However, to revert, I can in a spirit of genuine charity thank both the present dean, who survived the Spanish flu, and, to a lesser extent, the precentor, for independently recommending to me À l'étourder, because this blend is especially good. M. Aziz calls it Five Hundred Nuns, so as to avoid confusion. I gather he adds a type of local *tabac à priser* that has certain medicinal qualities. I cannot say I notice the benefit, or even any difference, but the flavour is exceptional. Would you like to try some?" He reached for the leather pouch in the inside breast pocket of his frock coat.

"Thank you. Yes, I would. This has been a most unusual morning. A second pipe is called for. You are very kind." Sir George knocked the bowl of his pipe on the heel of his brightly polished boot. To the glassiness in Bishop Stanley's eye that Sir George had picked up on a few moments earlier, he thought he detected a sort of curious inertia as well, a stasis, a slight woodenness as he held out his tobacco pouch. The bishop looked a bit like the statue of Mr Gladstone in front of Bow Church.

"Nothing serious, I hope?" inquired the bishop.

"Nothing at all serious, no."

"I hope Sir George, you will feel able, if ever you should need to do so, to call upon me at any time if I can be of assistance to you—or any member of your household."

"Thank you, bishop."

"It's just that your predecessor didn't—ever—which was unfortunate."

"If I may ask, why?

"I could have implored Strickland to stop spending so much money, especially on that enormous motor car, although it did at least give H.M. government at the time the perfect excuse to pave a few more roads, for which one does give thanks."

"I gather we can thank Old Sock for frustrating Sir Henry's plans for a tennis court."

"Indeed. For weeks, silently and at night, Sock singlehandedly altered the topography of the site—over there. It used to be flat. Now it looks like a gorge on the Yangtze; after that a tennis court simply wasn't viable. That's what can be done with a Scot, a spade and a wheelbarrow. Have you had a chance to spend any amount of time with Sock?"

"Not yet."

"A dear, good man. Presbyterian, of course."

"What brought him here?"

"No-one is quite sure. It was a long time ago. I suspect Mrs Huntingfield knows but she is most confidential. Fellow Scots. You know what they're like. Although Mrs H. has 'the gift,' so she says. Dabbles in that Theosophy nonsense, spiritualism, table-rapping, horoscopes. Mme. Blavatsky has a great deal to answer for. Mrs Huntingfield came here from India after her husband died. He was something minimal in Madras. One thing I can say, Sir George, is that your domestic and local staff are fiercely loyal."

"Yes, I sense it already. Half the battle." The Bishop's tone continued to have a serene and meditative quality throughout their discussion. Sir George had liked him since they first met in Port Louis prior to embarkation aboard the *Dormouse*. He was a sound man, and nothing in this conversation had shaken that belief, on the contrary. What he had not quite grasped until then was that Bishop Stanley was a saintly man as well, a godly man, a man with probity, heft, and spiritual depth, in other words a prelate with bottom. He felt therefore that their meeting today was little short of providential. Having taken loose tobacco from the pouch that Bishop Stanley proffered and re-filled his own pipe, Sir George rummaged in the pocket of his waistcoat for his matches, struck one, and lit up.

Passamanana is a narcotic substance derived from the sap of the St Edward coastal pine (*Casuarina concitatii*). Its consumption affects mood, perception, and emotional state. All of these effects are modulated through the brain. The three most common routes of administering this psychoactive, mood-changing substance are oral consumption, that is, after it is stirred or cooked into a comestible, liquid or solid; intranasal consumption, that is, in finely powdered form and taken as snuff; and inhalation by smoking. When swallowed, passamanana goes to the stomach and easily passes through the digestive tract and into the bloodstream. When sniffed, however, the powder adheres to the lining of the nasal passages, the nasal mucosa, through which the molecules released by passamanana also enter directly into the bloodstream. When inhaled into the lungs, which provide a large surface area, the smoke produced by burning passamanana quickly passes, as before, directly into the bloodstream. Once in the bloodstream, these molecules are transported to the brain. To enter the brain, they must first cross the blood-brain barrier. There, they begin to exert their psychoactive influence.

"Very good," said Sir George after a few puffs. "Capital. My word. Yes, I do see what you mean."

"I'm very glad you like it. I would, I think, be lost without it."

Those of his many *Church Times*-reading acquaintances, Sir George pondered while quietly puffing, gentlemen who had any amount of influence at Lambeth or in Whitehall, really ought to beseech the Prime Minister to translate Stanley. He was wasted on St Edward. After all, Colombo was vacant. So was British Honduras. On the other hand—Sir George noticed for the first time a certain quite extraordinary depth of colour in the largest amethyst on the bishop's pectoral cross, that superb lustrous cabochon stone in the middle, a richness of colour with somehow treacly saturation, made the more glorious by the sun in its present equinoctial position—on the other hand ... He took another long and contemplative puff.

"Remarkably good."

On the other hand, thought Sir George—noticing, as if for the first time, it seemed to him, the *intense* blue of the sea—on the other hand, Bishop Stanley might well turn out to be one of his most valuable assets here in Port Charlotte. The vacancy created by his departure might very well be filled by a dotard, half-wit or cad. In these troublous days, notwithstanding for the time being a reliable Tory government in Whitehall, that possibility seemed to him very real. Sir George changed the subject.

"Is this not a most spectacular position for any vice-regal establishment?"

"It is, Sir George, yes most certainly, and I am afraid the Church of England secured for herself the better view of the ocean from Bishopscourt. Quite unobstructed and spectacular, although the price we pay for that is greater exposure to storms and gales in the season."

"Have you been to Government House, Rangoon?"

"Alas no."

"Enormous pile, absurd. They call it Queen Anne Renaissance. Whoever coined that phrase must have been wearing dark glasses. It was like living in a large metropolitan railway station, a very hot and sticky one."

"Poor you."

"Millicent's bathroom was the size of St. Mary Abchurch."

Sir George chuckled affably, and puffed a little more. "Still, to live in such a lovely place will surely ease any future burden. I see what you mean about the colour of the sea."

The bishop turned to Sir George and smiled faintly. "Yes, beautiful isn't it?"

"Such an intense velvety deep, *deep* blue," Sir George continued, puffing. "A resonant blue. A particular blue that possibly outstrips all other attempts at blueness."

"Yes, I know what you mean."

"Millicent once remarked upon the cool clear sapphire blue of the deep reef water around the Nicobar Islands, but they pale by comparison, literally." Sir George was becoming somewhat more reflective.

"Yes?" The bishop continued to smile faintly.

"My word, yes. A cloudy blue, I should say, and of course that cloudy, paler blue gets gradually cloudier and dirtier and, frankly, less *blue* the nearer you get to the Irrawaddy Delta. I should say that on the whole, compared with this, the Andaman Sea looks like a cheap opal."

"Well, another benefit of this particular spot"—the bishop suddenly careened in an entirely different direction—"is that I usually come here with a very serious, merely serious or even only potentially serious or very serious problem. A vicar and vestry suspected of conspiring to embezzle, for example."

"Good Lord."

"Or a vicar up before the magistrates again for indecent exposure or surplice-lifting or interfering with livestock or fiddling his expenses or having committed the common law misdemeanour of obscene libel, that sort of thing."

"No!"

"Yes. You'd be surprised by the number and regularity. To the extent that sometimes I'm inclined to give thanks to Almighty God that it's *only* indecent exposure."

"Really?" Sir George, calmly and occasionally puffing, was a little distracted because he was beginning to notice, and with not a little pleasure, ever more intense and delightful colours in everything around him. To say, for example, that the grassy sward upon which they were standing was green: why, one might as well describe Stonehenge as old or the Firth of Forth as a bridge and not a miracle of modern engineering. No, this was green as of a flawless emerald prized with the tip of a dagger from the gilded forehead or eye socket of a terrible heathen deity ...

The main functioning unit of the brain's vast web of circuits is a specialized cell called a neuron, which conveys information both electrically and chemically. The neuron receives signals from other neurons, integrates and interprets these signals, and in turn, transmits them on to other, adjacent neurons. Within the brain, signals are carried from neuron to neuron in the form of electrical impulses. But when signals are sent from one neuron to another, they must cross the gap at the point of connection between the two communicating neurons. This gap is called a synapse. At the synapse, the electrical signal within the neuron is turned into a chemical signal and sent across the synapse to the target neuron. The chemical signal is conveyed by messenger molecules that are called neurotransmitters that attach to special structures called receptors on the outer surface of the target neuron. The attachment of the neurotransmitters to the receptors consequently triggers an electrical signal within the target neuron. Neurotransmitters may have different effects depending on what receptor they activate. Some increase a receiving neuron's responsiveness to an incoming signal—an excitatory effect—whereas others may diminish the responsiveness—an inhibitory effect. It has long been understood that, unique among psychotropic substances, passamanana releases molecules that stimulate in the brain both excitatory and inhibitory effects, apparently at random, and sometimes both at once and in different measure or combination. We do not yet understand why this is so. What we do know, however, from studies of animals, is that generally speaking the excitatory effect is increased tenfold with every successive doubling of the amount of passamanana consumed.

"And then there are all the doctrinal matters," continued the bishop, "an altogether different set of ... problems. Unorthodox dogma, erroneous dogma, blasphemous libel. Not long ago, I had to deal with a curate who thought it might be, in his words, 'a lark' to join the Communist Party—Liverpool branch; I gather they adhere to Mr Trotsky. I don't quite know how he thought that might work for him in the parish of Baie du Diable."

"I'm sure I cannot imagine." To the extent that this was ever possible, Sir George was awestruck by the unctuous smoothness of the colour of the sandstone of Government House from this angle and in this light, a sort of Naples yellow; no, an eggy Nash yellow, yet throbbing with the merest hint, the tiniest additional admixture and blush of pale but warm pink ...

"Special Branch put me onto him, and I put Archdeacon Pearson onto the curate. Did the trick. Moved him sideways, but it does take up so much of one's time."

"Of course."

"And since the War you'd be astonished by how many clergy wives seem to regard the Ten Commandments as no more than advisory," Bishop Stanley turned to Sir George, "if that."

Sir George, his heart gradually filling with compassion, sensed in the bishop more serenity and more pain, but mild.

"One encounters such things all over the Empire, of course." Sir George—to say "red brick" is almost insulting, he thought, glancing in the direction of Bishopscourt, certainly the wrong expression, more of a tomatoey but, at the same time, dry and somehow dusty, powdery *cardinal* sort of colour—Sir George was sensing that the bishop was slightly distracted, his thoughts perhaps somewhat disjointed. This was no doubt part and parcel of an oracular and holy mind, a soul quite obviously endowed with purity. "In Rangoon," Sir George continued, "the bishop's chaplain ran off with the wife of the harbour master. She was ten years older. Tricky."

"When I come here, though," continued Bishop Stanley, holding the bowl of his pipe and laying emphasis with the stem, "to this place, and when I have my second or third pipe—the problem tends to go away. At length it simply vanishes. But completely. And that is, I think, why my wife insists that I come here to smoke my pipe." Again, the Bishop looked at Sir George rather emptily, but still smiling faintly, and with an expansive gesture of both hands.

"I do envy you, bishop. Do please remind me, what was the name of that tobacconist?"

Even in broad daylight Surgeon Commander Clark's stuffy upstairs room was made unsettling to his infrequent visitors by the empty eye sockets, the uncertain lurid shapes, and, above all, the musty odours of the doctor's collection of medical and other curiosities, and by the even greater obscurity of the contents of his many glass specimen jars, submerged in cloudy preservative spirit. Late at night, however, the effect of Clark's crowded shelves and cabinets was further lifted into the realm of the lurid. Yellow light, occasionally flickering, was emitted by a single bulb that hung from the flamboyant plaster ceiling rose. This, the naked bulb, afforded only the thinnest pallor, caressing Clark's neatly labelled bottles with all the zest and playfulness of a Caernarfonshire wake. Dark shadows filled the corners of the room; further shadows played across the foxed engraving of *The Charge of the 21st Lancers at Omdurman* that hung over the mantel. Shadows danced across the broad window sill, and over the floorboards, bare but for a balding animal skin of uncertain provenance. Both Norman and Colin had, of course, experienced environments far more sinister than this, above all certain military hospitals and convalescent homes, but, equally, Clark's room would have been exceedingly uncomfortable without their having, at the same time, to anticipate the grisly task that lay before them. It was not by any means a cool night, nevertheless the room evinced more than a suggestion of coldness.

The potentially dangerous manoeuvre of bringing the headless torso upstairs from its temporary place of repose in the laundry was accomplished immediately before dinner, when every member of the Governor's household could be relied upon to be dressing. Mrs Huntingfield had, without any hint of surprise, furnished a large stout canvas bag with which partly to conceal the object of Surgeon Commander Clark's inquiries. Solange had likewise answered Mrs Huntingfield's unusual request for the large bag without question, as indeed these two redoubtable women had earlier met without hesitation the challenge of providing to a headless torso temporary accommodation in the laundry. Clark had cleared a space on his work table. He had extracted a modest array of surgical and other instruments from his locked bag, and had privately agreed that Norman and Colin would re-join him after dinner when the Governor's household eventually disbanded as usual—being quite sure, of course, to leave a suitably discreet pause, and to use the servants' staircase and the back corridor so as not to disturb Miss Lettice, Miss Harriet, or, above all, Miss Davies, whose bedrooms all gave onto the upstairs landing.

"Come in," called Clark rather brightly, when Norman knocked softly at his door. The doctor had removed his tail coat, and was wearing a blue and white-striped apron over his starched shirt-front. The earpieces of his inexplicable stethoscope clung to either side of his starched collar, framing a dusty white tie. He was already wearing a stout pair of bottle-green rubber gloves. In the circumstances, Norman thought Clark's appearance could perhaps inspire a little more confidence. He looked like the head waiter in the middle of an acrimonious plongeurs' strike. Colin slipped quietly into the room a few seconds later.

"Ah, Campbell. Here we all are."

"Commander," acknowledged Colin, who looked around him with wary interest, alighting eventually upon the engraving.

"Omdurman," said Clark with a hint of drama. "I was present."

"Ah."

Clark took a deep breath. "And now, to work," he said, clasping his gloved hands with that form of glee that is often associated with members of the medical profession when faced with something especially gruesome. "Well, well, well—let's see what we have here." Clark craned over the torso for a few moments, his sharp professional eye scanning every contour. "You, gentlemen, will take notes. I hope you will not hesitate to make any pertinent observations; alas pathology was never my forte." Clark glanced at his clock. "I see the time is twenty to eleven p.m. And the date ..."

Norman looked at Colin, who produced a small notebook and a pencil from his breast pocket. He jotted a note.

"March the fifteenth, Sir."

"The Ides of March, eh?" said Clark, with antiquarian

satisfaction. "Right. Overall appearance suggests that the deceased was originally hirsute, and obviously male. Much of the hair has been singed; such of the remnants would appear to have been dark. Am I going too fast?"

Colin shook his head. "Not at all, Sir." His pencil hovered expectantly.

"Hand me the magnifying glass ... Thank you. Let me see." There was a lengthy pause. "Head ... lacking; severed at the ... neck; certainly above the fifth or sixth cervical vertebrae, whichever that one is." He gestured vaguely with his rubbery bottle-green fore-finger.

"Sir."

"Arms ... mostly lacking. Legs ... ditto."

Norman and Colin glanced at one another.

"Numerous cuts and scratches, several of these post mortem. *Copious* loss of blood prior to that. You follow?"

"Yes I think so, Sir," said Colin.

"Let us now free the deceased from this extraordinary pink encumbrance. Might I have your assistance, Threlfall?" With considerable awkwardness Clark removed the foundation garment in unnecessarily complicated stages, each of which did much to disturb what remained of any viable forensic evidence. Clark folded it roughly and set it to one side. Norman noticed something wispy trailing from the hem. In its undressed state the torso assumed an even more alarming prospect than before.

"Physique ... powerful. Note, for instance, the advanced development of the *pectoralis major*—the chest muscle." Clark prodded rather insensitively with his percussing instrument. "Genitals ... hmmm ... certainly male."

"A pretty safe hypothesis, if I may say so, Sir," said Colin with a nervous chuckle.

Clark glared at Colin with considerable hostility. "There will be no irreverence during this procedure, is that understood? I will not tolerate irreverent language or laughter."

"Yes, of course, Sir. I'm awfully sorry." Colin blushed.

Clark sighed impatiently.

"Obviously uncircumcised?" offered Norman.

"I fail to see the relevance of that observation, Lieutenant Threlfall," said Clark.

"I'm so sorry, Sir ... I simply thought ..."

"Quite all right," Clark's tone was terse. He resumed his close inspection, at length muttering to himself: "*corpus cavernosum*; *corpus spongiosum*."

"Sir?" Norman wondered if Surgeon Commander Clark was, at last, usefully sharpening his focus.

"Nothing." Clark stood up straight, and placed his hands on his hips. "Race ... Caucasian; nationality ... not, I think, English."

"Oh?" If not sharpening his focus, Norman wondered if instead Clark had groped towards some substantial conclusion.

"Looks foreign. Yes, *distinctly* foreign—a slight greasiness of the skin. Note that please, Campbell."

"If I might, Commander?"

"What is it Campbell?"

"Terrible, grievous wounds to be sure, but are those not traces of high explosive? It's those quite distinctive burns ... here, here, and again, here." He gestured as precisely as he was able. "It's just that one often saw similar in Flanders."

"Ah yes, very good: very observant," said Clark, his eye

simultaneously alighting upon Colin's patch. He experienced a twinge of embarrassment. "Yes, very good."

"One can therefore rule out ritual dismemberment?" added Colin, ignoring the lapse.

"Only if that shocking, terrible end were *not* itself achieved with the aid of those self-same high explosives," said Clark, at the same time making with the rubbery bottle-green forefinger of his right hand an irritating gesture of mental fastidiousness. "The identifying mark on the shoulder; the fragment of crude tattoo. Might we accept Foster's suggestion that it relates in some way to the French Foreign Legion?" Clark sounded dubious; he pored over the motto with his magnifying glass.

"Yes, I do think so, Sir." Norman was quite sure.

"Let us now turn him over … carefully."

Norman and Colin duly joined in this distasteful operation, which they carried out in short order.

"Hmmm," said Clark, resuming his careful inspection with the magnifying glass.

"Nothing much more here, really, is there?"

"Sir?"

"Back and, er, bottom … male. *Gluteus maximus*; again, in this instance, well developed." Clark paused for a moment. "I have always taken the view that one bottom is very much like another," he said sniffily.

Norman absorbed this extraordinary remark as best he could, for, if pressed, he would have admitted privately that, on the whole, bottoms intrigued him—and that some were strikingly different from others. Norman thought wistfully of Paris. Colin, meanwhile, was rapidly concluding that Surgeon Commander

Clark was severely touched. He noticed an impressively large jar next to Clark's locked bag marked *tincture of laudanum*. "Far fewer signs of burns, abrasions and other damage, though, Sir."

"Ah, yes. Which would suggest that the impact of the explosion was almost certainly frontal?"

"Yes, Sir."

"*Very* good." Like all masters of condescension, Clark built a head of steam. "Time of death, meanwhile ... time of death ..." Clark hovered on the brink of an observation. "Time of death ... well, certainly very *recent*," said Clark.

"Less than twenty-four hours, Sir?" offered Colin.

"Perhaps," said Clark, with non-committal oracularity, no less terse. "Age of deceased ... somewhere, in my opinion, between twenty-five years and forty-five. A *very* mature twenty-five, or else a forty-five year-old in superb condition—and, I suppose, anything in between." The efficient scratching of Colin's pencil fell silent.

"I wonder, Sir, might those be animal hairs adhering to the hem of the foundation garment ... just *there*?" Norman pointed.

"Well done, Threlfall, yes, I believe they might."

"Should we perhaps preserve them in an envelope?"

"Ah, yes. A clue—yes, of course."

"And might I ask Mrs Huntingfield to launder the lady's foundation garment? Craddock seemed to think it might be in some way distinguished."

"If you wish. Can't myself see the point; it's not as if it *belonged* to the deceased."

Norman shook his head. "I think you may be mistaken, Sir. Did you notice how many of the small abrasions corresponded exactly with very small blood-stained holes in the garment? Holes, not tears. I think he was probably wearing it when whatever happened to him ... happened."

"Good God. You mean ... he was a *nancy*?"

"Not necessarily, Sir," said Colin, concentrating upon deepness of tone. There was a little pause.

"Theatrical? Ballets Russes sort of thing? Ye-es, I do see your point."

"Possibly, Sir," said Norman doubtfully.

"He may simply have liked to wear such things next to the skin," said Colin, who had from time to time caught wind of such habits. There was Jumbo Cheevers, for a time military attaché at Brussels, and also Midget Hargreaves at G.H.Q., who apparently wore stockings. It was not unknown. "Concealed, of course," he resumed. "Only a hypothesis, you understand, Sir."

"Never heard of such a thing." Clark muttered.

"Quite," said Colin, casting down his eye.

"Of course, we may never know," said Norman, although he was fairly sure that they would.

Earlier that evening, at around the time, just before dinner, when Norman, Colin and Surgeon Commander Clark were discreetly hauling the headless torso up the servants' staircase at Government House, M. Orlando was reclining on the sofa in his office.

The premises of Orlando *et Cie.* only partly disguised the consul's great wealth, for the building originally housed a bank which had failed in the nineties. Facing Queen Victoria Quay, the front was duly muscular, and deployed the classical orders with workmanlike but admirable sobriety—but for an incongruous pair of fruit-laden urns, oversized masonry ornaments that perched atop a fussy balustrade running along the top. Two large sash windows flanked the front door. Consistent with the style of the town, the façade was painted a gay colour—in this instance eau-de-nil. The upper floor was occupied by Peeble, Cartwright, Peeble & Co., a firm of solicitors; their name was inscribed in tarnished gold paint on all three of their front windows. The interior of Orlando's principal trading room below resembled that of a small post office. It was large and airy, but plain. The floor was covered with durable linoleum. Several clerks worked at raised wooden benches down one side, while, seated at a modest desk and busying herself with a large typewriter, Orlando's secretary stood weary sentinel at the frosted glass door to his office at the rear. A large counter ran down the other side, behind which more clerks carefully inscribed with steel-nibbed pens upside-down ticks in the columns of dusty ledgers under the watchful eye of the head clerk. The furnishings were hard; few decorations obtruded. Towards the end of the working day M. Orlando's trading room continued to thrum with commerce; agents, speculators and freight forwarders still came and went, though in diminishing number. Beyond his frosted glass door, however, the thrum of commerce gave way to the faint music of the senses. Persian carpets, fuchsia-coloured lampshades, a plump ottoman, his comfortable sofa, rich curtains, and an enormous Chinese bronze incense-burner declared to his many callers that M. Orlando aspired to the condition not of a successful financier so much as that of an oriental satrap. Vulgar scent mingled with the fragrance of his little black cigarillos from San Sebastian.

Only the very large cast-iron safe, emblazoned with the revered name of Chubb & Sons, Wolverhampton, which stood where a mantelpiece would normally be, alluded to the consul's business affairs.

With that special brand of cupidity which is the province of the self-made rich—for whom large sums of money are never large enough—M. Orlando had been absorbing a summary of the previous day's transactions, but his mind strayed. He put down his papers and reclined on his sofa, basking in the pleasant recollection of Miss Harriet Sutherland—such an exquisite, unspoiled English girl; the perfect complexion, the exquisite embonpoint! Not a distinguished beauty, to be sure, but was there not an irresistible charm in that particular combination of plainness, plumpness and strident bossiness? And, though certainly large, he mused, being English, young Harriet was surely athletic, a *strong* girl, and no doubt possessed of the qualities of an incipient tigress. Such qualities, which Orlando found very exciting, merely awaited ignition at the hands of an appropriate Svengali. The obstacles were daunting. Lady Sutherland was watchful, and would never permit her younger daughter to accept even the most formal invitation to go on a guided tour of Orlando's guano warehouse, and afterwards to take tea. It might take time, but Orlando savoured the prospect of systematically overcoming such obstacles as stood in his way. Meanwhile he pictured Harriet naked, much like Marie-Louise O'Murphy in Boucher's famous picture, lolling playfully among the soft cushions on his sofa ... A knock at his door disrupted Orlando's fevered imaginings.

"What is it?" he called with irritation.

"Excuse me, Monsieur. There is a young man who wishes to speak to you, a M. Beck, M. Jacob Beck."

"Thank you, Gabrielle. Please show him in." As Beck was led into Orlando's inner sanctum, the head clerk glanced up and watched the young man enter, then returned to his work.

Orlando rose with disquiet. "Ah, M. Beck. I do not believe we have met—but of course *Professeure* Hodgkinson has told me all about you."

"How do you do, M. Consul. Do please forgive this intrusion."

Gabrielle closed the door, and returned to her desk. Jacob advanced into the room.

Orlando continued to speak with elevated volume, his eye fixed on the frosted glass. "Such a pleasure. Do please sit down, Monsieur. How can I be of service?"

"Thank you, Monsieur."

Orlando lowered his voice, turned towards Jacob, and leaned inwards. "What is the meaning of this? You know the protocol: No contact, *ever*." Orlando spoke quickly and made no attempt to disguise his annoyance. Then, raising his voice once more, "Do me the honour, please, of joining me for an aperitif. The day is nearly done."

"I'm sorry, Sir," said Jacob, sotto voce. "But I had no choice. There has been a disaster."

"What is it?"

Speaking swiftly, but at considerable length, Jacob reported to Orlando the events of the day; the disastrous outcome of the landing; the peremptory departure of the *Marianne*; the loss of the dynamite; the death of the hero of the Mandingo Wars, among several others; the deeply embarrassing detail of Di

Bartolo's headless torso having been placed by his men in the rear compartment of the Governor's Rolls Royce, still clad in the pink lady's foundation garment that he was wearing at the time of his sudden death. In vain Jacob attempted to cast this last item in a positive light—suggesting that it constituted the opening up of a daring new front in the struggle; an opportunity seized in the chaos of adversity so as to prosecute against the perfidious occupiers a new and daring form of psychological warfare. Regularly mopping his brow, Orlando asked a number of extremely terse questions, for clarification, in tones of rising incredulity. Jacob answered them all as best he could.

"Fools! You have risked everything," hissed Orlando. "And now you have dared to come to my office! You *know* you are being watched. Do not come here again, do you understand? I shall instruct you by the usual method. Now get out of my sight."

Orlando strode to his frosted glass door, opened it, and, as he showed Jacob out, said, in his most unctuous manner, "Do please send my compliments to *Professeure* Hodgkinson—so thoughtful of him to send you in person. Good evening M. Beck."

"Good evening, Monsieur."

Orlando returned to his divan, took a deep breath, and contemplated the situation with dismay. The loss of Di Bartolo would have been a grievous one without most of his remains being delivered directly into the hands of the British; the rest having been foolishly consigned to coastal waters dangerously close by. But what, he wondered, was going on at Government House? They had obviously decided to keep the discovery a secret—for the time being, for, had the constabulary been called in, that sensational news would already have spread throughout

Port Charlotte. They were obviously operating according to the absurd English principle of hush-hush; so predictable. But had they in fact bitten off more than they could chew? Could this extraordinary turn of events even be advantageous? It is not easy to dispose of a headless torso, Orlando reflected. The available options were few. Exposure, even ridicule, could be infinitely more damaging to Sir George than what could be achieved with any amount of dynamite. Nevertheless, Orlando had no choice but to report these unwelcome developments to his masters in the Deuxième Bureau. Normally he would have done this by sending an apparently innocuous commercial telegram: Your order of 19th inst. arrived, stop. Damaged beyond repair, stop. Something, something, something. In the circumstances, however, now that Beck had so recklessly beaten a path to his very door, he could not possibly run that risk. Beck pays a call, after which Orlando sends a telegram. One might as well report the interview, and the entire situation, directly to Tabby of the Port Charlotte *Truth*. No, a far better, safer option was close at hand—an option that was by universal consent held in reserve for dire emergencies.

The Church of St. Aloysius Gonzaga on the corner of Gordon and Kitchener Streets was empty but for a handful of elderly penitents who were muttering prayers, saying the rosary, or else patiently waiting for the evening mass. Several of the nuns from the adjoining convent knelt motionless in the choir amid the gathering gloom. Although his large white suit positively glowed in the half light, M. Orlando's was a familiar presence and not therefore conspicuous. As usual he waited his turn, whereupon, with slow and somewhat implausibly pious gait, he squeezed himself into the meagre space afforded by the confessional and drew the curtain. After a few moments, and with disconcerting sharpness, Monsignieur Lebecq threw open the little shutter. The perforations in the grille on Orlando's side represented the Sacred Heart of Jesus. This, he noticed, emitted other-worldly rays of light, while an especially lethal-looking crown of thorns encircled the disembodied organ, a flame rising from its neatly severed arteries. In the circumstances this symbolism was a little unnerving.

"*In nomine Patris et Filii et Spiritus Sancti. Amen*," intoned Monsignieur Lebecq in his weary monotone.

"Bless me, Father, for I have sinned," said Orlando rather breathlessly. "It is two weeks since my last Confession. And I have an extremely important message for the Mother House."

"Go on, my son."

"You are to send a telegram on behalf of the nuns as soon as possible. You will advise the Mother House that they have informed you that the new set of vestments was delivered on schedule, but that they are damaged beyond repair."

"Damaged?"

"Ruined. Completely destroyed. It will be necessary to make alternative arrangements."

"That is all?"

"No, Monseigneur. You will indicate that the nuns also now beg leave to know when they may expect the next Apostolic Visitation, which will greatly assist them in solving the problem of this and, indeed, similar matters of ordinary procurement on St. Édouard."

"I see."

"That is all. For these and all the sins of my past life, I ask pardon of God, penance, and absolution."

"Aren't you forgetting something?"

"Monseigneur?"

"Lulu and Valérie."

"Ah, *mon vieux*," chuckled Orlando quietly. "You are well informed."

"Ten Hail Marys."

"The spirit is willing but, *hélas*, the flesh is weak." For a moment Orlando thought of Miss Harriet Sutherland, fervently hoping that in her case the opposite would be true.

"So you said last time. And the time before that."

"Yes, Monseigneur."

"Don't do it again."

"Non, Monseigneur."

"*Et ego te absolvo a peccatis tuis in nomine Patris, et Filii, et Spiritus Sancti.*" The shutter slammed shut.

Orlando returned to his pew, knelt for a moment, mopped his brow, and then rose and quietly slipped out of the church. He had urgent business to transact in Madame Beck's establishment above the Café des Artistes.

Late that same evening a warm breeze caressed the palms and hedges of pittosporam in the garden of the Villa Les Humeurs. Gene was fast asleep in his room, but Mrs Hodgkinson was sitting up in bed. The French windows stood ajar; the whispering of the ocean was making her drowsy. In his basket on the verandah, Fang was quietly gnawing on a very large bone. Mrs Hodgkinson lit a cigarette, and re-read the crucial opening passage of *Do What Thou Wilt* by Gwladys Baring.

> ... what a lark what a plunge for Cecilia, the air, heavy now with harvest dusty heat Sir Ephriam's massive shoulders his thighs his arms his back—precious manly—faintly she could hear the songs of the farm hands working on the estate, in Plymouth town there lives a maid she recalled the distant tolling of the Little Mainwaring church bells sweat sweat—marrow pudding—her lips quivered slowly raised and the village green at tea time father she gasped her thoughts fingernails traced circles, so hard. She was alone, invisible. Fingers buttons laces bodice chemise drawers corset petticoat stockings *"duello magno dirimendo, regibus subigendis,"* very good young man, heaving freed the boy trembling oh mother is that you thrusting tearing ripping throbbing in Plymouth town there lives a maid. Oh Sir Ephriam (that methodical nicety which is the essence of true elegance!) with a hey nonny no throbbing oh the throbbing she shuddered slow slow now now now—if I should die before I wake a line of sweat rolled down her spine and she felt, standing there at the open window, that something awful was about to happen ...

Smiling to herself, Mrs Hodgkinson set aside the pages, and lit a fresh cigarette.

Foxtrot

Mike and Sharon
2020

Shag?

> Better be good

Fuck

> What?

Elysee Palace *and* Daily
Mail seeking clarification
from Downing St about St
Edward file. Just got txt from
Nob in Downing St

> What do you
> mean clarification?

Neither buys the Blitz
bullshit. Think its a cover up

> Funny that

Want to know exactly how
do we know it was destroyed
in the Blitz. PM wants

unequivocal statement
ASAP. Having kittens

What did you expect me to
say, that I fed into nearest
shredder?

Never use that word, not
even here. No such thing
as end to end encryption.
NSFW

Wevs. Fact 1 it was destroyed.
Ask yourself Q. When was a
shitload of shit destroyed? A.
in the fucking Blitz

Youd better be able to prove
it Sharon

*　　*　　*

1926

Paris.

Norman was not given to introspection, was never one to
dwell on the past. Yet from time to time he felt a twinge of ...
what? Guilt? Remorse? Certainly of melancholy.

He was a very junior member of the British delegation to the
Paris Peace Conference. They had arrived in time for the great
Victory Parade, and the magnificent fetes, dinners, soirees and

balls that followed in quick succession. The city was draped in bunting, flags, garlands, coloured lights. The crowds were alive, surging, cheering, wild with relief, frantic to celebrate the end of the terrible war.

Norman was present at the opening of the Conference at the Trianon Palace, standing on the very fringe of the vast hall, the huge central table packed with sombrely attired old men. The work over the next few weeks was dull. Many hours standing around, ready to answer a call for assistance from his masters, which rarely came. Nonetheless, he was happy. His duties were not onerous, and he had plenty of time to himself, time with which to explore the city. He loved the dance halls of Paris, the red lacquered walls, the coloured lanterns, the taxi dancers of Le Perroquet, Chez Florence, Florida, Gaya, Bricktop, Delli's, and the fascinating rhythms, tango, ragtime, jazz, the new dances, La Java, the Brazilian samba, and of course the foxtrot. The wartime ban on public dancing had been lifted and Paris had gone dance mad. Norman was captivated, the mood of post-war exuberance was so different from the quietly respectable tea dances of the London season, and the genteel orchestras that played at Queen Charlotte's Ball.

One of his principal tasks—loosely defined, yet important— was to look after the wives while their husbands thrashed out details of realigned borders and the reparations to be demanded of the defeated Germans and their allies. That was how they met. It was the great fete given at the Hotel Doudeauville for the benefit of the Polish Red Cross. Clusters of men, some in evening dress, others in uniform, engaged in informal discussion, brokering deals, negotiating perhaps the reallocation of a border in the

Middle East, or manoeuvring for a greater share of Germany's dismantled Empire. The Great Game, diplomacy played out in shimmering ballrooms and salons.

Béatrice Auerbach was standing alone in the vast ballroom that was hung with flags of all nations—except, of course, those of Germany and the German allies. Glittering chandeliers hung from the ceiling, urns of Oriental design were ranged along the walls containing spiky tree ferns. Béatrice was a pretty Jewish woman, a little older than Norman, stylishly dressed in a shimmering cape of orchid moiré. She looked bored.

"Can I get you a drink madame?" Norman asked politely.

"Non, merci."

"A seat perhaps?"

"I don't think so."

"Nothing I can do for you then?" He smiled.

"No."

"Perhaps I should leave you alone."

"No, please stay. I am sorry, I was being rude."

"Not at all."

"You are being very attentive."

"It's my job."

"You are with the British delegation?"

"Yes. And your husband?"

"That is him over there, General Auerbach, talking to the Italian Prime Minister and those other men."

"He looks very distinguished."

"Oh, he is. Very distinguished."

"You must both be pleased that the war is over."

"Of course, although my husband quite enjoyed it I think.

And he loves ... all this." She gestured around the room. "But please, tell me about your job at the Conference."

"Nothing exciting. I take notes. Carry papers for my superiors, who rarely call for them. Arrange for the cars to turn up on time, book hotel rooms, tickets to the Opéra, the Louvre, you know, keep them amused. And amuse those wives who have been abandoned by their husbands at functions like this."

"You are good at your job then."

"My superiors only notice me if something goes wrong."

She smiled. "Nothing is going wrong at the moment."

"Well now, at the moment this doesn't feel like work."

The discussion between General Auerbach and the group of diplomatic nabobs was breaking up. The general strode briskly towards his wife and Norman.

"Meet me for a drink," she whispered hurriedly, recklessly. "The bar of the Hotel d'Angleterre, Saint-Germain-des-Prés, five o'clock, Tuesday. Perhaps best ... not in uniform."

"Lieutenant," boomed the general. "Thank you for looking after my wife."

From the other side of the great ballroom Fitzroy Bancroft, head of Paris station at the British Embassy watched as Norman chatted politely with one of the most powerful men in France.

She was seated at a small table in the corner of the bar wearing a simple slate blue chinchilla wrap when he arrived. Norman, tall and slender in his dark suit, still managed to look as if he was in uniform.

"Can I get you a drink *this* time madame?"

She smiled. "Please, champagne I think."

Norman returned with two glasses from the bar.

"This place. You should feel at home here. It was once the British Embassy."

"I know. Benjamin Franklin refused to step inside."

"I'm glad you came. I wondered if you would," she said

"I wondered if you would be here."

"It was indiscreet to ask you. I hope it doesn't get you into trouble."

"Why should it?"

"Well, I have taken a room."

"Oh." Norman smiled. "I am flattered."

"I shouldn't have asked you to meet me here."

"I am glad you did."

"I was so bored, you see, and you were so kind. It was an impulse, wrong of me."

"I don't think so, but I will leave if you wish."

"No, please stay. Let us just talk."

"Does your husband know you are here?"

"No, he prefers not to know."

"Does he mistreat you?"

"No, he is a perfect husband, generous, thoughtful. But he is a military man, and he has a taste for other military men, preferably from the lower ranks. He needs a wife, you see, but merely to maintain appearances."

"Are you lonely?"

"I have my work, he allows me that."

"What work do you do?"

"I teach. *La petite école*. The little ones, they give me such joy."

"Do you have children of your own?"

"No." She drained her glass.

"Another?"

"No, I don't think so."

"Shall we go dancing?"

"Afterwards, maybe," she said, taking him by the hand and leading the way upstairs to their room.

In the event they did not go dancing, nor, to Norman's regret, did they ever go dancing. At seven the church bells started ringing, Béatrice got out of bed and started dressing.

"Can't you stay a little longer?"

"Non, cheri. Tonight is the great ball, given by His Royal Highness Duke Lois d'Orleans-Bourbon at the Ritz. I have to go. The General will expect me to be there."

Thus began an affair that lasted the whole time he was in Paris, and would no doubt have continued had he been permitted to remain. But it never progressed beyond their brief meetings, two or three times a week if his duties allowed, at the Hotel d'Angleterre. A glass of champagne in the little bar, then to their room. Béatrice always left at seven. Norman always longed for her to stay a little longer, but he accepted that these were the terms of their *liaison*.

"Will I see you again?"

"Perhaps this evening at the Ritz, but from a distance, we must not be seen together."

"Of course."

She kissed him. "And here, if you wish, same time on Thursday?"

"Let me take you dancing."

"Maybe next time."

Norman was sitting at a small table in the corner of the bar at L'Hotel Angleterre with two glasses, and an unopened bottle of champagne in an ice bucket. He had been early. She was late. The door opened. Norman glanced up. It wasn't her. It was, however, Fitzroy Bancroft, head of Paris station and Embassy fixer.

"Threlfall, old chap. Mind if I join you?"

"Of course not," Norman replied warily. "Sir."

"Champers, eh? A little rich on lieutenant's pay. May I?" Without waiting for an answer Bancroft removed the cork from the bottle, filled Norman's glass, and poured one for himself. "Cheers."

Norman raised his glass resignedly.

"Nice place. Of course Jefferson wouldn't set foot in here when it was the embassy."

"Yes, I know."

"Tricky business, diplomacy. Particularly with the French. Prickly bunch."

"I imagine so."

The door opened, Norman glanced around. It wasn't her.

"It's the general, you see. Won't fuck his wife, but doesn't want the world to know someone else does."

"Oh."

"Won't do, d'you see? Won't do at all. The Peace Conference. Peace, ha! Not peaceful at all, not a bit of it, all of them fighting over German territories. And Ottoman. A mandate here, another protectorate there, a few favourably realigned borders in Europe. Americans not interested. Britain, France, carving up the world like children looking for sixpences in plum pudding at Christmas. We need the General, you see, part of the great *Alliance*

Angleterre/Francaise. Make sure they don't get too greedy, at least no greedier than we are. Make sure we don't miss out on our sixpences. You understand? Of course you do old chap."

"Yes. I suppose I do," Norman muttered.

Again the door opened. Two middleaged commercial travellers entered, shrugging off their overcoats, lighting cigars.

"You will return to Portsmouth immediately. You will not, under any circumstances, come back to Paris. Your luggage will be waiting for you at the station. Here is your passport. Your ticket. Train leaves in three hours. You are never to set foot in this hotel again." Bancroft got to his feet. "You do understand, don't you, old boy?"

"Of course. Sir." Two bright spots of colour were burning on Norman's cheeks.

Bancroft got to his feet and drained his glass. "Thanks for the drink." He touched Norman's shoulder briefly. "I am sorry, lad. Orders. The greater good and all that." As he reached for the door it swung towards him. He held it open and graciously ushered the newcomer into the room, turned back to Norman. "Three hours, Threlfall."

Norman gazed helplessly at the General's wife.

Two hours later she said: "It's time to get dressed. You mustn't miss your train."

"You could come with me."

"Oh, Norman."

"No, really."

"Run off together and *au diable les conséquences?*"

"Yes. Oh yes."

"You would desert? Do you British still execute deserters, or is that just in wartime? That would make a dramatic and romantic end to our doomed love. They would write an opera about us."

Norman smiled. "Yes, *L'Hotel Angleterre* by Puccini: they lived for love, they died for love."

"We *both* must die? Surely the British would not execute me as well?"

"Don't be too sure, we are a vindictive race."

"I will never forget you Norman."

"I love you."

"I know. But believe me, my love, there will be someone else. There always is."

"Pssst," said a pile of laundry. Nathalie was folding sheets.

"What is it Yvette?"

Yvette the pretty blond Venus Butterfly emerged from behind the laundry.

"Let's go dancing!"

"Non, ma mere won't allow it, you know how she is."

"Don't tell her. We can slip out while she's doing the accounts."

"I have nothing to wear."

"Voila!" Yvette held up a shimmering gown in beaded and fringed crepe de chine. "It is Lulu's. And this ..." She flourished a pink feather boa, "... is yours! That beast Orlando brought it back for me. You must keep it."

That evening Norman took advantage of his night off and once more strolled aimlessly through the old town, gradually becoming aware of music. He picked up his pace and followed the sound to a large dance hall, with an illuminated sign above the entrance that read as follows:

DREAMLAND BALLROOM
noté pour sa respectibilité.

A roughly printed poster proclaimed in bold type: CE MOIS-CI SEULEMENT, L'OISEAU CHANTEUR DE SAINT EDOUARD: CLAUDETTE MOREAU AVEC ANDRÉ DEVEREUX ET SON CAFÉ ORCHESTRA!!!

Norman walked up to the handsome glass panelled doors, pushed the polished brass handles, and entered. He was met by a wall of noise, a rush of heat, clouds of tobacco smoke, swirling colour and movement. It wasn't Le Hot Club, he thought, it was better, vibrating with life and energy. The polished timber floor was oak inlaid with circles of a darker timber, well sprung and ideal for dancing. Panels beneath the Moorish arches were decorated with Oriental landscapes and colourful scenes of island life in the previous century. A huge yellow moon hung from the ceiling, which was painted midnight blue, and decorated with little fairy lights, twinkling on and off like stars. An orchestra shell in the shape of a peacock's tail framed the stage, which was surrounded by small potted palms, and where Claudette Moreau in a sequinned tail coat, top hat and white gloves was singing loudly to the accompaniment of the Café Orchestra.

Norman stood beside the dance floor watching the dancers, so lithe and athletic, so different from the tea dances, balls and soirées of London, and with something of the wild abandon of the apaches in Paris, although none of the violence.

He very much wanted to dance.

Nathalie and Yvette were dancing together.

"Oh, Yvette, look, that young man by the wall, he is the one I told you about, the one I saw dancing with his shadow."

"I don't recognise him."

"I thought all men on the island came eventually to Mme Beck's."

"Sooner or later."

"Isn't he handsome? Doesn't he look like Ivor Novello?"

Yvette had a low opinion of all men, but agreed that, yes, he was very handsome.

"He danced so beautifully."

As if he'd heard, Norman looked in their direction.

"*Bonté moi*, he saw us."

"Yes, he did."

"Is he coming?"

"Yes, he is."

Yvette spun away, laughing, leaving Nathalie alone on the dance floor as Norman approached.

"It is you, I thought it was."

"Oui monsieur."

"I have scared your partner away."

"She is very shy."

"Since she has deserted you, may I have this dance?"

He took her in his arms. She was a natural dancer, instinctively following Norman's lead. Together they moved through the crowded dance floor—Norman steered her adroitly past farm workers, bankers' servants, guano miners, off-duty soldiers, sailors on leave and weary taxi dancers.

"You dance beautifully."

"So do you."

"I knew you would when I saw you."

"Yes, I remember. You danced with your shadow."

"I am sorry, I was rude, I felt I was intruding."

"It is nothing."

"The music that night, I bought the recording from M. Aziz."

"Really? You remembered?"

"*Sur cette terre, ma seule joie, mon seul Bonheur*

C'est mon homme ..."

Nathalie laughed. "... *J'ai donné tout ce que j'ai, mon amour et tout mon cœur*

À mon homme ..."

"And here she is, the songbird of Port Charlotte, Claudette Moreau with the Café Orchestra."

"Visiting, they will leave soon. To Paris."

"Then let us enjoy them while we may."

Norman spun Nathalie around and they danced into the crowd.

There was a pause in the music, the glass-panelled doors swung open dramatically and M. Orlando moved onto the dance floor like the great French battleship Richelieu pulling out of Marseilles. He set course through the dancers and hove to next to Nathalie and Norman.

"Ah, Mademoiselle Beck, it *is* you. The boa—so chic. And the dress, where have I seen it before? Never mind—wherever it was, on you cheri, it looks so much better." Orlando bowed. "Lieutenant, so good to see our rulers reaching out to the local communities—hearts and minds, is that not so *n'est ce pas*?" The debonair Frenchman's lips came together in a moist little moue, he raised an eyebrow knowingly, and with that he continued suavely on his way through the crowd, which parted to make way for him.

"Ah, I do not like that man. Monsieur Orlando."

"I know who he is. How do you know him?"

"He visits my mother's … café, the Café des Artistes."

"Ah."

"He will tell maman. I will be in trouble, my mother, she does not like me to go dancing."

The music started up again.

"Well, there's nothing we can do about that now. Let us keep dancing."

"What did he mean 'rulers'?"

"Well, no, not rulers." Norman was embarrassed, and worried himself, wondering if Orlando would perhaps inform on him as well. Who knew what his new superiors would think of him frequenting the Dreamland Ballroom. A memory of Béatrice Auerbach flashed in his mind. "Administrators maybe. But yes, I do work at Government House."

"You dance so very well. Is that one of your official duties?"

"No." He laughed. "And no one at any official function I have attended dances as delightfully as you." Again the image came back to him of the little bedroom at the Hotel d'Angleterre, an empty champagne bottle, clothes scattered across the floor, then the memory left as quickly as it had come.

So they danced. He taught her the foxtrot, working some stylish moves (the turn and reverse, the natural weave, the open telemark, the hover cross) into the modern syncopated beat of the Café Orchestra. She taught him *La Bébée*. He taught her the beguine. She taught him *Les Gars de Senneville*. They danced and talked and danced until Claudette Moreau announced that the evening's entertainment was concluded.

"May I drive you home?"

"*Mais non*. I must find Yvette."

But Yvette had disappeared, last seen with one of Monsignieur Lebecq's maids.

"I will drive you home."

Norman pulled up outside the darkened Café des Artistes.

"Can I see you again?"

"*Peut être éventuellement*. As long as Monsieur Orlando has not informed on me. Perhaps next week at the Ballroom." Natalie slipped elegantly from the little car. She turned, hesitated, and raised her fingers to her lips, before running lightly to the side door of the building.

From an upstairs window Colonel Pole gazed out, reflectively lighting a cheroot. He wondered who was driving the vice-regal Austin.

PORT CHARLOTTE TRUTH

"Cats' Whispers," by Tabby

Yankee "hootch" parties have very little—if anything—on the merriment that nightly turns our own Dreamland Ballroom into a screamingly "futuristic" impression of lurid blues and crass vermilions. It's hard for a sweet young church mouse just in from Gwern to hold onto her illusions, when, coming hither for a much anticipated week-end—quite thrilled up at the thought of jazz parties, orgies of shopping, a trip to the movies, and all the splendid people she might meet—instead she leaves the Dreamland Ballroom or the Café des Artistes at the break o' day with a sore head, torn garments, and an aching heart. No amount of eggs and bacon scoffed soon afterwards in the Scotland Room, if you please, at the Grand Hotel can mend it. She wishes for nothing more than to be "in the swim." It all starts out decorously enough, although Tabby is yet to see any of our Grande Domaine Damsels deigning to join our English girleens in throwing round the crockery. Our Frenchies are far, far too Grande for us (thank goodness), and if not too Grande then certainly too Buxom, owing to their diet of pastries, we suspect. No, at the Dreamland Ballroom Tabby sees only gay slender young things who patronize more toney demesnes of King Jazz than would fill the Domesday Book, and then leave a good bit over. Mostly these are coatless and hatless male flappers, lolling and lounging and hustling about, and even, Tabby is told, accepting gifts—even of silk 'jamas—and from *much* older ladies. How thrillingly nauseating! As the flowing bowl circulates, and the fun waxes wilder, and the crazy jazz orchestra sets their faerie bower a-swayin' and a-jerkin', no doubt our excitable young lady just in from Gwern indulges too freely in her favourite tipple, if indeed she has had time enough to fasten upon a favourite! Mixing at length with energetic flappers who could even pass for landed gentry— and might Tabby dare to suggest there are quite a few others who couldn't, wouldn't, and don't?— she probably finds the hoochie coochie heat of the room, and the smoke-permeated cheek-to-cheek atmosphere, plus one or two more exhilarating cocktails of the mastise-leaning variety, a bit too much for the equilibrium. At length this girleen conceives a veritable "pash" for one very well-connected partner in particular—Tabby reckons she "falls" 'neath his "threll." With skill he steers her delightfully petite figure on the crowded dance floor, but, at various points in his eccentric fox-trotting career, manages (through no fault of his own) to get our church mouse bumped into, and heavily, by several other couples— each one prettier than the last! She succumbs to these combined influences at a little after four, and tumbles head over heels, affording a riotous glimpse of her "knickers"—which weren't even the frilly sort, just every day "plain Janes." She has to be carried out and plumped into the back seat of her new boy friend's car. He manages to convey her as far as Gordon Street without disaster, but with the swaying of the scenery and the jolting of the motor on the cobbles of Queen Victoria Quay, the voyage terminates with a volcanic tragedy—at the front gates of Government House, if you please!

Colonel Pole put down his pen, shifted in his chair, and scratched his head. At times he resented the long hours he spent drafting and re-drafting Sylvia's weekly "Society Notes" for the *Clarion*, but Tabby's column in *Truth* required far greater concentration. Not that he disliked either task. He had come to enjoy undertaking both—single-handedly. Indeed, they were very necessary.

"Hearts and minds, old chap. Hearts and minds." That was what Lord Axminster used to say back in the old Department of Information, admittedly under the desperate, black cloud of 1917.

Yet on St Edward, and in these times of peace and plenty, the point about hearts and minds was doubly true. And, of course, Pole was in the unique position of being able to survey both spheres accurately. Sylvia's was, of course, his own. Indeed he found to his surprise that her lengthy commentaries on blistered satin, rose pink charmante and petunia triple georgette flowed as easily from his pen as did the Governor's regular cables to the Colonial Office—far more easily, in fact, because the cipher, once extracted from the safe, was too tightly bound, and was therefore almost impossible for Pole to navigate between pages without it snapping shut, and causing him to break into a sweat of annoyance. In fact, Sylvia had become a welcome diversion; and he was rather good at her. Tabby, on the other hand, required far more careful thought, greater discretion, and, occasionally, informants—besides employing language that Pole would die before uttering himself. True, Tabby picked up almost everything at Madame Beck's. There was little that escaped the girls' notice, and it was mostly reliable. He mused. Actually it was *always* reliable. He couldn't fault them.

Contriving to place Sylvia and Tabby with their respective editors had proven laughably simple. In exchange for the *Clarion*'s modest fee and a tacit undertaking that the local constabulary would turn a blind eye to *Seraglio Governess* by Gwladys Baring, which, though banned throughout the Empire, was circulating widely on St Edward, Mrs Hodgkinson had graciously agreed to stand in for Sylvia. The *Clarion* had absolutely no cause for suspicion. This arrangement had even survived Magnolia's prolonged absence in London; she was an inveterate and extravagant cabler, and the Cincinnati Ohio & Delaware Banking Corporation generally paid the bills. Madame Beck, meanwhile, was only too pleased to perform the same function in respect of Tabby and the Port Charlotte *Truth*—on comparable, mutually satisfactory terms. His only vulnerability, it seemed to Pole, was the risk of exposure and embarrassment. That, or some spontaneous intervention or alteration by the editors over whom of course he had no direct control, although it was deeply satisfactory that both frequented Madame Beck's establishment—and were therefore bound by Gordian knots of discretion. Besides, the editor of *Truth* could see for himself how easy it was for Tabby to assemble her tawdry gleanings and cheap tittle-tattle. So far, the system had proven most effective, although Miss Davies had started making unwelcome inquiries as to the identity of Sylvia, which were sure to lead eventually to Mrs Hodgkinson, but fortunately no farther. No, any and all such risks, Pole concluded, were negligible.

Naturally, Mrs Huntingfield knew. It was she who discreetly conveyed Sylvia's finished drafts to *Les Humeurs*, and Tabby's to Madame Beck, downstairs at the Café des Artistes, merely slotting these in amongst her usual round of weekly errands in town.

Without fail, at half past ten Mrs Huntingfield brought the Colonel his whisky-and-soda, and replaced his ashtray.

"Sylvia or Tabby this evening, Colonel?" said Mrs Huntingfield.

"Both, I'm afraid."

"Then I'll bring the decanter. You know you'll give yourself a turn, and no mistake," said Mrs Huntingfield with real concern.

"Thank you, Mrs Huntingfield. I'll be all right."

"If I may say so ..."

"Please do."

"That Miss Davies is very inquisitive."

"Of that I have no doubt."

"You know I have the gift, like my poor late mother before me."

The Colonel knew this. He reached for his cigarettes.

"And, sure as I stand in this room, that woman is not above casting her eye over other people's desks," she continued. "I thought you should know."

"Thank you, Mrs Huntingfield. Then I daresay we must make sure there is always something there for her to notice." He struck a match in his ingenious way.

"Oh, Colonel," said Mrs Huntingfield good-naturedly, turning to leave. "You are a perfect devil. Mind you get some rest now."

"Thank you, Mrs H.," said Colonel Pole, lighting a fresh cigarette.

Mrs Huntingfield hesitated at the door.

"Colonel?"

"Yes, Mrs H.?"

"Tabby wouldn't say 'knickers'. 'Undies' is better."

"Really?"

"Yes."

"Good-oh. Thank you, Mrs H. Good-night."

"Good-night, sir."

Pole took up his whisky-and-soda, and thought for a moment. It was time for Sylvia.

> The cream of Port Charlotte society flocked to an extraordinary meeting of the Royal Society of St Edward in the Chapter House last Tuesday evening, which His newly-minted Excellency and Lady Sutherland graced with their presence. Bishop Stanley presided. Wearing a magnificent peach-coloured kasha gown for evening, set off by tiny black-and-white buttons down the front and on the sleeves, Her Ladyship lent to the occasion her incomparable dignity. His Excellency's suite were in attendance, and Miss Maud Davies was wearing a demure frock of putty ninon. At last, ladies, it seems we shall see the formal establishment, under Lady Sutherland's august patronage, of our very own branch of the British Ornithologists' Union, a scheme that was

prompted, we are told, by the sensation lately caused in London by the arrival of Sir Henry Strickland's blue-helmeted parakeet. After some lively debate concerning a disputed sighting of Townsend's Shearwater near Mount Raglan, such a rarity never before seen so far north and west, Mr Beck—the well-known young engineer just now employed on the construction of new premises for the Cincinnati Ohio & Delaware Banking Corporation—was at length elected President. Such an unusual, modern choice, we are bound to say. Fascinating young ladies, exquisitely frocked and partnered by youthful cavaliers, exhibited the most affecting determination to subscribe to this new scheme, which will in due course arrange outings to sylvan corners of our island home to learn easy methods of cultivating the friendship of birds. It seems a veritable mania for ornithology has been discovered among the ladies of Port Charlotte that we hardly knew we had— such fun! One cannot omit to mention that seated next to Mrs Stanley, who was wearing a sweet frock of shell pink georgette, were Professor and Mrs Gene Hodgkinson, of Les Humeurs. With characteristic flair, that handsome lady was wearing a sumptuous apple-green gown of crêpe-de-chine, boasting a wide gypsy girdle beaded in white and red, and a hem of quite daring length that was the envy of the room. Mrs Hodgkinson was gracious enough to propose Mr Beck, which unexpected endorsement no doubt persuaded many other, naturally reticent ladies to follow her courageous example. Dear Colonel Pole, always so gallant, yielded in the second ballot with superb magnanimity, and threw his own support behind Mr Beck—not a hint of dismay, embarrassment, or rancour; such a noble English gentleman. For the benefit of our dear catholic Plantation ladies, who so rarely come to town, might one go so far as to trill in liquid notes from the branch of our new and verdant tree, *"Annuntio vobis gaudium magnum: Habemus Presidentam"*?

Colonel Pole yawned, looked at his watch, and drained the last of his whisky-and-soda. It was half past midnight.

In a small apartment in the Rue des Poitevins in the Sixième Arrondissement, not far from the Monnaie, behind an unmarked door at the top of a steep, sinuous staircase, a pneumatique clattered into the wicker basket with its characteristic whoosh and thump.

Moments later the duty officer brought the unopened cylinder into Colonel Truffe's small office.

Dusty sunlight filtered through the dirty panes of an open dormer window; dusty pigeons gathered on the sill. The Colonel was feeding them crumbs from his morning croissant. A dusty Persian carpet had long been permitted to lie carelessly wrinkled on the floor. Open files littered the desk.

Truffe was seventy. He was a veteran of *le Deuxième Bureau de l'État-major general.* He managed not only to survive each successive stage of *l'affaire Dreyfus*, but also, despite many, often traumatic manoeuvrings through the intervening decades, to reach the top of his service.

The Colonel wore his dusty black frock coat like a uniform. The only adornment, in his dusty lapel, was the chevalier's rosette of the *Légion d'Honneur*.

The duty officer handed him the pneumatique. The Colonel attached his pince-nez, opened the cylinder, and extracted the paper slip from the Bureau of Signals—it was blue, indicating the highest degree of urgency. He read. The Mother House. Vestments. Apostolic Visitation. After a moment's reflection, removing his pince-nez, he murmured:

"Ah! *L'Angleterre, la perfide Angleterre.*" He turned abruptly back to the window, and clasped his hands behind his back. "Tell the Nuncio I wish to make my confession. Go through the sisters. And contact Monsieur Baiser. Immediately."

CHAPTER 10

Bird Watching

Mike and Sharon
2020

Youd better be able to prove
it Sharon

Last entry on third last index
card indicated file borrowed
by strategic command July
1940. There were 2 more
cards after that but I shredded
them too

Im serious Sharon. No
S word

Grow some balls Mike

Fuck you

Anyhow thats point 2, last
documented July 1940.
Point 3 last surviving entry
on newest (surviving) card
also indicates file located on
shelf F31

So

> So, sunshine, shelves F29
> to F35 incinerated in
> Whitehall on night of 14
> Oct 1940. See Times 15 Oct
> 1940, cross-check against
> relevant confidential but now
> declassified memo to war
> cabinet. Online scan on Kew
> Archives website. QED unless
> you want a fucking affidavit
> from the Luftwaffe pilot

Piss off. How come it
wasn't incinerated then

> NFI. Must have still been
> with strategic command,
> which is quite interesting

Why

> Strategic? 1940?
> Wakey wakey

*   *   *

1926

Thanks to Miss Davies' efficiency, and the fact that Her Ladyship's social calendar was still sparse, it was not too hard to arrange Lady Sutherland's first bird-watching expedition. Of course, Maud did not know the real reason for it. Sir George was firm on this point, and so too was Millicent Sutherland. Not long after Jacob Beck's election, over their daily morning chat about letters and the diary, Lady Sutherland asked Maud, please, to write to Mr Beck on her behalf, congratulating him most heartily upon his recent election as President of the Royal Society of St Edward. She should indicate that were he, in that capacity, to issue an invitation to Her Ladyship to join him on one of his next bird-watching expeditions to the lower slopes of Mount Raglan, or to any other neighbourhood on the island that was rich in avian treats, Her Ladyship would be delighted to receive it in Her Ladyship's own capacity as the Society's newly-minted Patron. As to the logistical arrangements, Mr Beck need not fret—Foster would drive them as far as he could in the Governor's motor car, and Her Ladyship could think of nothing pleasanter than to walk some considerable distance if necessary.

In situations of this kind the general pattern was long established at Rangoon, and Lady Sutherland was well aware of it. When Millicent Sutherland wished any such correspondence clearly to convey warmth and friendliness of mien, in the subsequent letter, drafted, typed and posted as quickly as possible, Maud made sure she turned down the temperature. Phrases such as "would be delighted to receive" were replaced by "would make every effort to consider it favourably," although her nib usually hovered with uncertainty over the word "favourably." More often than not she would change her mind and scratch it. "Most heartily" and "nothing pleasanter" obviously went, and the sense of "need not fret" was thrown into reverse. Finally, Maud laced the final document with little hints that served to lay emphasis upon the concept, familiar in all vice-regal circles, that Lady Sutherland's demarche should not be taken as a sympathetic expression of lively interest, but rather as a command any failure to comply with the whole or even only a small part of which could and would not be tolerated. Maud concluded by listing a number of dates on which Lady Sutherland was still available, and urged Mr Beck, please, to make every effort to respond with dispatch lest any of those dates became impossible in the meantime. That "command" concept, of which Maud Davies was such an effective lieutenant and mouthpiece, neither rang bells with the talented young engineer employed by the Cincinnati Ohio & Delaware Banking Corporation, nor, for that matter, with the courageous covert instigator of a popular insurrection and uprising. So, when he received this prolix, high-handed and, frankly, confusing letter, Jacob Beck wondered what to do, and went to seek the advice of Gene Hodgkinson. Although he was a man of the world, being an American Gene had to read Miss Davies's letter twice. He then explained to Jacob what he *thought* it meant.

"Those folks' idea must be that you, Jacob, have to invite Lady Sutherland to go on a bird-watching caper—on one of those dates, because that's what she wants, see?"

"But if that is what she wants ..."

"Point is, she can't ask you. *You* gotta ask *her*. And it'll have to be the eleventh, son. Because we need you right here on all the others. Understood?"

"Yes boss."

In due course, Jacob managed to write his letter, and all these and many other obstacles were overcome through a long series of telephone calls that were trying for Jacob, and trying for Maud. They were trying for Jacob because the only telephone to which he had access was bolted to a wall in the builder's busy office. Noise was a problem, as well as there being no adequate surface on which to write. They were trying for Maud because Mr Beck didn't seem to grasp the essential character and components of a vice-regal occasion. To her he seemed all vagueness and indecision. Maud was, of course, an absolute stickler for accurate timings and other points of meaningless vice-regal protocol, for example "Lady Sutherland alights from the left hand side of the vice-regal motor car." After many twists and turns it was finally agreed and arranged that Jacob should present himself at Government House for a bright and early start on the appointed day.

Jacob's modest home consisted of two small rooms at the rear of a small Williams & Gosling warehouse close to the Port Charlotte docks. Gene Hodgkinson had helped him find it when he commenced work on the viaduct. It was simply furnished. His tiny kitchen was barely large enough for a small table and a single wobbly bentwood chair. A paraffin stove and a chipped enamel basin sat on the table at which he worked, cooked and washed. The other room contained a neatly made single bed, a small chest of drawers, and a book case that held several well-thumbed engineering manuals, the works of Marx, Locke, Montesquieu and Rousseau, a bible, and copies of *Tropical Birds* by Sacheverell Sitwell and Crabtree's *Birds of Mauritius and St Edward*. On one wall there was a cracked mirror, a small wooden crucifix and an engraving of St Francis; on another were photographs of Jacob's two brothers in uniform, his *certificat* from the École Catholique d'Arts et Métiers at Reims, and a faded engraving of Gustave Eiffel. The other two walls were bare. On the floor was a simple rug of Basque design. Under the rug was a loose floorboard. And under the floorboard was a locked box containing a stack of used, small denomination St Edward pound notes, a British officer's Webley revolver, and a complete set of Jacob's own drawings for the new prize-winning viaduct. He would not have needed to store them there, had his more recent plan not been to blow it up—a plan that, for want of dynamite, was for the time being put on hold.

It was the break of day. Jacob brushed his hair. He was neatly but practically dressed, because they would be walking some distance into the woods. Jacob took up his binoculars. Along with a few other necessities, he tucked his copy of Crabtree into his neat knapsack and a medium-sized, somewhat battered old pewter flask—filled from a stoneware demijohn with a big cork stopper that sat on the floor in the corner. One last thing. He retrieved his Webley revolver from under the floorboard, checked the lock, and put it, too, into his knapsack. Glancing at his watch, he closed his door behind him and quietly set out on foot, but at a brisk pace.

Half an hour later Jacob presented himself at the gates of Government House, and was duly admitted and made his long ascent to the forecourt at the appointed hour. This was the first time he had ever been inside the grounds of Government House, but he knew more than he wished to know about what had gone on there in recent days. Rounding the last corner of the gravel drive near the top of the hill, Jacob was unprepared for the conflicting emotions awakened in his breast by the sight of the enormous Rolls Royce motor car, black and gleaming in the early morning sunshine—the weather was unusually fair that day—with Foster in his smart bottle-green livery standing to attention at one side. Jacob knew far too much. He was about to enter a hearse, a chapel of repose, a shrine to the memory of a great hero of the Mandingo Wars, but he could not mourn, he could not kneel and give thanks, he could not lay a wreath even if he had had one to lay; he could not and must not shed the hot tears that the *patrie* positively demanded of a manly patriot in acknowledgment of a great hero who, though he liked to wear elegant camiknickers next to the skin, had given his very life in the struggle against the perfidious occupier for nothing less than *la liberté*.

Through the front door sailed Lady Sutherland, dressed apparently for an ascent of the Matterhorn but for a stout pair of agricultural binoculars swinging from her neck, and Miss Davies in attendance. Mr Craddock and a number of the footmen followed them carrying a well-stocked picnic basket, several thermoses, and a small cargo of rugs, folding stools, a card table, neatly folded tablecloth, large umbrellas for the sun, and a butterfly net. Together with an elaborate Army and Navy first aid kit marked with a large red cross, everything was crammed into the boot, an amenity almost as large as Jacob's quarters behind the Williams & Gosling warehouse near the docks. Nobody could have hoped for more plentiful supplies, or would have been better able to cover the contingencies of a Shackleton or a Livingstone.

"Dear Mr Beck, *Monsieur Président*! Good morning to you," boomed Millicent Sutherland while pressing upon him a crushing handshake.

"Good morning Lady Sutherland."

"I cannot tell you how excited I am about our excursion this morning. You know Miss Davies, I think?"

"We have never met, Ma'am, but we have spoken on the telephone."

"Good morning, Mr Beck," hastened Maud in her clipped, slightly less enthusiastic way.

Jacob noticed that even the process of entering the vehicle was overladen with mysterious ritual, requiring Foster to carry out a series of gymnastic movements in order to open doors and close them, first Lady Sutherland's—rear left.

"Mr Beck, now I will *not* take no for an answer: You shall ride beside me because we have so much to talk about— Columbiformes, Psittaciformes, Passeriformes. Today I want you to find them all for me, *everything*.

"I will try my hardest Lady Sutherland."

"Maud, you sit in the front, beside Foster."

Maud's heart sank. Normally, of course, when in attendance, Maud would sit silently beside Lady S. on the right-hand side. Indeed, she could not recall an occasion when she had not. This was not merely unexpected; it was a rude awakening, and to be bumped by ... Not for the first time in recent days did Maud experience not mild irritation but downright anger. Her neatly typed brief for the day had, as usual, *clearly* stated the car seating arrangements, to which Lady S. had made no objection, yet now she had peremptorily thrown them into disarray. Contemplating, as well, the very different character of travel in the open air and outside the closed rear compartment and therefore the imminent destruction of her Marcel wave, she clambered into the front seat next to Foster and they set off.

From his upstairs study window, Sir George watched and chuckled to himself as the Rolls lumbered down the drive.

Jacob had recommended as an ideal setting for that morning's bird-watching a glade he knew, not unlike the one from which he and Mimo had witnessed the arrival of the new Governor. However, it was farther away and higher up, a clearing in the woods you could reach along a relatively easy footpath at the end of the only road worthy of the name that leads up the eastern slope of Mount Raglan. It was, he reckoned, about an hour's drive. He knew it was a good place to see a lot of birds—he had been there often—although he also knew that a number of his men lived in the villages that they would pass through on their way, in L'Étang-Salé les Bains and Le Tampon and La Plaine des Poivres. Nonetheless, this would possibly be a good dress rehearsal, because if the day went off well, Lady Sutherland might want to go back. La Plaine des Poivres was closest to their destination, and also offered the amenities upon which Maud had insisted in their, to him, increasingly tedious planning discussions on the telephone. Covert leaders of resistance movements, naturally accustomed to any degree of hardship in the pursuit of *la liberté*, are perhaps uniquely ill-equipped to assess the suitability of ladies' bathrooms, much less to take into account the particular requirements of English ladies. In any case, he had also chosen that spot because they could be sure they would not encounter anyone else who might just be there already, or indeed be disturbed by new arrivals. Maud had insisted upon this, being a non-negotiable precondition of any vice-regal picnic.

"What worries them about other people?" he asked, when a few days earlier Nathalie brought him a single word from M. Orlando: Proceed.

"They are not like us," she sighed, nevertheless thinking of the handsome young man with whom she had danced at The Dreamland Ballroom. "Be careful, brother." She kissed Jacob on the cheek and hurried away.

This was Lady Sutherland's first real glimpse of the countryside of St Edward any distance beyond the outskirts of Port Charlotte, and combined with her natural curiosity, the pretty scenery, her excitement about all those bird treats that lay in store, to say nothing of the dear little village folk with their quaint customs, for her the drive took no time at all. For Foster, Maud and Jacob that journey of about hour and half, as it turned out, flashed past in just ninety minutes.

Throughout, Foster was concerned about the parlous state of the winding dirt road. *Route de la forêt des ramparts Raglaniens* was its rather grandiose name. Galway tinkers wouldn't risk the axle of their worst caravan on it, he thought, doing his best to avoid the biggest potholes. His greatest fear was for the Rolls Royce.

Maud was concerned not about the volume so much as the

regularity of Lady Sutherland's outbursts of laughter emanating from the rear compartment. I really don't know how she does it, mused Maud. Her laughter has none of the brightness of bells of perfect clarity and pitch—her mind strayed towards cousin Cynthia—not like Rudhall of Gloucester or the equivalent, no. It has more of the deep resonance of that 16½-ton bronze boomer, the Great Paul in the City of London. This clever, wicked thought prompted Maud to let out one of her spontaneous but infrequent mews of incipient laughter.

Having attained control of his initial flood of emotion with respect to mourning the glorious dead, Jacob was more concerned about which specific portion or general area of the generous and extremely comfortable calfskin upholstery, which seemed clean enough, had lately played host to some of the mortal remains of a great French hero of the Mandingo Wars. Lady Sutherland must surely know, but she didn't seem to mind, so far as he could see. Perhaps she didn't know. He was also concerned about Maud's head, which, viewed through the pane of glass that separated them and thoroughly disturbed by the breeze at this high speed, easily twenty-five miles per hour on the least bumpy stretches of road, looked exactly like the crest of an especially effulgent grey-crowned crane (*Balearica regulorum*). At the same time, he was doing his best to keep up with Lady Sutherland's rapid-fire requests for information, for facts that she so obviously craved but tended to know anyway. She seemed happy enough doing most of the talking, and laughed a lot.

Finally, after a steady climb they arrived at the little cul-de-sac with which the road reached its dead end.

"Now then, Mr Beck and I shall make straight for our bird-hide. Maud, be a dear and help Foster with the things."

Maud began the journey, these unconventional seating arrangements having been forced upon her, thinking that this just might happen; by the time they got there, however, she was certain it would. She was not pleased. However, she was at least mentally prepared to disguise her displeasure, and with what she regarded as supreme professionalism. Thus, Maud managed to shine just sufficient brightness upon:

"Certainly, Lady Sutherland; I'm sure we can manage."

"Come, Mr Beck. Lead the way! Oh, Maud. Give me one of the picnic rugs. That's it. Lovely. Off we go!"

When at last Maud and Foster reached the little glade, staggering under the weight of the picnic basket and all the bits of folding furniture, Jacob and Lady Sutherland had taken up a position overlooking a gentle wooded slope that dropped away to the north and afforded an excellent vista of the surrounding woods. They were both lying side-by-side on the picnic rug, not inappropriately near, but not exactly all that far apart either. Foster had to suppress a really ludic guffaw, so vividly did the sight remind him of something he saw not so long ago in one of the smutty illustrated magazines Craddock got posted to him from Berlin. It was the contrasting silhouettes that did it—large and not large—as well as Lady S.'s mannish brown lace-up shoes. She and Jacob were propped on their elbows, their binoculars scanning the tree canopy. Evidently, they were finding much of interest for Lady Sutherland's ejaculations were frequent.

"Look," she boomed, "a red-tailed tropicbird. But so far inland, Mr Beck. Surely that's most unusual?"

"We are not more than four or five miles from the northeastern coast, Ma'am. It is possible."

"Those tail feathers must be twice the length of its body. How remarkable, and what a lovely red."

"According to Crabtree, Ma'am, this is not unusual. *Phaethon rubricanda*."

"Phae-*ton*, Mr Beck. The second h is silent ... But don't they eat fish? What's it doing here?"

"They nest on the rocky cliffs and escarpments up there," said Jacob pointing at the higher slopes of Mount Raglan, "and they fly long distances, so it is possible they feed in the ocean."

Maud and Foster busied themselves with the rather complicated task of preparing the al fresco picnic luncheon. Cook and Craddock had filled the hampers not only with enough food to feed a small army, but also filled it in such a way that Maud could see that putting everything back in again would be akin to solving a jigsaw puzzle, quite a hard one.

"Look, up there! A raptor, is it ... yes it is: a Western marsh harrier, a magnificent male, and what a beauty. Look at him wheel."

With every sighting, and there were many, Jacob struggled to find the right page in Crabtree.

"*Circus aeruginosus*, he definitely has his eye on something down there that he means to snatch, kill and eat, Ma'am. He sees himself as the rightful owner of this side of the mountain."

"Rath-*er*. But has he ever been spotted outside The Azores?"

"Only once before, by me. It was here, Ma'am."

"So I am making history! Jolly good."

There were lengthy pauses, of course. Bird-watching requires much patience, something of which Maud was only too aware.

Although from knowledge reluctantly acquired over her many years in vice-regal service, Maud often wondered how it was possible Lady Sutherland ever *saw* a bird when she insisted on making such a racket. Weren't you supposed to be quiet? And just what was that Mr Beck up to? In her extensive experience of compulsory bird-watching, she had never yet encountered a handsome young man who entered upon that voluntarily. It followed that there must be an ulterior motive.

"Where will you have your sandwich, John?" Maud liked Foster because he was English, athletic, dependable and clearly in no way interested in bird-watching.

"I'll be happy over there. Don't worry about me, Miss."

"Where?"

"On that stone."

"Oh, that would never do. You might get the piles. Take one of the folding stools. I'll bring you a big plate presently, before we sit down. There's so much."

"Thank you, Miss."

A long pause supervened.

"Ma'am," Jacob whispered, "if you turn your binoculars thirty degrees to the left, not far away, against that brighter green shrubbery ..."

"No," gasped Lady Sutherland, loudly.

"Yes," whispered Jacob even lower.

"*No!* The grey-headed lovebird, what a heavenly green."

"*Agapornis canus*. I have not seen it before."

At last Maud finished laying out on the card table this splendid picnic luncheon with plates, knives, forks and all other necessaries. It took longer than she had hoped because as the contents of the hampers gradually disclosed themselves in ever greater profusion through the late morning, she was oppressed by the need to follow cook's prompts, as well as Mr Craddock's. If any unused or at least undeployed comestibles were returned untouched—which would have been Maud's preference—the ramifications in the kitchen and pantry were too horrible to contemplate. In this regard, Foster was a boon, because onto his overladen platter of extra food Maud was able to heap those items she knew from experience held less appeal to Lady Sutherland than certain of the others. She did not think of herself, and she did not care about Mr Beck. She wondered why Craddock thought it necessary to send four large thermoses, thus furnishing *oceans* of tea.

"Luncheon is ready, Lady Sutherland," said Maud, who was by then hungry.

"Wait a bit. Wait a bit, the Pink pigeon—a pair! You see, over on the branch of that tree?"

"I see them, Ma'am: *Nesoenas mayeri*. According to Crabtree, they sift with their beaks through the leafy matter on the forest floor. They use their beak to turn over dried leaves in search of grubs."

"Just marvellous, isn't it, Mr Beck? And the loveliest of greys. I must remember to write and ask my milliner if he needs any. Well, come along Mr Beck we must feed you or you will starve."

It was, to some extent and broadly speaking, merely a conventional picnic, but upon getting up and turning around Jacob couldn't believe his eyes. The card table was heaped high. Over a crisp white tablecloth embroidered with the badge of St Edward, together with a neat stack of Royal Doulton plates and silver knives and forks and cake forks were arranged on plates and stands and in bowls and baskets cold salmon with mayonnaise, cold pheasant, Scotch eggs, pressed tongue, pork pies and pastry sandwiches. There were curried eggs, cucumber sandwiches and chicken sandwiches, not too gooey, not too lumpy, just right. And there were lemon sponges, little custard tarts and several large thermoses of tea.

"Oh, dear Maud, isn't this place simply beautiful? And Mr Beck has found me the most glorious array of treats. You have *not* disappointed."

"Very beautiful," ventured Maud, lacking conviction but making up for it with her wonted brightness. This place reminded her of the coppice beyond the bicycle shed at school where she and Cynthia used to go and scoff illicit boiled sweets after Mrs Hall's calisthenics lesson before prep.

It has been suggested that the English upper class has never been at all interested in food, merely shooting at it. That may be true but it is irrelevant. Neither Millicent Sutherland nor Maud Davies belonged to the English upper class so it is not surprising that one of the few things they had in common was a deep love of eating. They ate a lot, and they ate quickly and appreciatively. Foster, meanwhile, liked his grub. Jacob was slightly overwhelmed by eating so much food at lunchtime. Nevertheless, he took full advantage of the opportunity. In a way, Jacob had exchanged a morning of bird-watching for a morning of English-watching. Afterwards and somewhat sheepishly, Jacob produced the flask from his knapsack.

"May I?"

"Of course, Mr Beck, but only if you tell me what is in it."

"It is a fine old Gwern wine that Maman Beck has kept aside in the cellar of her café all these years."

"It looks as though you are enjoying it, Mr Beck."

"Yes, Ma'am. It is good."

"Maud dear, pass me the cup off the top of the thermos. I simply must try. Is there enough?

"Of course, there is plenty."

"Are you sure?"

"Yes."

"You see, I am beginning to find the cellar at Government House—perfectly agreeable, of course, and very adequate—slightly dull. There is a certain sameness. I must speak to Craddock. And now I learn that excellent wine is available from Gwern. How useful!" Lady Sutherland burped. "Gracious, do please forgive me. It must have been those Scotch eggs. I simply adore them. One or two is never enough and three is too many. Where can one obtain this delightful drink. I must ask Craddock to get some."

"Some comes to the islands by ... informal channels."

"Oh!" Lady Sutherland exclaimed with a shriek of delight. "Smugglers! How romantic."

"However this was produced legally in the Bailiwick Ma'am," said Jacob hastily, "from the vineyards on Gwern. They were all planted by French refugees of the *Révolution*. It is much cooler there, and the vines have always been sheltered from the prevailing wind."

"Oh I see. Yes, quite. No, no, just a drop. Plenty, thank you. To absent friends!" At first, Lady Sutherland sipped with caution.

"Heavens! That *is* pungent, isn't it? But so *interesting*." She sipped again. "Sharp but sweet."

Maud munched aggressively into the flank of her pork pie, feeling very much as if she too would have liked to taste this unusual cordial had the opportunity presented itself, which clearly it wasn't going to. Tea would have to do. Lady Sutherland drained the rest of her cup much as, following the destruction of Elphinstone's army, having staggered into the sanctuary of Jalalabad, Assistant Surgeon William Brydon, its sole survivor, drank clean water for the first time in days.

"Delicious!"

Aback does not even begin to describe what Maud was privately taking.

"You must have a little more, Lady Sutherland."

"Well, I really shouldn't, Mr Beck, because that flask of yours is not very big."

"I insist."

"Are you quite sure?"

"Of course." Jacob decanted a sizeable slug of maman Mastise into the thermos cup, and Lady Sutherland drank.

In her boarding school in England, Millicent Sutherland had been a bright girl, very fond of Latin. She had taken to it, in fact, like *Anas platyrhynchos* to water. In later years, after Lettice and Harriet were packed off to the same boarding school, old and respectable, certainly, but more affordable than most, she was still inclined to chide Sir George from time to time with playful Latin mottoes such as, whilst wagging her finger, "*De minimis non curat lex*." Or, in rare moments of heightened tension—no marriage is without them—something along the lines of "*Acta exteriora indicant interiora secreta*: George, I do mean it," a fact of which he was well aware. She had also made it her business to explore Pliny, and was familiar with his famous dictum *"in vino veritas"*, and she was starting to see the truth in a great many things, all at once.

Furthermore, following upon such an enjoyable series of bird treats that morning, and such a pleasant picnic lunch in this most beautiful glade, almost Arcadian such were its charms, its softness, its Cytherean quality—and the view!—Lady S. was beginning to look upon Mr Beck with brighter, somewhat dreamier eyes of affection. With every sip from her cup she felt the weight of decades falling away. With every sip, one by one her residual vexations evaporated; one by one, the awful responsibilities associated with supporting her husband in the exercise of his solemn vice-regal office were ever so slightly alleviated. In other words, every sip brought strange but entirely pleasurable vibrations. In her mind's rapidly adjusting eye, the vessel from which she drank ceased to be the top off a thermos in sensible bakelite. It was, if you will, a sort of chalice, a royal stoup, to which only the finest wine may ever be entrusted on a day as beautiful as this.

"And what is the name of your delicious wine, Mr Beck?"

"'*Domaine des Sept Vallées*,' Ma'am."

"How *poetic*."

"Maman Beck likes it very much also."

"I'm sure she must." Millicent Sutherland was by then remembering that famous episode in the *Historia Naturalis* in which Queen Cleopatra laid a wager with Mark Antony, claiming that she could easily outstrip, and by a considerable margin, his preposterous efforts at show and extravagance by serving a single simple dish that cost 10 million sesterces. Cleopatra took a crystal goblet charged with vinegar and, removing one of her not quite priceless pearl earrings, dropped it into the liquid. Slowly but surely, the pearl dissolved. With grand disdain, and surrounded by Mark Antony's Babylonian display of waste and decadence, Cleopatra triumphantly proceeded to drink this concoction, a concoction that, after all, cannot have tasted all that different from this most ravishing *Domaine des Sept Vallées*, because of the sharpness, you see, and the lightness and joy that it imparts also. Queen Cleopatra won the bet. Further, it then suddenly occurred to Lady Sutherland that the other parallels were too numerous, obvious and amusing. However, the tables were turned, weren't they? Because it was she, for the time being a *vicereine*, who had provided this gorgeous picnic lunch, but dear Mr Beck who had with only a little of this quite breathtaking wine, and from that ugly little metal container, outshone it.

"I think if *I* had barged down the Nile, I'd have sunk," said Lady Sutherland, and burst out laughing.

"Are you all right, Lady Sutherland?" Maud suddenly wanted to go to the lavatory.

"I'm marvellous, thank you Maud. Never better." Lady Sutherland again burst into gales of laughter. "Oh dear, do please forgive me. It must be the emotion. Galliformes, by Jove, Falconiformes. And the mountain air and such an excellent picnic. Do please tell Craddock when we get back that cook really has excelled himself today."

"Of course, Lady Sutherland."

"It was the pearl!" she exclaimed, clapping her hands. "Is there a secret ingredient? Some old Alsatian vintners' technique happily marooned on Gwern ever since the French Revolution but since then entirely forgotten at home? Come, come, dear Jacob, you must tell me."

"I do not know."

"How is that possible? You know so much!"

"If you say so, Ma'am."

"In any event, George and I must visit Gwern as soon as possible and be graciously pleased to allow them to present to us some crates of this quite ravishing *Domaine des Sept Vallées*—more please—no, more than that, please don't stop. Thank you. Where was I?"

"You mentioned a pearl."

"Oh yes, quite. Maud, dear. Write this down while I think of it. If I ever needed to do it—and I certainly never shall—but if I did," Lady Sutherland was attempting to keep a straight face, "the very last method I would choose is to clasp a bloody asp to my bosom." Again Lady Sutherland roared with laughter. "You know?"

Not only did Jacob not know; Jacob had no idea what Lady Sutherland was talking about. However, the phenomenon he was observing was well known to him. Therefore, he was quite pleased with himself. She resumed.

"Now I see Foster is looking shifty over there, aren't you, Foster? *Shifty*. And Maud, you've packed up all the things. Well done you." More laughter. "Is it nearly time for us to go back?"

"I am afraid so, Ma'am," said Jacob. "But we shall return."

Maud looked daggers.

"Return, Mark Antony, return! Oh yes, *please*."

The little party duly retreated down the footpath to the cul-de-sac, where the Rolls Royce motor car awaited them. By then, to Maud's infinite relief, Lady Sutherland had decided that having stretched her legs, yes, she would very much like to avail herself of the amenities at *La Plaine des Poivres*.

This and all the villages like it in the more arable north of St Edward mostly existed to accommodate people who worked on the nearest French land owner's great estate. The bigger the estate, the bigger the village. *La Plaine des Poivres* was smaller than most, so its amenities were basic. However, it did have a little pub that Jacob assured Maud during the planning phase would if necessary be more than willing to afford Lady Sutherland the opportunity to refresh. Few motor cars, much less the Governor's Rolls Royce, ever passed through *La Plaine des Poivres*, only mules. Therefore, the return of this enormous glossy black conveyance, which had, of course, passed through earlier without stopping, and the fact that this time it did stop, was remembered there for many years afterwards. Villagers converged from all sides. Many of them greeted Jacob with particular warmth, and for the first time that day Jacob felt uneasy. Would Lady Sutherland notice the high esteem in which he was held by people who should really have been strangers to him? But equally, would the people misconstrue the easy familiarity with which Jacob consorted with the enemy—riding in luxurious state, if you please, while the rest of them laboured under the yolk of *la tyrannie anglaise*. It seemed to him that in *La Plaine des Poivres* he was walking a tightrope.

"How charming! Now, while Maud and I are gone, dear Jacob, please thank them all very much indeed for coming to see me."

"Of course, Lady Sutherland."

"Come, Maud."

As they approached the front door—a small crowd parting deferentially like unto the parting of the waters when Moses led the people of Israel out of Egypt—the somewhat dessicated-looking publican of the *Hôtel les Roches Grises* was waiting to receive Lady Sutherland, and his plump and breathless wife was making ready to present Her Ladyship with a cheerful but rather wilted posy. Their appearance alarmed Maud, who was trotting along behind, to the extent that it offered no reassurance about the state of *les toilettes*. Still, it was too late now. In Burma, Lady Sutherland had become a dab handler of large gatherings of local people mainly because their physical disparity, hers and theirs, allowed her effortlessly to command the sort of respect that a blue whale automatically receives from schools of sardines. It was not a skill after which she had ever hankered, nevertheless it came naturally. Fearlessly, and with much continuing merriment, she accepted the publican's welcome; pretended to admire the bouquet before lobbing it to Maud; strode inside and nodded affably, smiled brightly to all the customers in the tiny front bar. Under normal circumstances, Lady Sutherland would never have run the dreadful risk of addressing any such hostess or gathering in French. Hers was functioning, certainly, but she realized it lacked beauty and rhythm. However, these were not normal circumstances. That was before mastise. Instead, she turned grandly to the publican's wife.

"*Madame, où est-ce que je peux aller me repoudrer, me rafraîchir,* spend a penny, *comme nous anglais disons, hein?*"

"*S'il vous plaît,* Madame." The publican's wife led Lady

Sutherland down a narrow damp corridor strongly reminiscent of Zola and gestured to a rather narrow door.

"*Voilà, Madame.*"

"*Merci bien.*"

Many years later, it was still remembered of that occasion that upon entering the designated booth or hutch Millicent Sutherland burst into fits of laughter so loud that they might easily have been heard as far away as Le Tampon. These effusions continued throughout the duration of her quite lengthy withdrawal. She re-emerged comparatively refreshed and, wiping from her eyes tears of mirth, rejoined the publican's wife. Maud then discreetly took her turn. Instead of laughter, however, there was a sharp scream, followed by an eerie silence from within. It was never discovered what in particular brought forth the laughter, or elicited the scream, for afterwards Lady Sutherland mentioned the matter only once, and Maud never did. Passing back through the tiny front bar, its many patrons broke into spontaneous applause, as did the attentive crowd of villagers outside.

"How touching," Lady Sutherland said to Maud, whilst nodding and waving with dignity in acknowledgment of the people. "I must ask George to get them a lavatory, or at least something to sit on," with which, once again, in her rich baritone Lady Sutherland erupted into yet more fulsome laughter.

Maud felt sick, but soon they were on their way back to Government House. Not even Elizabeth Woodville, flying with her daughters into the safety of Westminster Abbey upon the readeption of Henry VI, could have yearned for sanctuary more than Maud did.

The only other thing that unnerved Jacob that day overlapped with the first. It was what Foster said. Both men were standing expectantly beside the idling Rolls Royce while Lady Sutherland and Maud were performing their ablutions inside the Hôtel les Roches Grises. Having been chatting affably with a few of the villagers whom he obviously knew, Jacob turned and found that Foster's solemn, steely eye was fixed upon him. The chauffeur's arms were crossed, and he was motionless. At length, at very great length, Foster said:

"I've got my eye on you, lad, and don't you forget it."

Earlier that morning, after the conference with Sir George, Norman hurried through the grounds and down past the mews, as inconspicuously as possible. He was beginning to lose count of the number of times he had done this through the previous forty-eight hours, so he doubted whether it made much sense even to try to look scarce. Old Sock was busy layering his compost and seemed not to notice Norman, although of course he did. Foster was cleaning the Rolls Royce, inside and out, with far more than his customary zeal; just then he was worrying over the calfskin upholstery in the rear compartment.

It was, as usual, a beautiful morning; the sun was strong, but its radiance was softened by a gentle sea breeze that rustled through the branches of two splendid horse chestnut trees on the Bishopscourt side. Norman passed through the lychgate, trotted up the stone path to the front door, and rang the bell. Just then he reflected that in a more conventional location—Wimbledon, for example—Bishopscourt would resemble any other spacious suburban villa erected in the past twenty years; but the position it shared with Government House, high upon the northern end of the Observatory Bluff, surrounded by the magnificent park and gardens, conferred much dignity. Smith, the Stanleys' maid, ushered Norman into the parlour, and, after a brief absence, led him along a number of long dark corridors and into the study, where Bishop Stanley was intent upon solving his crossword puzzle.

"Good morning, Threlfall. Do sit down. Thank you, Smith."

"My Lord."

Smith evaporated.

"Good morning, Bishop," said Norman in his most business-like manner.

"'Roast Mules go topsy-turvy,' in ten letters," said the Bishop. "Something, something, *M*, something, something …"

"It's obviously an anagram, Sir." Norman pondered.

"Yes, quite," muttered the Bishop. "Roast Mules … Something, something, *M* …" he repeated thoughtfully.

"'Somersault'."

The Bishop looked up and blinked. "Well *done*! You must pay a morning call far more often, Threlfall. What can I do for you?"

"I bring the compliments of His Excellency, Sir, and a slightly unusual request."

"It has been twenty-five years since I was ordained and consecrated a bishop in the Church of God—Old William Cape Town did the honours. Since that day I have found most requests that find their way to my doorstep are unusual, more often preposterous. Tell me all about it." The Bishop reached for his pipe.

"The Governor wonders if you might be in a position to conduct a discreet burial."

The Bishop blinked. "I see. Who is the deceased?"

"I'm afraid we don't know. Not yet."

"But I take it the body has been released for burial. Is the undertaker Mr Murray? What about the next of kin?"

"That's just it, Sir. The body was found yesterday morning in the rear compartment of the Governor's motor; we believe it was placed there on purpose, but we know nothing more about it—him—than that."

"On purpose, you say?" The Bishop was momentarily baffled.

"Deliberately," said Norman. "It—he—may even have been put there with the particular aim of embarrassing the government."

"In which case, whoever put him there obviously succeeded." The Bishop crossed his legs. "You're quite sure he's dead?"

"Quite sure, Bishop. In the circumstances, the Governor wishes the matter to be treated with circumspection."

"No fuss?"

"None."

"Yes, well, that's probably for the best."

"Sir?"

"Mr Murray makes a great deal of fuss; undertakers generally do."

Norman absorbed this as best he could.

"'I am the Resurrection and the life, saith the Lord,'" continued the Bishop, rather wearily.

Norman cleared his throat, and pressed on. "Yes, Bishop, but now His Excellency is anxious for the remains to be given a decent burial—as discreetly as possible."

"Was the deceased baptized?"

"I assume so, Sir, but to be honest there is much about him we simply do not and, at this stage, cannot know."

"What on earth do you mean?"

The conversation proceeded in this awkward manner, no less difficult than Norman's discussion with Lady Sutherland some days earlier. Norman felt that it was only proper to make a full disclosure of the present condition of the headless, limbless torso.

"Might this have something to do with the lumpy child's mattress that, from her bedroom window one morning last week, Mrs Stanley observed Surgeon Commander Clark, Mr Craddock and Foster removing from the Governor's motor, and then deposit most secretively in, I believe, the laundry? My wife can be very ... observant."

"Ah, yes. Quite so." Norman had not taken account of the uninterrupted line of sight from the south side of Bishopscourt. In the circumstances, he felt he might as well go on to describe the pink lady's foundation garment in which the headless torso was clad. The Bishop was troubled by this detail.

"There is no other hint at religious affiliation?"

"Bishop?"

"I mean, he doesn't *sound* Church of England."

Norman did not necessarily think the deceased sounded significantly less Church of England, or markedly more so, than any other headless torso that had ever been discovered dressed in nothing but ladies' smalls. Prudently, however, he kept his counsel. "It is possible, Bishop, that the remains were merely wrapped up that way."

"Is that your own view?"

Norman, at this point, felt the full moral force of the Bishop's kindly but shrewd gaze.

"No, Sir."

"I didn't think so." The Bishop continued to puff with reassuring calm.

Norman found himself wondering how many communicating members of the Church of England, apart from defrocked clergymen, ever found their way into the French Foreign Legion, and, of these, how many were likely to acquire a tattoo. He guessed rather few.

"There are canonical difficulties, Threlfall," said the Bishop, apparently for the moment setting aside the matter of the foundation garment.

"No doubt, Bishop."

"In the first place, 'Man that is born of woman hath but a short time to live, and is full of misery. He cometh up, and is cut down, like a flower ...' but he is not often divided into separate pieces, of which only a limited selection is, in due course, made available for burial;" the Bishop gestured with the stem of his pipe, "'... in sure and certain hope of the Resurrection to eternal life through our Lord Jesus Christ; who shall change our vile body, that it may be like unto his glorious body, according to the mighty working, whereby he is able to subdue all things to himself.' This is an important point, Threlfall."

"Yes, of course."

"Second, 'Thou knowest, Lord, the secrets of our hearts;' but I, for one, would need to know a little more about the secrets of *his*—I mean, of course, that of the deceased—before I could in good conscience commit his mortal remains to the ground. I mean, of course, the bits of him that you are, at this stage, sitting on—and, besides, ideally one would wish for a closed coffin."

"Yes, naturally," said Norman, attempting to grasp the three-way connection between secrets of the heart; the missing portions, and a closed coffin. "I should perhaps add that we are sitting on one bit only, but it does constitute the majority."

"And third," continued the Bishop in his methodical way, "there is the question of the ground itself. My chapel here is of course at the Governor's disposal—provided I can get rid of my chaplain for the day—and I suppose I could consecrate some suitable plot, but, you see, Mrs Stanley is rather fond of the garden."

"Ah."

"These are formidable obstacles."

"If a suitable spot could be found on the Government House side?"

"Possibly, yes," The Bishop puffed thoughtfully for a moment. "Had you thought of consulting Monsignieur Lebecq? In my experience, there's hardly anything they won't bury."

Of course, he hoped the Bishop would appreciate that for a number of excellent reasons Norman was not in a position to do this.

"No, of course you can't." The Bishop pondered further. "Burial at sea? I'm sure Bracegirdle has the wherewithal."

"Tricky."

"Yes, but far less tricky than having to explain how a headless torso came to be buried in an unmarked grave on the grounds of Government House, when, at some future date, it is accidentally exhumed by the gas man's trench digger. Still, all credit to Sir George for exploring the available options."

"Thank you, Bishop," said Norman, rising to leave.

"Don't mention it. Oh, Threlfall, before you go …"

"Yes, Bishop?"

"'Amundsen's Forwarding Address,' in four letters: something, something, something, *H*."

"South Pole?"

"I assume so."

Norman thought for a moment. "Mush."

"Well *done*!" said the Bishop with a twinkle. "Do let me know what you would like me to do," he said. "I'm sure one could overlook the register of burials; but there will of course, be a modest fee."

In a small antechamber outside Colonel Truffe's office a small man waited patiently. He wore a black overcoat, rather tightly buttoned across his tubby form. A bowler hat sat on his knees, and a battered briefcase rested next to his feet, which did not quite meet the floor.

"Ah, Monsieur Baiser," said Colonel Truffe. "Thank you for coming, *mon vieux*. There is work to be done."

After dinner, in the airy drawing room of the Les Humeurs, Mrs Hodgkinson and her husband were arguing—parrying would perhaps be the better word. The ocean sighed through the French windows, which were propped open, and a light, warm breeze caressed the palms and flowering shrubs outside. From time to time the gauzy curtains were set in gentle motion, and, on the side-table, her carnivorous-looking potted orchids swayed and nodded in unison. Mrs Hodgkinson was artfully draped over the chaise longue, sipping Turkish coffee from a tiny gilded cup. Fang was similarly arranged on the floor adjacent. Pacing the room, Gene was expressing concern about the direction in which his wife's work appeared to be going. He pointed out the vast gap between her sales, particularly of *Seraglio Governess*, and the pitiful sums that had ever been earned by James Joyce. Hell, it was right there in *Publishers' Weekly*; she could see for herself. That was all very well, but Mrs Hodgkinson objected that sales were not always the fullest measure of success, although she was obliged to admit that they *were* among the more reliable. What about art? Mrs Hodgkinson could lecture Gene about art as much as she liked, once she discovered, in due course, the extent to which her readers would feel betrayed—for this was Gene's gravest fear. Mrs Hodgkinson freely acknowledged, but with impatience, that Gene *might* have a point. He went on to urge his wife not to be seduced by the arch methods of those pansy Bloomsbury types, but to take his advice and go for a more robust style, as exemplified by Zane Grey, author of *Riders of the Purple Sage* and other novels Gene thought were pretty damned good. Mrs Hodgkinson's mind raced. She sat up straight, crossed her legs, lit a fresh cigarette, and considered aloud the possibilities of the Western Romance, for example *Lambs to the Slaughter*—the twin daughters, perhaps, of a wicked cattle baron, who both fall in love with a retired gunslinger turned sheep farmer—let us call him ... Johnboy Valentine; the dull sheen of gun metal, the worn leather chaps, the twin daughters' tight-fitting *chaquetilla camperas* falling to the rude floor of an adobe hut in an out-of-the-way corner of their father's vast ranch; the saddle, the harness, the jingle of spurs, the riding crop … That, urged Gene, with a commercially astute snap of the fingers, which startled Fang, sounded exactly like the kind of sure-fire thing Mrs Hodgkinson's readers would seize upon. *Yes*! Did he mean the unbearable dry heat of the *American Cordillera*? That he most definitely did. The hopeless desolation of stones, baked under a relentless, unforgiving sun—not a blade of grass; only the occasional wrinkled, thorny cactus? Now she was talking. Lured into a jealous rage thanks to the devious machinations of one of the sheep farmer's proud half-breed servants, a shapely older woman of Navajo and Spanish descent, might not the twin sisters fight viciously, tooth and nail, even in the dirt outside a sordid tavern—at the last minute dragged apart by the handsome Reverend Doc Armstrong? Gene knew, he just *knew*, goddammit, Mrs Hodgkinson would see things his way. Perhaps, perhaps. However, Gene needed to understand that Mrs Hodgkinson really did feel the call of *Do What Thou Wilt*? This, she was quite sure, was something Mrs Hodgkinson needed to follow as far as it took her. It was, Gene warned, mighty strong medicine. Strong medicine, responded Mrs Hodgkinson, was exactly what these parlous times cried out for. If she said so. Yes, she most certainly did. Very well, but Gene implored Mrs Hodgkinson at least just to think about it. Of course she would; Gene's was the opinion she valued above all others, as of course he knew perfectly well. And, without question, she promised to introduce a lean, suntanned gunslinger to her next Southern romance, bringing a touch of the Old West to the Spanish moss, the antebellum mansions, the swaggering plantation owner; he *was* such a treasure. Gene feinted, turning as if to leave, and then pounced, emitting the growling noises he wrongly presumed Mrs Hodgkinson enjoyed so much.

"Oh Gene."

Fang slunk out of the room, and crept into his basket on the veranda outside the bedroom—where, patiently, he began to gnaw at yet another very large bone.

As Professor and Mrs Hodgkinson were discussing the possibilities of the modern western romance, Colonel Pole was walking down a narrow alley in the *Vieux Carré*. A sea mist had come in, the few electric lights emitted no more than a dim glow. The colonel stopped at a darkened doorway, a pair of worn but carefully polished shoes were all that was visible of the man standing in the doorway. The colonel extracted a cheroot, and lit it, as always, one-handed. The match flared, briefly lighting the face of M Orlando's head cashier.

"What do you have for me André?"

"Monsieur Orlando had a visitor. It was Beck. I don't know what they discussed, but Orlando looked most displeased, and left shortly after Beck."

"Good work lad." Colonel Pole tucked a folded St Edward five pound note into André's breast pocket, and walked back the way he had come.

CHAPTER 11

Mousseline-de-soie

Mike and Sharon
2020

Strategic? 1940?
Wakey wakey

You are seriously fucking
annoying me today

ILY2. Think I worked it out.
Went to London Library.
Theres this amazeballs
librarian there. Shes been
really great. Deirdre. Love
her. Can find anything in 5
minutes. Figured out what
happened St Edward in 1940

1940?

Nazis occupied Channel
Islands and St Edward? Not
liberated until 1945? Did you
even do the entrance exam?

Fuck off

Anyhow they did. St Edward
must have made it onto
agenda for the first time

Havent got time for
history lessons

Shut up. Thing is, I read the
file. A few things jumped out.
Theres an *unofficial* paper
trail as long as your arm

Jesus

All you need is a brain. Thats
comforting in the short
term but even dumb phone
hacking Murdoch morons
at Daily Mail will work it
out eventually. There will
be a story Mike. Question is
what story?

Just get me something to
flick to Downing Street per
kind favour Nob

Need to get hold of old
memoir entitled Hush
Hush (not joking) by
Cynthia Gribble

*   *   *

1926

CABLE TELEGRAPH

MOST SECRET REFER CIPHER
JENKINS—COLONIAL OFFICE WHITEHALL
REQUEST URGENT ASSISTANCE STOP
REMAINS UNIDENTIFIED MALE DEPOSITED
IN GOVERNORS MOTOR STOP PART TATTOO
BELIEVE FRENCH FOREIGN LEGIONNAIRE
STOP POWERFULLY BUILT STOP APPEARS
PERISHED IN EXPLOSION STOP DECEASED
WORE PAIR LADIES CAMI-KNICKERS STOP
PINK MOUSSELINE SOIE STOP VERTICAL
STRIP TUCKS DECOLLETAGE STOP FINEST
VALENCIENNES LACE STOP SMALL ROSE
EMBROIDERED EACH SCALLOP KNICKER
PORTION STOP HIGHEST QUALITY STOP
LAUNDRY MARK UNMISTAKABLY FRENCH STOP
READS HERSANT SDB 144 PLEASE IDENTIFY
CLIENT STOP RSVP STOP POLE

"You're quite sure mousseline-de-soie is strictly relevant, Craddock?" Colonel Pole was struggling with the cipher book. "Apart from this extraordinarily fiddly bit of code, there is also the added cost to consider."

"Would you like a hand, Sir? Oh my goodness, I'm so sorry."

Norman was doing his best to assist the Colonel; Craddock stood nearby.

"Quite all right, thank you Threlfall." The cipher was inclined to snap shut, but Pole had mastered the technique of using a paperweight and a pair of scissors to prop it open.

"Oh, yes, Colonel. Mousseline-de-soie is extremely fine, and most distinctive," said Craddock. "Milled, I believe, in Lyon."

"And the lace?"

"Unmistakable. Now produced by hand in Belgium, among the costliest."

"As you said yourself, Sir," said Norman, "we have two avenues of inquiry. The launderer's mark, and the garment itself. Craddock, you are quite sure?"

The three men turned their attention to the dainty article that was draped somewhat frowsily on the Colonel's desk.

"Quite certain, Sir. The genius of the new step-in cami-knicker is that the camisole and the knicker portions are combined so as to guarantee that waist slimness which is so desirable in long-waisted frocks." Craddock's tone was verging on the dreamy. "This model is so delicate that it could almost be threaded through a wedding ring. Fairy fingers must have been at work to produce such delicate, almost microscopic stitching—such tiny pleats and pipings and drawn-thread designs. *Beautiful.*"

"Could one pin it on a particular dress-maker?"

"Without doubt. Such a model could only have been made under the close supervision of a distinguished Parisian *lingère*—a rare artist employed by Callot Soeurs, Doeuillet-Doucet, Rouff, Philippe et Gaston, Chéruit, Louiseboulanger, those sort of people. Of course, their clientele will be treated with the utmost discretion ..."

"You mean?"

"Personal preferences—shrimp pink, apricot, buttercup, or pale mauve. Certain specifications. And, above all, measurements. The Queen of Spain, Frau Krupp, Madame Gulbenkian, Pavlova, Melba—none would wish these or, er, any other particulars to be broadcast, much less the terrific cost of such exquisite under-garments to be made known. The Aga Khan would not flinch at receiving an account for £600 or more from the Maison de Chéruit, but his eyebrows might well leap skywards if he knew that £450 of that went on the Begum's cami-knickers alone—capacious though they undoubtedly are."

"And, I suppose, the same would be doubly true of our French Foreign Legionary." Colonel Pole was a man of the world. "There *are* ways it could be done," he mused.

"Sir?"

"'Ah, Monsieur. Such a pleasure to see you again.' 'Mademoiselle is too kind.' 'How may we assist Monsieur?' 'A very special gift for Madame, a surprise. She has been very good. Something *intime*, you understand. She is most partial to little tucks, and scalloped lace ...' 'Does Monsieur think Madame might look with favour upon something of ... this quality?' 'Madame undoubtedly would.' 'Would Madame's figure—do please remind me—closely resemble that of my colleague here ... Mademoiselle may I borrow you for a moment?' 'I daresay Madame's figure is very nearly identical.' 'Very good. Does Monsieur wish to order a variety of shades and styles, and to which of his usual addresses shall we have them delivered?' Easily done."

"Yes, I do see." Norman pondered.

"However, the launderer's mark is, perhaps, the more likely to yield treasure." Colonel Pole returned to the realm of the practical. "But I suppose Jenkins will use his best judgment, and of course such of his resources as may be conveniently deployed in Paris." He reached for his cigarettes. "I wouldn't mind laying a wager on 'S. D. B.'"

"You mean that 'S. D. B.' is our man's initials?"

"Or those of the lady who will surely beat a path to our man."

"Quite so."

"Marvellous thing, the telegraph cable," Colonel Pole leaned back in his chair.

"Miraculous," said Craddock.

"Our station on Gwern is a vital link in the All Red Line—joins the Cape to Perth, Singapore, and on to Vancouver. Thousands of miles of British copper cable laid right the way across the ocean floor."

"More or less instantaneous test match results throughout the Empire." Norman was genuinely moved by the thought.

"All manner of uses," said Pole. "Including, now, secret inquiries about women's underclothes. Get rid of that pink thing, Craddock, there's a good chap."

The following day, in Whitehall, Jenkins received and carefully deciphered Colonel Pole's message from St Edward, Gwern and The Thimble Isles. Such communications, though relatively infrequent, rarely disappointed. At once Jenkins perceived that certain pieces of a puzzle, the dimensions of which had hitherto eluded him, were beginning to fall into place. What had caught his attention? It was insubstantial—shadows, rumours, ghosts; nothing he could yet present to his superiors in black and white. And yet, and yet ... His instincts told him Colonel Truffe was on the move. Gossip had been picked up by a British sailor in a bar in Marseilles. Whispers from an Algerian prostitute of a certain Foreign Legionnaire with very particular tastes in underclothes who had lately gone off the map. A report of cargo moved with great care from a seedy warehouse in Barcelona, and loaded late at night onto an even seedier steamer, the *Marianne*, registered under a flag of convenience, that of Liberia. Light had been seen to be burning late into the night in Truffe's office in the rue des Poitevins. And a source at the Bank of England told of a money trail running from the Champs Élysées branch of Crédit Commercial de France, through shell companies in the Netherlands Antilles and the Belgian Congo, thence to a certain Monsieur Orlando, guano trade, banker and financier on St Edward. The game was afoot, such as it was. Jenkins wired the embassy in Paris. It was, of course, known only to a few officers of the Secret Service that Fitzroy Bancroft, Second Secretary (Commercial), doubled as Head of Station.

CABLE TELEGRAPH

MOST SECRET. REFER CYPHER.
BANCROFT—H.B.M. EMBASSY, PARIS.

REQUEST URGENT ASSISTANCE STOP REMAINS
UNIDENTIFIED MALE RECOVERED ST EDWARD
GROUP STOP PART TATTOO BELIEVE FRENCH
FOREIGN LEGIONNAIRE STOP POWERFULLY

BUILT STOP APPEARS PERISHED IN EXPLOSION
STOP DECEASED WORE PAIR LADIES CAMI-
KNICKERS STOP PINK MOUSSELINE SOIE STOP
VERTICAL STRIP TUCKS DECOLLETAGE STOP
FINEST VALENCIENNES LACE STOP SMALL
ROSE EMBROIDERED EACH SCALLOP KNICKER
PORTION STOP HIGHEST QUALITY STOP
LAUNDRY MARK UNMISTAKABLY FRENCH STOP
READS HERSANT SDB 144 PLEASE IDENTIFY
CLIENT STOP RSVP STOP JENKINS.

More perhaps than most British missions abroad the Embassy in Paris existed in a bubble, as if the thrum of accordions, the fragrance of Gauloises, and the clatter and coughing of unreliable French automobiles did not exist immediately below her haughty façade above the rue du Faubourg Saint-Honoré. The offices of the Second Secretary (Commercial), were situated behind its upper windows, and on this particular morning Fitzroy Bancroft sipped his cup of tea and studied the latest cable telegraph from Jenkins in Whitehall. He re-read it with considerable distaste. His Service was not often called upon to penetrate quite so forensically into the sphere of ladies' foundation garments, but clearly Jenkins knew what he was doing, and it was also true that the gravest matters of counterespionage occasionally lurked beneath trivial snippets of information. He had an idea.

"May I have a word, Miss Gribble?" said Fitzroy Bancroft through the half-opened door to his office.

"Yes, of course, Sir." Cousin Cynthia rose from her desk,

which stood in the airy vestibule, took up her notebook, and briskly entered.

"Do sit down."

"Thank you, Sir."

"It seems we have another little conundrum."

"Goodness, Whitehall *is* keeping us on our toes," said Cynthia brightly.

"I am asked to identify the putative owner of ... this," Bancroft handed Cynthia a blue slip on which he had jotted down the particulars.

"Cami-knickers?"

"Yes."

"Rather a detailed description, isn't it Sir? Sounds *lovely*." For a moment Cynthia thought with dissatisfaction of her own rather dreary two-way stretch girdle, and shifted on her chair.

"Bit of a mystery to me, these things, Miss Gribble."

"Naturally, Sir."

"The laundry mark might help in the first instance."

"Quite. Powerfully built French foreign legionary killed in an explosion whilst wearing cami-knickers. On St Edward. How interesting."

"I suppose one shouldn't be surprised by that sort of thing."

"Happening on St Edward?" Cynthia was thinking of Maud.

"I really meant the cami-knickers."

"Ah yes, quite."

"And you see ... down here ... the presumption seems to be that the client and the deceased are one and the same. Do you think that is possible?"

"Technically possible, but rather improbable I should say, Sir."

"I gather Foreign Legionaries do occasionally come at it from odd directions."

"Odd enough for cami-knickers?"

"Evidently in this instance, yes."

"Beg, borrow or steal," gushed Cynthia. "Or did he run them up himself?"

"Jolly good," muttered Bancroft, unimpressed by the joke. "No, but the question is whether he bought them in Paris or had them laundered in Paris or both—or whether the previous owner, if there was one, can lead us to him."

"Yes I do see, Sir."

Fitzroy Bancroft pondered for a moment. "Do you think you could track down this, er, garment for me?"

"Quite easily I should think. One would start with the Eighth, and fan out from there. I should have thought, though, that this type of expensive hand-made thing would be entrusted to a rather grand *blanchisserie*."

"See what you can do."

"Certainly, Sir."

"Very hush-hush, mind."

"Of course, Sir. Thank you so much!"

"That's all."

Cynthia Gribble was rarely entrusted with a task as "active" as this, and such a task filled her with excitement. It took her very little time, consulting her well-thumbed Didot-Bottin, to deduce that the launderer's mark HERSANT probably corresponded with the daunting Maison de Blanchisserie Hersch at 76, rue du Faubourg Saint-Honoré, an establishment known in the highest circles of society to have been, on occasion, entrusted with the most delicate batches of fine intimate apparel shipped by the Maharani of Jaipur, Princess Bibesco, the Begum Aga Khan, among other ladies of demonstrated chic. Cynthia was therefore faced with a particular dilemma. She hurried home to her little flat. Looking in the mirror over the basin in her bathroom, she knew without any shadow of a doubt that it was quite impossible to pretend that she was not an English gentlewoman of a certain age, currently employed in His Brittanic Majesty's Embassy. There was no reason, she mused, not to wear this distinction with her customary pride, or, in this instance, exploit it, somewhat ironically, as a handy cloak of official secrecy—one that nobody in their right mind would think to question, since it was obviously true. She therefore put on her tweediest suit, her most sensible shoes, and a plain but smart hat that positively shrieked Home Counties, and strode out along the Faubourg Saint-Honoré, armed with a mannish black umbrella, expertly rolled, feeling rather like a powerful British and North American Royal Mail Steam-Packet endowed with the precious gift of being able to outrun those lesser, dirtier craft of the Compagnie Générale Transatlantique. She aimed to achieve results.

Though small, the vestibule of the Maison de Blanchisserie Hersch resembled that of a small but exclusive bank—all veined marble, Louis XVI *mirroir*, and a complete absence of signage—but for the letters H, wrought in gilt bronze, which formed the handles of the extremely heavy front doors. Cynthia found herself facing a sleek young man wearing a morning coat. He rose from behind an impressive tulipwood *escritoire*.

"*Bonjour*. Gribble from the Embassy. Now, look here. I have a particular problem."

"*Oui, Madame*?"

"It seems an elegant item of ladies' apparel has gone missing; it was laundered here. I believe the mark is HERSANT SDB 144."

"Gone missing?"

"Lost."

"*Lorst*?"

"Yes, lost."

"Ah, *disparu*. Most regrettable. One moment, Madame." The sleek young man retreated to the small *bureau*, and returned with an enormous register bound in red morocco leather. "Let me see. HERSANT SDB 144." He scanned the pages.

"Any luck?" Cynthia craned forward as far she dared, but the writing was far too small.

"Madame is quite right," said the sleek young man. "That order was carried out here several months ago, but it was definitely received by our client in good order. We are very particular in that regard."

"I see. Who was it?"

"*Pardon*, Madame?"

"Who was the client?"

"*Hélas*, Madame. I am not at liberty to say," said the sleek young man, firmly closing his register.

"Why not?"

"It is simply a matter of ... discretion, Madame. I am sure you understand."

"Not particularly. Never mind. I shall need to replace the

item for the lady in question. You see it was a gift. A gift from *him* to *her*."

"If you say so, Madame." The sleek young man gave Cynthia a look of undisguised scepticism.

"What?"

"I am sure I cannot say."

"Do you remember the order?"

"But how could one forget? Items of the most exquisite workmanship and *qualité*."

"Really?"

"Incomparable. Of course, one comes to recognize the artistry of the seamstresses, the *couturières distinguées* of the Maison de Paquin. Stitches one would attribute not to human fingers but to *les fées*, how do you say it?—the fairies."

"Paquin. In the Place de Vendôme?"

"Yes, Madame. Number 20."

"Right. Lovely. Thank you so much, you've been moderately helpful."

"We are at Madame's service."

As she stomped out, Cynthia could not help but feel irritation. That *nancy* at the Maison de Blanchisserie Hersch was completely intransigent. On the other hand, she reflected, striding determinedly back the way she came, she was simply loving this, one of only very few bits of undercover work that had ever been entrusted to her. She couldn't wait to write to Cousin Maud and tell her all about it; Aitken in Chancery would toss her letter in the bag, as usual—St Edward, such an undistinguished posting, poor darling Maud—embroiled no doubt in the matter of this deceased Foreign Legionary in cami-knickers, too strange.

At the same time, Cynthia pondered the particular problem of the Maison de Paquin. If the Maison de Blanchisserie Hersch could be so very cagey about their clients, God alone knew what could be done to prize information out of the Maison de Paquin. She needed leverage, the type that gives one real purchase. She smiled faintly, as, with private amusement, she seized upon the right strategy.

A little rain began to fall shortly before Cynthia reached her destination. As she sailed through the front doors of the Maison de Paquin, she shook her umbrella rather violently, and sniffed.

"Bonjour, Madame." An immaculately dressed *vendeuse* materialized.

"Bonjour. Gribble from the Embassy. Ladies' underclothes, please."

"But of course, Madame."

Cynthia was led upstairs, and through an apparently endless suite of elegant salons over which there hung an atmosphere of sumptuously perfumed hush. Naturally they struck Cynthia as rather vulgar, and not quite clean. Whereas from place to place various other lady customers conferred in confidential tones, each attended by one of the vendeuse's soignée colleagues, occasionally examining dainty articles of intimate apparel, gliding silently from *mode* to *mode*, Cynthia was inclined to bustle noisily—much as a really mature gnu makes her way into unfamiliar terrain, only dimly aware that she is disturbing entire herds of lithe gazelle. Reaching an especially spacious *boudoir*, dotted with divans and two or three large low frosted glass cases, daringly modern, the soignée *vendeuse* besought an equally immaculate Mademoiselle to assist Madame Gribble from the

Embassy. Mademoiselle was only too pleased to assist Madame; offered to relieve Cynthia of her scratchy coat and umbrella, and invited her to sit. How, then, could Mademoiselle be of service?

"Too kind," said Cynthia. "You see, Mademoiselle, I have a particular problem to solve, and I do hope you may be able to assist me."

"I shall do my best, Madame."

"Look here. For reasons that need not detain us, I need to replace a pair of lady's cami-knickers, which I gather were purchased here not long ago by a gentleman. The model was rather lovely, in mousseline-de-soie, with a strip of little vertical tucks in the décolletage. There were embroidered roses on each scallop around the knicker portion; point de Valenciennes, just perfect. *Pink*. But, you see, they have gone missing."

"*Gorn?*"

"Gone missing."

"Ah, *disparu?*"

"Yes."

"*Biensûr*, Madame. That particular article, *Rêve de Printemps*, forms part of our spring collection, most sought-after; a triumph of the most intricate workmanship. It is, of course, made to order—but I fear there is a long waiting list."

"*Rêve de Printemps*. Splendid. Well, that solves that." Cynthia scribbled in her little notebook, and snapped it shut. "I wonder if you could possibly just confirm for me the identity of the gentleman in question?"

"Madame?"

"The gentleman who bought the cami-knickers."

Mademoiselle regretted most sincerely that she could not possibly discuss any such matter with Madame Gribble.

"Why not?"

"Our clients insist upon the highest degree of discretion, and the Maison de Paquin prides itself upon meeting that obligation. *Je suis desolée*, Madame."

"You mean privacy?"

"Of course, Madame."

"Ah yes, naturally."

"*Oui*, Madame."

"I do wonder, though."

"Madame?"

"Well, it sort of depends on the circumstances, doesn't it?"

"I am not sure I understand, Madame."

"Yes, well, of course I quite see that the House of Paquin treats with utmost circumspection large orders placed by the Queens of Spain, Norway, Roumania, and of the Belgians, the Hellenes and so on ... By appointment, and all that. Also, I daresay, frightfully rich Americans such as Mrs Frick, Mrs Whitney, and so forth."

"I cannot comment, Madame."

"No, of course you can't. Good girl. Magnificent. It's just that ..." Cynthia leaned forward confidentially.

"Madame?" Mademoiselle was slightly alarmed by Cynthia's face, large and faintly yellow, as it advanced suddenly, the brim of her putty-coloured hat jutting like an inverted shovel.

"Well, the view of my Embassy might well be that, *equally*, the Maison de Paquin could ill afford to let it be known, *publicly*, that they purvey ladies' cami-kickers to discerning gentlemen for their own private amusement—as a matter of routine. Models,

I daresay, nearly identical with those supplied to the Queens of Spain, Norway, Roumania, and so on? I mean, Good Lord—think of the scandal!" Cynthia laughed in her hearty way, and looked around.

A well-known *vicomtesse*, assisted by one of Mademoiselle's soignée colleagues, was seated some considerable distance away, thoughtfully comparing several superb negligées.

"I say, Madame. *Madame*. Yes, you. Sorry to intrude, but, my dear, have you ever heard of such a thing? Gentlemen purchasing dainty cami-knickers for themselves! Actually to *wear*? Too funny. Next we ladies will be shopping for elasticized sock-suspenders! What do you say?" Cynthia's renewed chuckles loudly permeated neighbouring boudoirs.

The *viscomtesse* smiled politely, nodding her head several times in bewildered assent, and then rose and glided somewhat guiltily out of the boudoir. Other ladies farther distant hastened to escape from the appalling Englishwoman with the loud baritone.

Mademoiselle became deeply anxious. "Madame, *s'il vous plait*!"

"But you see? Such an immediate effect!" Cynthia's eyes narrowed. "The gentleman in this particular case—how can I put it?" resumed Cynthia. "Well, he is somewhat eminent, and it is a vital question of some delicacy for me to confirm his identity so as to take steps to prevent the gutter press from getting hold of it."

"Eminent?"

"Exceedingly. Obviously the Embassy can assure Madame Paquin that any such information will be treated with the strictest confidentiality."

"You say it is vital, Madame?"

"Without question."

"But Monsieur Baldwin is a most respected client."

"I *beg* your pardon?"

"Is that not the gentleman to whom you refer?"

"Mr *Baldwin*?"

"Lilac cami-knickers, always lilac—he is most particular."

"Mr *Stanley* Baldwin, the Prime Minister?"

"*Absolument.*"

"You must be mistaken."

"*Mais non*, Madame."

"Really, the very idea."

"Forgive me, Madame—but I thought ..."

"Never mind. At any rate, no, I was not referring to Mr Baldwin. No, no, no, indeed *no*. The gentleman of whose identity we are seeking confirmation had ... has, we believe, a *tattoo*. A relatively young French military gentleman, with refined tastes."

"*Militaire*?"

"Yes. He has, I believe, mainly served abroad."

"There are many gentlemen who patronise the Maison de Paquin."

"No doubt, but do please think. Young, possibly dashing— serving *abroad*."

Mademoiselle suddenly acquired a distant quality. "Ah yes, I think perhaps Colonel Di Bartolo."

"French?"

"*Mais oui*, Madame. A gallant *officier*."

"Di Bar ... do please spell it for me."

"Colonel Di Bartolo ... Dear Serge, so strong."

"S. D. B.," muttered Cynthia, scribbling in her little notebook once more, and with unalloyed feelings of triumph.

Mademoiselle recovered her composure. "Madame will place an order for the *Rêve de Printemps*?"

"What?"

"Pardon, Madame. But did not Madame wish to replace the *Rêve de Printemps?*"

"Good Lord, no. Far too expensive and impractical. One might as well freeze to death. Best to press on with Army and Navy."

Cynthia Gribble hurried straight back to the Embassy and reported her discovery to Fitzroy Bancroft.

"Well done, Gribble."

"Thank you, Sir," gushed Cynthia.

Bancroft then wired Jenkins.

CABLE TELEGRAPH

MOST SECRET. REFER CYPHER.

JENKINS—COLONIAL OFFICE, WHITEHALL.

BELIEVE SUBJECT INQUIRY COLONEL SERGE DI

BARTOLO STOP PURCHASED CAMI-KNICKERS

MAISON PAQUIN PLACE VENDÔME STOP

MODEL RÊVE PRINTEMPS STOP MERELY PART

LARGE ORDER STOP VERY COSTLY STOP

LAUNDERED MAISON BLANCHISSERIE HERSCH

STOP POSSIBLY EVEN MORE COSTLY STOP

BANCROFT

CHAPTER 12

An Order for the Burial of the Dead

Mike and Sharon
2020

Need to get hold of old memoir entitled Hush Hush (not joking) by Cynthia Gribble. Stupid cow later prosecuted under Official Secrets. Court transcript was in file with no explanation. Did time in Royal Holloway. Something to do with the Fitzroy Bancroft scandal

Nightmare. What makes you think that

Oh I dont know Mike, only court transcript of six hour cross examination in High Court of Justice about exactly when in 1927 did she learn Bancroft was Soviet mole. Why didnt she tell grownups

until 1951, that sort of
thing. Apparently it was
blackmail. Something to do
with a smutty novel, serious
customs infringements and
diplomatic bag irregularities.
Thing is, she was likely also
protecting her cousin Maud
who was actually working
at Government House St
Edward. Thought she might
bring shame on the family.
Shedve been right about that
wouldnt she? LOL

OK Fine. Look dont dig
any further. Just focus on
drafting me something new
(and good) on St Edward
file and Blitz. Now

On 30 Jan 2020, at 2:37 pm, Sharon Julius <sharonj@fcoff.gov.
uk> wrote:

Dear Dr Carter

Further to the recent application 5552391 under the Freedom
of Information Act, a second application, 5552391-1, has been
made for access to any and all documents that "will either confirm
or cast doubt on the claim that" Foreign and Commonwealth
Office records relating to the British Crown Dependencies of

St Edward, Gwern and the Thimble Isles (the Bailiwick of St Edward) were destroyed during the Blitz.

We regret that for reasons of national security we are unable to accede to this new request.

However, we can confirm that the relevant file was among approximately 1,800 that were incinerated during a Luftwaffe bombing raid over Whitehall on the night of 14 October 1940, a raid moreover in which many dozens of innocent British lives were lost.

We would respectfully refer any and all future or related inquiries to the relevant personnel in MI5 and/or MI6.

Yours sincerely,

Ms Sharon Julius
Second Assistant Under-Secretary, Political Affairs
Foreign and Commonwealth Office
Whitehall

Please consider the environment before printing this email message.

Got it?

Genius, especially bit about
national security followed
by bit about innocent lives
followed by bit about MI6.
Implicit linkage. Nice work

Jesus Mike. I think I know what Im doing. Patronising bastard. More KPIs.

Shag at mine?

Fuck off

*   *   *

1926

Well before dawn, under cover of pitch darkness, the gentlemen of the household made their extremely conspiratorial way down past the mews to the compost heap. Colonel Pole led the party; Commodore Bracegirdle and Surgeon Commander Clark followed, and, bringing up the rear, Norman, Colin, Foster and Mr Craddock carried between them Norman's steamer trunk, somewhat incommoded by the heavy contents. Old Sock stood disconsolately a little distance from the large deep hole he had, with great difficulty, been persuaded to dig right through the middle of his carefully tended mound of compost. Bishop Stanley waited patiently at the head of it. Had they been clearly visible, the two men might have resembled a sort of socially inverted Daniel and Nebuchadnezzar—the latter complaining about a dream which had made him afraid, and of the thoughts upon his bed and of the visions in his head, all of which troubled him.

"Bishop," said Colonel Pole, briskly. "Lovely morning for it."

"Don't be so silly, Pole. It's dark, damp and unhealthy.

Everyone here?" Without further preliminaries, Bishop Stanley intoned the rite of consecration—in record time. "O God, Who hast taught us in Thy holy word that there is a difference between the spirit of a beast that goeth downwards to the earth, and the spirit of a man which ascendeth up to God who gave it ..."

Norman could hardly believe it was possible to recite so quickly, whilst retaining absolute clarity of diction.

"... and likewise by the example of Thy holy servants, in all ages, hast taught us to assign peculiar places where the bodies of Thy saints may rest in peace, and be preserved from all indignities, whilst their souls are safely kept in the hands of their faithful Redeemer: accept, we beseech Thee, this charitable work of ours in separating this portion of ground to that good purpose, and give us grace, that, by the frequent instances of mortality we behold, we may learn and seriously consider how frail and uncertain our condition here on earth is, and so number our days as to apply our hearts unto wisdom; that in the midst of life thinking upon death, and daily preparing ourselves for the judgment that is to follow, we may have our part in the Resurrection to life with Him, who died for our sins, and rose again for our justification, and now liveth and reigneth with Thee and the Holy Ghost, one God, world without end. Amen."

"Amen," said the little congregation.

The Bishop blew his nose. "There," he said. "More or less fit for purpose."

"Thank you, Bishop," said Colonel Pole. "That was very fine, very beautiful."

The first light of dawn was indeed beginning to lend the palest blush to the horizon.

"Rubbish, Pole. And I am far from sure that you should be thanking me for consecrating Sock's compost."

"A most unusual exigency, Bishop. His Excellency is most grateful."

"'Preserved from all indignities,' Pole. I shall hold you to that."

"Yes, Bishop. Sock has undertaken not to dig deeper than ..."

"Yes, yes, I'm very pleased to hear it. And now to the consequent matter at hand. Threlfall, where is the deceased?"

"Here, Bishop."

"Ah, yes," said the Bishop, regarding Norman's steamer trunk with general disdain, and the White Star label with particular displeasure; it read *Not Wanted On Voyage*. "Did I not specifically mention a coffin?"

"Yes, Sir. I'm so sorry, but this the best we could do."

"It is sealed?"

"Locked."

"I suppose that will have to do," said the Bishop. "Shall we proceed?"

The congregation shifted uneasily in the darkness, vaguely aware of the Bishop's stole flapping in the breeze.

"Forasmuch as it hath pleased Almighty God of his great mercy to take unto himself the soul of our dear brother ..." The Bishop trailed off and turned to Norman.

"Serge, Bishop."

"*Serge*?"

"Yes, Bishop."

"Very well ... to take unto himself the soul of our dear brother," the Bishop cleared his throat, "*Serge*, here departed"—he uttered the name with marked absence of relish—"we therefore commit his body to the ground; earth to earth, ashes to ashes, dust to dust; in sure and certain hope ..."

That night Bishop Stanley was in his study reading a well-thumbed Gwladys Baring, *Drink To Me Only*. He was an admirer of Baring's work, such depth, such profundity, such wise appreciation of the ubiquity of sinfulness. Perhaps there was something here for this Sunday's sermon. His wife was playing patience. The streets of Port Charlotte were empty. The ballroom was closed. Above the Café des Artistes it was a slow night. There was only one client, Colonel Pole, who was engaged with the athletic Agmaya in a tantric congress of such complexity that it involves all seven available limbs. Lulu and Valérie slept, their arms entwined. Madame Beck studied her accounts. And in her little room Nathalie lay in bed, reading by candlelight, thinking of the young Englishman who so closely resembled Ivor Novello. He was a lovely dancer. And he had such nice hair.

At Les Humeurs, Mrs Hodgkinson lit a cigarette and put another sheet of foolscap in her small portable typewriter. Gene Hodgkinson lay awake in his bedroom, unable to sleep as the staccato rattle of his wife's new Corona No. 4 rose to a crescendo.

In Government House all was quiet. Cook and Craddock were still awake, drinking Sir George's brandy in the butler's pantry. *"Mon Homme"* drifted faintly from Norman's open bedroom window. All other members of the vice-regal household were asleep.

Old Sock sat in his room, staring through the window at the dark shape of Mount Raglan, from which distant drumming could just be heard.

"Aye," he muttered. "I have been all things unholy."

Later that night Miss Davies lay under her bedspread, curtains tightly draw, torch in her hand, reading avidly:

> ... sublime arrogance, Ali Bey stood upon the top step, magnificent in his uniform as colonel of the Circassian Guard. The hilt of his sword glinted in the warm moonlight. He turned to his escort. "Adnan, Ramzi, Nubar: That will be all; leave me at once and admit no-one," he barked.
>
> As the great ebony door slammed shut behind him, Cynthia heard the turn of a key in the latch. Her mind raced. Her heart beat faster. In her semi-nakedness, she cringed farther into the suffocating depths of the Sultana's scented cushions. They were quite alone.
>
> "I am innocent!" she cried.
>
> Ali Bey advanced slowly.
>
> "I see into your very soul, my child," his cruel bass baritone echoed the length of the imperial apartment. "At last you are mine once more. Your precious major is dead, *dead*," he rasped.
>
> Cynthia cried out.
>
> "There are no more British to rescue you now."
>
> A deep blush mounted upon Cynthia's heaving

bosom. More than her desperate protest, more than her scream of despair, that blush, that bloom, betrayed how far, yet again, the sight of Ali Bey ignited an exquisite, terrifying flame in Cynthia's heart and kindled that shameful, mad desire she had desperately tried to smother, out of higher devotion to poor Harold. Yet the flesh is weak. What was it about Ali Bey? His coal-black hair? His flashing eyes? The vicious flare of his nostril? His superb swagger, the tight buckskin breeches and glossy riding boots? The sheer, fascinating insolence?

"Get out! Or I swear I shall ..."

"What?! You *dare* to defy me?" Closer still, and closer, came Ali Bey, his powerful shoulders looming high over Cynthia's soft divan.

"Come no nearer, do you hear me? You, you ... *fiend*!"

"And what if I refuse?" he gritted, moving ever closer. "When I bought you from the Sultan of Huffuf—10,000 pieces of silver, and worth every one—I was not expecting such rebelliousness." He threw his head back, and laughed again— wildly. "I am my father's son!"

"Beast!"

Cynthia seized the dagger concealed under her pillow and, half mad with rage, flew at Ali Bey, lunging at him with all her might, but with lightning speed he seized her pale wrist and shook the dagger from her clasp. It scudded over the gorgeous carpets and came to rest under the Pasha's throne, distant and irretrievable.

"Vixen," his hot breath seared her cheek. "First you attempt to escape, and now this? That I should even want you at all ... But did you think you could overpower Ali Bey? He who is master of this palace, and all within? This is your fate. It is your destiny."

Cynthia almost swooned.

"*Brute*! You will never own me. Harold was twice, three, ten times the man you are," she panted.

Ali Bey laughed again and, laughing, gathered Cynthia into his powerful embrace.

"Such milk-white skin," he murmered. "Such golden tresses. Kiss me."

"*Never!*"

"Foolish child, you know perfectly well that I possess you, but completely. Kiss me again," he breathed.

"Let go of me!"

"And again."

"I would rather die!"

A gust of hot desert wind through the open latticework caressed Cynthia's lovely neck as once again, gasping, she succumbed to the prince's diabolical, thrilling touch as, with a single manly stroke, he tore the thin gauze from ...

CHAPTER 13

The Dreamland Ballroom

Mike and Sharon
2020

Fuck off

Nob reckons everyone in Downing Street now has keen interest in Mandingo Wars and the ancient religions of the Bailiwick of St Edward they never knew they had

Of course they bloody do. I got a shitload of stuff from Deirdre. Shes so great. You forget despite Entente, post WWI allied victory, Versailles etc. in the 20s the French really active against UK interests all over the shop. They financed hopeless local uprising thing on St Edward. Im talking gold, arms. They wanted the islands. They wanted the guano.

Great. PM will love that.
Gotta ask yourself why they
wanted it so much

Yes Mike *you* do. The rest
of us dont. Commodity
prices bonkers, off the scale
in 20s before Wall St crash.
Big agriculture basically
everywhere gagging for
nitrogenous fertisers. Plus
postwar soldier resettlement.
Fuck the environment. US.
Australia. Canada. South
Africa.

What about the wiccans?

Theleman. Ancient religion.
Nature worshippers. Fertility
spirits etc Solstice rituals. Lots
of sex

Sex?

Deirdre reckons pre
Christian, pre Roman, pre
everything. Been worshipped
St Edward thousands of years.
Bastards in Quai dOrsay
didnt hesitate to exploit it
against us (ie you)

God here we go again.
Someone got sand in
their vag?

*   *   *

1926

A week later Norman returned to the Dreamland Ballroom.

Nathalie was there. She had wondered if he would return. Her heart lurched as she saw him across the dance floor—elegantly sidestepping the sailors, farm labourers, gamblers and whiskey drinkers circling with the taxi dancers, the Saturday night hoofers clumsily attempting the Shimmy, the Lindy Hop, the Jitterbug, the Texas Tommy and the Shag.

"Shall we?" She smiled and nodded.

He took her in his arms. They glided across the floor, other dancers moved aside, made way for them. And when Claudette Moreau and the Café Orchestra stopped for refreshments they retreated to a quiet corner and talked.

"You work at the Café des Artistes?"

"I do the laundry. It is my mother's business."

"The laundry?"

"The Café des Artistes."

"When I saw you that night, you looked sad."

"Did I? Perhaps I don't want to be a laundry maid."

"What do you want?"

"I want my brothers to come back."

"Where are they?"

"They are dead."

"I am sorry."

"They were killed in the war. The British killed them."

"They fought for the Germans?"

"No, they were conscripted by the British. They had no choice, although it was not their fight. Your people killed them."

"I'm so sorry."

"I miss them so much."

"The war. It was terrible. So many dead."

"The farm workers say The Great Spirit Cernunnos can bring back the dead but no, my brothers will not return."

"Cernunnos?"

"Le Thelema. It's from the old times. Pagan. Before Christ. Before the standing stones." She laughed. "That's what the old ones say. The nuns try to stamp it out. And the British."

"You know I work for the British, at Government House."

"I know. You told me. And Yvette."

"How did she know?"

"Colonel Pole."

"The Colonel, but how ... ?

The band started up again, and again they danced. In silence.

She thought: He's with the British, but oh how he dances.

He thought: She hates us. But she's a good person. And a lovely dancer.

She thought: I should hate him.

He thought: She probably hates me.

She thought: They killed my brothers.

He thought: She's beautiful.

She thought: He is so handsome.

He thought: I'd like to see her again.

She thought: I'd like to see him again.

He thought: Should I ask?

She thought: Will he ask?

And when the music stopped their eyes met.

They did meet again at the Dreamland Ballroom the following Thursday night. He was wary. This could derail his career even more dramatically than it had previously been derailed. The band stopped at midnight, and they walked along the deserted streets of Port Charlotte, past the great guano warehouses. And under the towering, gloomy Norfolk Pines that lined the small beach next to the docks they sat, listened to the waves gently running up the sand.

"You look like Ivor Novello."

"You look like no one I've ever seen. You're beautiful."

"You English. Flatterer."

"Are you French?"

"No."

"But you speak French."

"My people were French, like so many on the islands. They escaped the revolution when they were children. Their parents did not. The British offered them sanctuary—the French wanted to kill them. So no, I do not think of myself as French. But you, you speak French so well."

"I lived in Paris for a while. I learned it from ... a friend."

"You were well taught."

"I had a good teacher."

"Tell me about Paris."

"It's beautiful. Much bigger than Port Charlotte."

"I know. My other brother Jacob told me. He went there, the nuns took him. Of course he was only interested in seeing the Eiffel Tower. He even met M. Eiffel himself, Jacob was so proud."

"The tower is quite something, but Paris, it's so much more. I think you'd love it, the cafés, the dance halls. Perhaps we'll go there one day."

"Perhaps," said Nathalie, a little sadly.

"I've been rude."

"How?"

"I haven't told you."

"Told me what?"

"That you dance divinely."

"You did mention it."

"Did I? Well it's true. You're a lovely dancer."

"So are you. But now I must go. Ma mere, you know."

"I'll walk you home."

A sea mist was rising, drifting in from the harbour. They walked under the Norfolk Island pines towards the Café des Artistes. Moonlight filtered through the trees, creating gossamer shafts through the mist.

"Look at that," she said.

"Moonbeams."

"Yes, like dreams."

"Like you."

They kissed.

"Where did you learn to dance like that?" Norman asked.

"I can't help it. It's the music. It does something to me."

"It must be some kind of affliction."

"It's a curse."

"And there's no cure?"

"No."

They stopped in a dark doorway. They kissed again.

"You should have told me."

"Told you what?"

Again they kissed, then walked arm in arm until they arrived at the Café des Artistes.

"The men here ... they only think of one thing."

"What's that?"

"Guano." She smiled, and in the shadows outside the Café' des Artistes, one last kiss.

"Goodnight."

Norman danced away.

"Bonsoir."

Nathalie blew a kiss.

CHAPTER 14

Charades

Mike and Sharon
2020

God here we go again.
Someone got sand in
their vag?

                Just saying. And fuck
                off Mike.

Thing is, we need to kill the
whole fucking story

                We? LOL. Good luck with
                that. Story will run

I dont want to know

                Yes you bloody do

Fuck

                Stop fucking and start
                listening. Theres a long
                passage in really boring posh
                memoir Vice-regal Days
                "on" St Edward by Lettice

Campbell. Emphasises the
hardship posting angle.
Spoiled cow

Get to the point

Plus 700-plus-page history
of long (unsuccessful)
struggle for freedom on St
Edward, Vers la republique
democratique mastisienne
by Giselle Beck. Very helpful
footnotes. Deirdre reckons
she had some sort of knocking
shop too. Tres Weimar.
Deirdres incredible.

Dont have time for this

*   *   *

1926

M. Orlando had been invited to join the household that evening
at the insistence of Sir George, and in the face of sustained
objections from his wife. The phrase he had used was something
like "necessary piece of diplomacy, my dear," to which at first
Lady Sutherland responded hotly by wondering if Sir George
had finally lost his mind. Not at all; if Lady Sutherland could
not grasp that it was plainly impossible for the Governor of St
Edward to avoid extending to the consul of France the courtesy

of an invitation to dinner at Government House, and as early as possible in their tenure, then Sir George wondered what on earth Lady Sutherland thought they were doing there.

"Fiddlesticks, George," had been Lady Sutherland's rejoinder, followed by many strong variants.

Lady Sutherland naturally accepted the principle, and would endure an evening in that frightful man's company provided it were leavened with a suitable admixture of the Chief Justice and his mousy little wife, Postmaster-General, Monsignieur Lebecq, Naval Station, Chamber of Commerce, Archdeacon Pearson, possibly one or two of the better planters (if ever they would deign to come), or Professor and Mrs Hodgkinson—but she hardly saw the need to absorb M. Orlando into the heart of what was effectively a family gathering. That, argued Sir George most persuasively, was the whole point of the exercise. Could Lady Sutherland not see that it was the very intimacy of the party that would itself amplify the honour of the invitation, and provide to the consul of France hard evidence of their bona fides? At length she had no choice but to accept that her husband was right. Sir George's single hard won concession to Millicent Sutherland had been to include the Hodgkinsons, for it could be argued that the Cincinnati Ohio & Delaware Banking Corporation was in many ways more important to keep close even than to feign doing so with M. Orlando. Besides, Mrs Hodgkinson was practically part of the household anyway.

Most reluctantly, meanwhile, Colonel Pole had had to excuse himself from that evening's entertainment, owing to pressing business in town.

Needless to say M. Orlando was unnerved. Discovering

upon his arrival that he was guest of honour, far from feeling warm gusts of gratitude, instead Orlando felt unease. There is somewhere nearby, he mused, a headless torso—presumably in rapidly deteriorating condition—the torso, moreover, of a great French hero of the Mandingo Wars. He was reasonably confident that even the English would not contemplate eating it, but the meal itself, which was endless and, to his eyes, lumpy and obscure, provided him with little reassurance. The social usage of the Governor's innermost circle, meanwhile, better resembled a clumsy game of football than that of a *banquet raffiné* in the noble French gastronomic tradition, with its unmatched eye for elegance and exquisite manners. As well, Orlando could not help but feel closely watched, as a visitor to the zoo is occasionally eyeballed from behind bars by a potentially hostile congress of baboons. Yet there was the fascinating presence of young Miss Harriet, a most welcome distraction.

After dinner, after the gentlemen re-joined the ladies in the large drawing room, and Mr Craddock distributed whiskies and soda from the drinks trolley, Lady Sutherland decided to marshal the household for charades. But before she did so, she was determined to take up a thread of conversation she had overheard quite clearly at the other end of the table. One of the particular skills of the hostess in those years, particularly the political hostess, was the capacity not only to speak and listen at the same time, but to speak and listen moreover to several other conversations all at once, some of them distant. So it was that evening with Millicent Sutherland.

"Dear Mrs Hodgkinson, did I hear you mention earlier that you and Lieutenant Threlfall have discovered a mutual fascination?"

"Dancing—specifically the foxtrot," explained Mrs Hodgkinson. "Too elegant, and I'm pleased to say quite the thing just now in Port Charlotte."

"Excellent news, Mrs Hodgkinson," said Norman, who knew perfectly well, since it was he and Nathalie who had introduced it at the Dreamland Ballroom.

"The foxtrot is danced with great flair at Madame Beck's salon, the Café des Artistes," said M. Orlando. "I am myself proficient," he lowered his voice, at the same time ogling in his slightly bug-eyed manner Harriet's décolletage. She blushed.

"I'm sure I've not seen it done," said Lady Sutherland, pretending not to notice. Suddenly she had a good idea—like her actions, Lady Sutherland's ideas were mostly sudden. "Norman, do please fetch your gramophone and show us."

"Now, Lady Sutherland?" said Norman.

"Yes, now Norman," said Lady Sutherland. "Fetch your gramophone and show us. Go on Norman. Chop, chop."

Norman glanced at Sir George, who nodded, and then at Campbell, who smirked.

"Your Excellency, Lady Sutherland, do please excuse me." Norman rose from the table and hurried out of the saloon.

"Such a dear," said Lady Sutherland.

Norman returned with his gramophone and gently placed it on the sideboard. With expert touch he wound it up and applied the cactus needle to the record.

"The Crazy Bone Rag," announced Norman, proudly. "Mrs Hodgkinson, may I have the honour?"

"Certainly, dear Lieutenant Threlfall, but the honour is mine," purred Mrs Hodgkinson, rising gracefully. She and Norman glided into the largest available space, and began to dance, her colourful fingertips firmly implanted among the aiguillettes strung over Norman's shoulder. Lettice tried her best not to notice this, for she had become very fond of Norman. Colin Campbell, in turn, noticed that Lettice noticed, as did Lady Sutherland, who was beginning to seize at the framework of what promised to be an excellent idea.

"Slow, quick, quick, Lady Sutherland," said Mrs Hodgkinson, "then slow, slow, quick, quick, slow. Oh, Norman you dance divinely." Norman was concentrating on smooth, sinuous motions, with which Mrs Hodgkinson seemed perfectly attuned. "The foxtrot must be danced very smoothly, with no unfortunate jarring movements," she continued. "Isn't that so Norman?"

"Quite so, Mrs Hodgkinson," said Norman, as the needle hastened towards the end of its scratchy path.

"Enchanting," boomed Lady Sutherland, clapping warmly, "Lettice, you must learn." The rest of the party joined in the applause, Gene beamed with pride, and Norman escorted Mrs Hodgkinson back to her place between Commodore Bracegirdle and Bishop Stanley.

"Now then, *charades*!" barked Lady Sutherland.

Earlier that day Lady Sutherland had asked Mrs Huntingfield to see that the contents of the dressing up box were freshened up.

"Normally, Aimee, as I have taught you, we soak the clothes overnight first. The next day they must be soaped, boiled or scalded, then rinsed three times—*three* times remem*ber*! Then wrung out, mangled, dried, starched, and ironed. Blue bag in the water for the whites. Cotton should be soaked first in buttermilk for a few days."

One by one Solange was removing the contents of the dressing up box and handing them to Aimee: an old sailor suit, a yellowing bridesmaid's dress from a forgotten wedding, a string of large wooden beads, a tambourine, a mismatched pair of spats, a pirate hat, a threadbare judge's wig, a tattered school blazer, a pair of angel wings. "But for these, a simple press will suffice. Sometimes they like to dress in disarray. It amuses them to dress like the poor."

Finally, from the bottom of the box, Solange removed a motheaten woollen robe embroidered with a flaming pyramid and other strange devices—a pentagram, a black sun, a horned serpent, a heart pierced by an arrow, a human skull—and, finally, from the bottom of the box, a stag's horn helmet, remnants of an amateur production of *La Damnation de Faust*, daringly staged at Harriet's boarding school by her dashing, forward-thinking sports mistress, Mrs Hall.

Aimee recoiled, and crossed herself. "La Thelema," she muttered.

The rules of charades are simple, but there existed many variations, so, in an informal but already competitive environment much, enhanced by port, brandy and general excitement, unfortunate misunderstandings between family and guests occasionally arose, and had even sometimes overshadowed entire weekend house parties. Therefore Millicent Sutherland liked to be absolutely clear about house rules before the commencement of battle.

"There will be two teams, red and blue," she boomed with her natural authority. "Teams will take it in turns to write a secret word or phrase on a slip of paper, to be acted out by one member of the other team *without* speaking, mouthing words, or pointing at objects. The dressing-up box may be resorted to if necessary, provided such items are not identical with the clue, or any part or parts thereof. Lettice be quiet, I am speaking."

"Sorry, Mummy."

"Now, the word or phrase will then be guessed by the remaining members of the same team. If the word or phrase is guessed correctly, the point is won; if not, the point is forfeited to the opposing team. And so on, until everyone has had their turn. Is that quite clear?"

The company voiced non-verbal assent in their jovial English after-dinner way. Lady Sutherland then proceeded to supervise the formation of teams; nothing so simple as allowing the company to remain where they were already comfortably settled, and dividing them down the middle. No, a far more astute division of talent required several minutes' cumbersome rearrangement. "Such fun!" she said, contemplating one final necessary adjustment. "M. Orlando, do please sit between Commodore Bracegirdle and Captain Campbell. Have you enough room? *There* we are."

<table>
<tr><td align="center">Red Team</td><td align="center">Blue Team</td></tr>
<tr><td align="center">Sir George</td><td align="center">Lady Sutherland</td></tr>
<tr><td align="center">Lettice</td><td align="center">Harriet</td></tr>
<tr><td align="center">Gene Hodgkinson</td><td align="center">Magnolia Hodgkinson</td></tr>
<tr><td align="center">Bishop Stanley</td><td align="center">Miss Davies</td></tr>
<tr><td align="center">Mrs Stanley</td><td align="center">Commodore Bracegirdle</td></tr>
<tr><td align="center">Norman</td><td align="center">Colin</td></tr>
<tr><td align="center">Surgeon Commander Clark</td><td align="center">M. Orlando</td></tr>
</table>

For charades, Orlando was completely unprepared. To be fair, it would not have occurred to Sir George, and even less to Lady Sutherland, that one of the wealthiest and most prominent colonists on St Edward knew nothing of charades. Nor could they have imagined that the usual courtesy of insisting that the guest of honour went first, would, in this instance, be interpreted as an especially hostile act.

"Dear M. Orlando, naturally you will start us off," said Lady Sutherland. Had she, screeching, accurately propelled the remains of a half-eaten banana through the bars of her cage, Lady Sutherland could not have proffered to Orlando a more unwelcome gesture. He blushed deeply.

And yet, and yet, Orlando had not made a fortune in the fiercely competitive guano trade without a degree of sly quick-wittedness.

The secret phrase, which he read on his slip of paper with irate partial comprehension, was "silly mid-on," the fielding position. This was chosen by Sir George, not entirely innocently. To his credit Orlando made every effort to act out his clue by paying particular attention to Harriet. He knew it must have something to do with cricket, but still the consul of France was temperamentally incapable of giving physical expression to the insulting concept of "silly." Scandalous, insufferable, *unacceptable*.

The blue team duly lost the first round.

Orlando was furious, but showed no sign of it. Of course, he was actually proud that he knew nothing, less than nothing, of this *stupid* English game—both of these stupid English games, in fact, cricket *and* charades. Outwardly he remained the charming *flâneur* of Port Charlotte. He deployed his expansive gestures of bonhomie; he uttered warm chuckles.

"Ah, Excellency—you English!"

Inwardly, however, Orlando seethed with a hatred of such intensity that it almost forced from his mind those fruity images of Harriet (sprawling naked on his velvet sofa, adopting, as we know, the pose of Boucher's Marie-Louise O'Murphy) that alone succeeded in bringing him to his feet in the first place. Only Harriet herself noticed for a moment the consul's eyes flash—black and dangerous—and a quite distinct flaring of those unusually disarming nostrils—she went so far as to remark upon these to Lettice early the following morning. "He does something with his nose, Let, haven't you noticed?"

Bishop and Mrs Stanley really should not have been on the same team, but that is how the numbers fell. Naturally they were old hands at the game. Several covert signals—the product of many years' subtle but, at times, urgent communication between the Bishop's throne and the front pew—passed between them undetected, so they made short work of the phrase that was handed to the Bishop, "son of perdition."

Magnolia Hodgkinson adored charades. She took up her position with considerable poise before launching into a most ingenious and effective performance—performance being the only word—of "Red Sails in the Sunset," but got a little stuck on the sunset part. Her idea was to evoke, arms stretched upwards, hands cupped, a great celestial orb slowly descending down and over the horizon.

"Circe Invidiosa," ventured Lady Sutherland.

"Archbishop of Canterbury," suggested Miss Davies, thinking of the last coronation. Daddy had been present, but being seated behind a column, saw nothing.

"Washing up!" cried Harriet, as usual failing to appreciate Mrs Hodgkinson's artistic side.

Further motions, measured and graceful, won Magnolia victory but from a most unexpected quarter. Most hideous voluptuaries are fairly quick on the uptake, and despite his best efforts to keep fanning the flames of rage that earlier burned in his bosom, some of them had gone out. Perhaps it was a moderately feverish desire to impress Harriet, and an undoubted appreciation for Parisian haute couture, that led M. Orlando suddenly to clutch at the correct answer:

"*Les voiles*! How is *en anglais*? Sails, yes, "Red Sails in the Sunset!" Suddenly realising that he was involuntarily edging towards a sort of precipice of enjoyment, M. Orlando took hold of himself and, once more, reignited those flames.

Bracegirdle dealt quickly with his secret phrase, "Deirdre of the Sorrows," by using a deftly disguised form of semaphore, which Colin picked up straight away. Lady Sutherland would normally have objected, but she was on the same team. Just as

Orlando's clumsy performance seemed embarrassingly directed towards Harriet, so too, in his far more cautious way, Bracegirdle verged upon solicitude in respect of Miss Davies. Ever alert to such possibilities, Lady Sutherland wondered if romantic sentiments, or the equivalent, could ever be coaxed from such gravelly soil without the careful provision of nutrients.

Being a mighty smart, certainly outgoing American, Gene Hodgkinson could be relied upon to throw himself into anything, a quality that delighted Magnolia—although perhaps a little less often—so he made short work of "Little Women." Gene's charming and surprisingly effective effort to project femininity especially delighted Mr Craddock who was as usual furnishing whiskies and soda from his position beside the drinks trolley.

"Red team three points, blue team two points," she boomed, before adding "Such bad luck, M. Orlando, but weren't you *clever* to guess 'Red Sails in the Sunset.' Well done you."

Harriet noticed that thing with M. Orlando's nose again, and Orlando noticed her noticing. It is characteristic of hideous voluptuaries that flames of rage tend to burn no less brightly than flames of lust.

Surgeon Commander Clark fluffed "Ride of the Valkyries."

Miss Davies struggled valiantly with "gin and tonic," which at last Commodore Bracegirdle guessed correctly, a fact of which, as before, Lady Sutherland took careful note.

The Governor's approximation of the hopping of a kangaroo nearly lost him his point for "Australia" because at first none of his teammates could fathom what on earth he was doing.

"St. Vitus' Dance?"

"Whirling Dervish?"

"Garter Day?"

"Constipation?"

In the end Bishop Stanley, a veteran of colonial dioceses and of the Society for Promoting Christian Knowledge, fastened upon the right answer.

"*Aus*-tralia," he said, placing emphasis upon the first syllable, which naturally rhymed with horse.

Merde, thought Orlando.

"Buddha" virtually handed Harriet her point on a plate—so said Lettice, very loudly, who proceeded to win an even easier point with "Antony and Cleopatra."

Lady Sutherland got hopelessly tangled up in *Was It the Lobster?* and would have forfeited had it not been for Miss Davies's shrewdness in seizing upon the pincer motions.

Mrs Stanley, by contrast, captured and conveyed "The Song of Hiawatha" with ease. Lady Sutherland was not by nature suspicious, nevertheless she did wonder.

"Well done Mrs S.," said Lady Sutherland. "Now let's see: Red team six points, blue team six points—neck and neck! Colin you mustn't let us down.

Fortunately for the blue team Colin scored an easy victory with "*The Pilgrim's Progress*," and then it was Norman's turn either to score a dead heat or to lose. His clue, handed to him by Lady Sutherland, was "wedding bells."

Norman's heart sank. He was distracted. He thought about Nathalie, about Paris, about the mysterious occupant of the rear compartment of the Rolls Royce. His heart plummeted farther.

His motions were misleading, awkward, half-hearted. All of a sudden, however, Lettice clapped her hands most unexpectedly.

"Oh Norman, you darling clever man—it's 'wedding bells!'"

Ever since their arrival on St Edward, Lettice Sutherland had felt a growing affection for Norman. He was, she felt, exactly the right sort of young English gentleman: well-bred—army family—polite, presentable, and he looked frightfully dashing in his naval uniform. Perfect in almost every respect except for the fact that he appeared to have had far too much education. There was also the difficulty, above all, that he seemed not to notice that she existed. Of course, Norman knew perfectly well Lettice existed. Even if he had been aware of her lively interest, which in fact he wasn't, Norman and indeed Colin were alert to the dangers of inhabiting a vice-regal household in which there were two unmarried daughters, and a fearfully shrewd châtelaine. With total correctness Norman invariably opened doors, pulled out chairs, and fetched glasses of water for Lettice, as he did when necessary for Lady Sutherland and Miss Harriet. So, when later that night there was a light tap on his door, Norman was startled to come face to face with Lettice, standing in the hall wearing nothing but her flannel nightdress, dressing-gown and slippers.

"Oh Norman, I knew, I *knew*, what you were saying to me. And to use charades, in the drawing room, with Mummy and Daddy right there! So daring, so romantic, so ... so *wicked*! I saw it, I saw it in your eyes. Oh, *Norman*, yes, yes, *yes*!"

Lettice planted a firm but chaste kiss on his cheek, and scampered noisily back to bed, leaving Norman to experience, first, astonishment, and, soon afterwards, a rising sense of panic and thoughts of an uncertain future.

Midnight in Harriet's bedroom: a pile of pillows under the bedspread cunningly arranged to give the impression of a sleeping girl, and an open window.

A cloaked figure hurried along Gordon Street, avoiding the dim pools of light cast by the new electric street lamps, stopped at Warehouse No 2, knocked twice on the door. It was very dark. Orlando opened the door, looked up and down the narrow street.

"You came, dear mademoiselle." He helped Harriet off with her cape. "Dear *séduisante* mademoiselle." Orlando regarded Harriet's breasts like a small boy watching a bowl of ice cream that might at any moment be snatched away.

"Gosh. Yes. Of course I came, silly." Harriet giggled excitedly.

Orlando pulled her through the door, checked the deserted street again, then shut the door firmly.

"This is my humble *établissement*."

They walked between towering crates of guano to Orlando's office. He ushered Harriet inside. It was not at all like the Palace of Huffuf. The reek of guano was overpowering, the floor gritty with its residue. Nor was Orlando, in his *robe de chambre* of velvet and cashmere, quite the dashing figure of the pitiless Sultan. Nonetheless, in the dim light from Orlando's green shaded banker's lamp, the room, with its dusty Persian carpet and overstuffed ottoman, did have a vaguely oriental appearance. And while Orlando's extra chins and puffy torso did not promise the kind of vigorous lovemaking that Harriet had been reading about in *Seraglio Governess*, he did have a suave sophistication that she had never previously encountered. And, as she had pointed out to her sister on a number of occasions, his eyes smouldered.

On the oak desk was a tray holding a carafe of milky liquid and two glasses. Orlando filled both, and handed one to Harriet.

"Crème de Cacao, my dear, the wine of love."

Harriet giggled.

"To abiding friendship and, as your English poet says, fertile reveries."

They drank.

He reached into the folds of his smoking jacket and removed a gold cigarette case.

"And now ... 'tobacco, divine, rare superexcellent tobacco, which goes far beyond all panaceas, potable gold and philosopher's stones.'"

"Another poet?"

"Indeed, *ma cheri*. A wise, wise man."

Harriet giggled again, blushing.

"Shall we have a cigarette on it?"

"Golly. Do let's."

Orlando removed two cigarettes from the case, placed them between his fleshy lips, and lit both, extinguishing the match with a flourish, then handing one to Harriet before drawing deeply on his own. Thoughtfully he examined the glowing tip.

"A sovereign remedy to all diseases."

Harriet herself drew deeply, suppressing a ladylike cough.

"And now ... shall we?" said Orlando, taking Harriet by the hand and leading her to the ottoman.

An hour later the door of Warehouse No 2 opened, and a caped figure emerged.

"*Au revoir, ma cheri. J'attendrai toujours ton retour.*"

The door closed firmly.

At breakfast the next morning Lady Sutherland asked Harriet if she was quite alright. Lettice sniggered.

As a major holder of shares in the Cincinnati Ohio & Delaware Banking Corporation, and a great believer in modern managerial practice, Gene Hodgkinson liked to maintain cordial relations with the bank's more senior employees and suppliers—not, of course, the actual depositors, whom he regarded with distaste bordering on horror (his constant, overriding fear, one he shared with all bankers, was that they might one day all demand their money back at the same time, which of course a few short years later they did). Thus it was that a dinner had been arranged in the great executive dining room on the top floor of the bank's striking new premises to celebrate the building's successful completion, on time and on budget. It had been designed, somewhat controversially, by the leading architect Reinhardt Foehkolb, of Berlin. Perched high above Port Charlotte, and unflinchingly eschewing ornamentation of any kind, the building was a daring assemblage of triangles, rhomboids and circles in steel, glass and concrete, arranged asymmetrically. The design reflected the bank's brief to the architect: unadorned, solid, functional, yet innovative, visionary and boldly confident. Jacob was the engineer assigned by his employers to the project, and he was seated next to Mrs Hodgkinson. She turned to him.

"Gene is so proud of the bank's new building," she said. "You must also be pleased."

"Indeed, Mrs Hodginson," Jacob replied politely. "It has been a fascinating project. Although of course I didn't design it. My job was simply to make sure it doesn't fall down."

"Oh, I am sure it will stand for hundreds of years."

"There *were* challenges," Jacob admitted. "The rock on which it stands is honeycombed with tunnels and chambers from beneath the fortress—originally Roman—that once stood on this site." And, he reflected, ideal for planting a large bomb with which to bring down this absurd edifice, although that would perhaps require more dynamite than he could reasonably expect to be delivered by his French masters.

"Tunnels and chambers you say Mr Beck? Torture chambers, perhaps?"

Mrs Hodgkinson's interest had been immediately aroused. After all, she prided herself on the historical accuracy, the *mise en scène* of her novels. She was a great believer in research, and ancient tunnels, dungeons and oubliettes sounded perfect, ideal material for the chamber she envisaged, illuminated by ghastly flaming torches, lurid shadows across the ancient, tattered wall hangings, in which the members of the fraternity of wealthy pleasure-seekers of her current work in progress would gather to indulge their intemperate fantasies. She leaned towards Jacob and spoke softly.

"May I ask, Monsieur Beck, are these 'tunnels and chambers' accessible?"

"Why yes, Mrs Hodgkinson, at the bank's request they have

been incorporated in the design for storage, old files, lists of debtors, trust accounts, mortgage documents."

"I write, as you perhaps know, novels of historical fiction, you may have read one or two of my works?"

Jacob replied that sadly he had not yet done so, but fully intended to remedy that at the earliest opportunity.

"I believe I owe it to my readers, and to history, to maintain the strictest level of accuracy, to respect the material. For even fiction, I maintain, must always reflect a deeper truth, in all its brutal reality."

Jacob agreed that, indeed, truth was very important, brutal realities notwithstanding.

"My current project centres around the forbidden love between a pleasure-seeking English aristocrat and the innocent young shepherdess who tends the flocks on his great estate. Sir Ephriam, my protagonist, belongs to a—how shall I put it?—a secret society—a brotherhood of like-minded individuals—a fraternity of aristocratic rakes, the motto of their association they have adopted from that of the Hellfire Club established so many years ago by the wicked Sir Francis Dashwood: *fais ce que tu voudras.*

"Do what thou wilt," Jacob said.

"Exactly," purred Mrs Hodgkinson. "My novel touches on violent themes, the violence, I believe, that lurks within the hearts of all of us. The steel fist within the velvet glove, if you will. You understand?"

"I'm not sure I do, Mrs Hodgkinson."

"And sex, of course."

"Oh," said Jacob.

"At the heart of the modern romance is verisimilitude. Authenticity. My readers demand it of me. Thus I must capture the reality, the closely observed expression, the tiny detail, the *chiaroscuro* that brings my characters and the worlds they inhabit to life. I need to see these underground chambers. I must see them. Will you escort me Jacob?" Mrs Hodginson laid her hand on Jacob's wrist. "May I call you Jacob?"

Two days later Jacob shepherded Mrs Hodgkinson through the massive plate glass doors, and into the grand atrium of the new Cincinnati Ohio & Delaware Banking Corporation building. From the vast polished floor a staircase rose to the upper levels in a series of uncompromising arcs. Beneath the first landing, discreetly set in the wall and shielded from public view, was a small grey door. Jacob selected a key from the ring he was holding, and opened the door. A stale basement smell rose to meet them both, a smell of new concrete and old paper, and dust, with an underpinning of something less easily identified: stone and earth, damp and decay, the smell of the underworld. Jacob pressed a switch and bare electric bulbs illuminated the rough concrete stairway that descended into the chilly gloom. He led the way, Mrs Hodgkinson followed gamely. At the foot of the stairs they found themselves on the unadorned concrete floor of a large basement room, its walls lined from floor to ceiling with gleaming steel shelves filled with files in Manilla folders. In a gap between the towering shelving was a battered timber door, obviously much older than the new building. Jacob selected another key, and, like a gaoler opening the cell door for the Count of Monte Cristo, heaved it open. The door creaked, protesting noisily, and opened on a tunnel cut out of the living rock. There were no lights now, and Jacob turned on his torch. Scuttling sounds, wind moaning somewhere in the dark, water dripping, an eerie hum. "It's just like daddy's wine cellar," Mrs Hodgkinson thought, unhappy memories flooding briefly back. She composed herself, and along the tunnel they went, coming eventually to another, even older door, this time of heavily studded rusting iron. It too protested loudly as it was opened, and they entered a large, yet somehow claustrophobic space. Gloomy light filtered dimly through two small and very dirty windows looking out towards the harbour. Jacob shone his torch around the cells, the rusting iron bars, the ancient chains still hanging on the walls, and the wheels, metal rods, worm eaten timber frames, rotten leather straps. Cobwebs hung everywhere. Water dripped. From the harbour came the sound of a pile driver working on the new docks. Mrs Hodgkinson could hear strange rustlings in the gloom.

"This is it Mrs Hodgkinson," said Jacob. "This is where the Romans held and tortured their prisoners, then the French, and more recently the British."

Mrs Hodgkinson ran her hand along the damp wall, the rusting iron bars. The clanking chains, the dripping water, the scuttling of rats, the wind rattling the cellar door, the angry call of seagulls in the harbour, echoed and reverberated, and among the echoes it seemed to Mrs Hodgkinson that she could hear the cries of the damned, the cracking slash of whips, the hateful voice of the scourge, the shriek of the iron maiden. Her head spun. Like Mrs Moore in the Marabar caves, the ou-boom of the torture chamber touched Mrs Hodgkinson profoundly. She felt she had brushed against something vast, timeless and wicked. She staggered, and reached out to Jacob for support, fell into his arms, and without thought kissed him violently on the lips.

And Jacob, being only human, returned the kiss with equal ferocity. Thus the slim but athletic Jacob was transformed through the potent magic of Mrs Hodgkinson's prose into the insatiable pleasure seeker, Sir Ephriam.

> Cecelia gasped Sir Ephriam tall and well limbed so hard muscle love love stones on her back wet chains wet the water dripping the chains the stones the whetstones your oysters pushed her down onto the stones venus shielding taboo shedding untied fingers hands breasts belly is it sin father please please black death thicket of curling hair rising hard lips open to receive his hands his lips his tongue his throbbing Cecelia was ready to faint the velvet bursting bursting bursting luscious

Gene replaced the page on the desktop. "Great Caesar's ghost Magnolia! You have surpassed yourself!" Mrs Hodgkinson smiled modestly. Gene approached in the usual sidling manner. "Where does your inspiration come from? Aw shucks," he said modestly. "Let me guess," and he growled his usual growl.

Mrs Hodgkinson smiled a private smile.

The streetlights were out. The Café des Artistes was in darkness, the upstairs revelry finished for the night. The house was silent.

Quietly they climbed the darkened servants' staircase. They paused at the landing. Smell of freshly laundered sheets.

Nathalie's bedroom. The old parquet clicked faintly under the thin rug as they crossed the floor—moonlight shone through the open window. Norman took her by the wrist and led her to the narrow bed, outside himself now, watching her, watching them both. For a moment he couldn't breathe. Soft skin, lips, eyelashes, breath. The shock of her touch, skin on skin. Her short dark hair. White shirt. Red beads. Pale skin. Straps. Buttons. Underclothes.

Norman stayed until the moon set. He stayed until they could hear the faint sounds of the fishing boats returning to the harbour. He stayed until the sea birds started their raucous dawn chorus and the stars began to fade and he was able to make out shapes of furniture in Nathalie's room, her small desk, her bookcase, her old reading lamp, their clothes on the floor, his shoes.

"I have to get back," he said. "My love."

Is this love, she wondered? I should know about love, all the movies I've seen, the books I've read, the love songs. Just words. Words that mean nothing. He is my heart now, my home. How did he find me, this strange boy, so graceful, so kind, who came from his cold island across the sea, with its rain and fog, its ridiculous rituals, its God Save the King? He is the moon, I am the sun. We dance, we're happy. He is beautiful. Is this love? Will he hurt me? Do I love him? Of course I love him, how could I not? I love him because I love him, she thought drowsily. *Mon homme.*

She could hear the cry of seagulls, the wind in the pines, the sea, and the door softly closing.

Then she slept.

On the landing Norman paused, shoes in his hand. The house was stirring, floorboards creaked, footsteps were approaching from the apartments at the front of the building. Quickly Norman tiptoed down the stairs, out the door, into the alley. Suddenly, as he was hastily lacing his shoes, the door behind him flew open.

"Threlfall!"

"Colonel Pole!"

"Here of all places." Pole chuckled and clapped Norman on the back.

"What were you ... oh ..."

"Rest and recreation old fellow."

"Sir ... I ... er ..."

"The daughter eh? Lucky chap." Deftly with his one hand the colonel removed a small cheroot from a case and lit it. "Smoke?"

Norman declined politely. "Sir, I don't know what to do."

Pole returned the cigar case to his pocket and puffed meditatively. "Quandary eh? Devil and deep blue sea?" He set off briskly in the direction of government house. Norman followed. "Devil, deep blue sea *and* Madame Beck eh?"

"Perhaps, sir, you could advise me."

"Hmm ... well ...

In the first grey light of dawn Norman and Pole, in step, marched up the government house drive, deep in conversation.

Mrs Huntington glanced out her window and raised an eyebrow, before returning to her planchette. Old Sock, working the compost, looked away, muttered to himself. Lettice, tucked up in bed, snored contentedly. Her heavily annotated copy of Marie Stopes' celebrated sex manual *Married Love* was discretely tucked under her pillow.

That evening Colonel Pole put down his whisky and soda, picked up his pen, and began to write.

Stop press my dears! It's all too too *too* shocking…

Then the Colonel paused, put down his pen and stared thoughtfully at his whisky and soda. A better idea.

"Come in Colonel," said Lady Sutherland the following morning.

"I apologise for this intrusion Ma'am, but I need to talk to you as a matter of some delicacy."

"Not another torso in the Rolls Royce I trust?"

"No, Lady Sutherland, but a matter of equal sensitivity."

"Really?"

"It concerns your daughter and her engagement to Lieutenant Threlfall."

"Go on," said Lady Sutherland, now on full alert.

"I am a military man, I will speak bluntly. I apologise if what I am about to relate causes distress."

"Do not concern yourself Colonel, but please, do come to the point.

"Lieutenant Threlfall's career has stalled. He will never be promoted. He will never serve in any capacity beyond that of aide to a Governor of any colony of greater importance—with all due respect to you and Sir George—than this one. Indeed he is likely to be exiled even further afield, to far less pleasant postings."

"But Norman has been so competent, so charming, so helpful. What has he done?"

"I am not at liberty to say Ma'am. Certain events which took place in Paris during the Peace Conference. No … please don't ask for further particulars, despatch from Fitzroy Bancroft in reply to enquiries made by self, hush hush, eyes only, you understand."

"Oh dear."

"By marrying Lieutenant Threlfall your daughter will commit herself to an itinerant life wandering from one lonely and frequently inhospitable outpost of Empire to the next, perhaps a short trip home to the mother country for a few weeks every ten years."

"And you're absolutely sure of this?"

"Absolutely Ma'am. I would not be having this conversation if I was not completely certain."

"Oh, heavens."

"And there is something else. I have to tell you that Lieutenant Threlfall has been spending time at the Café des Atristes."

"Is that such a bad thing?"

"*Upstairs* at the Café des Artistes."

"Since the engagement?"

"Yes. Old habits perhaps die hard."

"Ah."

"One last thing, if I may."

"Gracious. What now?"

"Lieutenant Campbell, excellent prospects, good war, fine family, and I have observed, strong feelings for your daughter. Far too honourable to act on them, of course, but strong feelings nonetheless. Excellent chap. Much more suitable match."

"Mr Craddock, can you find Lettice and ask her to come and see me?"

"Campbell, do you have a minute?"
"Certainly Colonel."

That night Colonel Pole picked up his pen again.

> Stop press my dears! It's all too too *too* shocking, a storyline straight from the wicked pen of Gwladys Baring, the devilishly handsome naval lieutenant and the innocent laundry maid ...

"Oh Norman. How could you? And I had to learn it from the Port Charlotte *Truth*—so painful, so *cruel*. I'm sorry, my darling, but our love can never be. My heart is broken. Mummy says I must return the ring." Lettice struggled to remove the ring.

"No, really, keep it."

"Really?"

"I insist," said Norman bravely trying to control his emotions. He felt like laughing. Like singing. Like dancing.

So Lettice did keep the ring, and in years to come she would relate to her children the romantic story of the ring, and her lost love before their father, Brigadier General Campbell, swept her off her feet that night so long ago under the glorious full moon of St Edward.

"Ah Norman," Lady Sutherland smiled. "Dear Norman, I am so sorry we have put you through this."

"Thank you Lady Sutherland. That's perfectly fine."

"I think you'll be much happier this way."

"Yes, I think so too."

CHAPTER 15

The Ubiquity of Sin

Mike and Sharon
2020

Dont have time for this

Plus chapter in sexy autobiography The Lines of Sin by Magnolia Hodgkinson. Trash novelist wrote under pen name Gwladys (not typo, really name, Welsh saint 6th century - thank you Dierdre) Baring. Bit of a feminist icon. No doubt youve heard of her

Piss off Sharon

Most important, two last things, Sea, Sand, Sex and Seduction in the Islands, sad sixties pioneering gay coming out thing by Nicholas Craddock, actually quite interesting

Sometimes you really get up my nose

Plus Archbishop of
Canterbury 58 vol Lambeth
Anglican Communion Sorry
Commission colonial era
injustice report

WTF

Fuck those bishops went on.
Case study St Edward alone
runs over 3 vols

*　　*　　*

1926

Bishop Stanley and Sir George met, as was by now their regular custom, on the cliff top to smoke their pipes and reflect on the trials of island life. The sound of drumming drifted faintly from Mount Raglan.

"A moving sermon this morning Bishop." Sir George puffed contemplatively on his pipe. "'The ubiquity of sin.' Something that must concern us all."

"Indeed it must. Satan's temptations are all around us, even in this island paradise. *Particularly*, I might say, in this island paradise. And particularly now."

"Why now?"

"Next week is the Summer solstice. It is celebrated—although 'celebrated' is perhaps not the appropriate word—as it is every year in the old French village at Baie du Diable. Passions become inflamed. All sense of decency or restraint is cast aside. It's a bacchanal, an orgy, a carnival of lust, a carnal itch that must be scratched every year. The revellers dance wildly until they fall into a trace under the influence not only of the driving, relentless rhythm of the drums, the chanting, but also strong drink, as well as powerful narcotics." Bishop Stanley sighed, drawing again on his pipe, swaying slightly, and unconsciously, to the persistent, but still distant beat of the drums. "And even more obscene practices occur, I am told, in the ancient stone circle on Mount Raglan. The lewd ceremonies conducted there under the influence of these varied stimulants are, I am assured, really quite shocking. Adherents of an ancient religion from ages past summon Cernunnos and his horned consort The Lady Hecate. Goodness knows what would happen if they really did succeed in summoning the great beast. It even concerns Monsignieur Lebecq ... there has been trouble, the nuns you know ... sometimes they ..." Bishop Stanley chuckled to himself, his head by now wreathed in fragrant pipe smoke. "Well ... you know what nuns are like when they let their hair down."

"Good Lord! We must put an end to this nonsense. I shall instruct Bracegirdle to call out the St Edward Rifles!"

"With respect, Sir George, I think not." Bishop Stanley inhaled deeply. "I think that would be a mistake. People come from all over the island, farmhands, fishing folk, timber cutters, women and children. It is an important event in their calendar. To curtail their enjoyment would be to invite trouble."

"Perhaps."

The two companions smoked meditatively.

"And besides, when you think about it, don't we all need to blow off a little steam from time to time?"

Sir George nodded thoughtfully. "Indeed we do," he laughed quietly to himself. "Yes, indeed we do."

Time passed peacefully. The Bishop and Sir George gazed out to sea in companionable silence, swaying gently from side to side to the increasingly insistent beat of the drums and drawing quietly and deeply on their pipes.

Later that evening Mme Beck was, as usual, working on her accounts when there was a firm knock on her door.

"Entrez."

Colonel Pole strode briskly into the room.

"Ah, mon Colonel. Un plaisir. Yvette is engaged this evening, but of course the twins are always delighted to amuse you. But please, do sit down."

"No Madame," said the colonel, coming smartly to attention. "I prefer to stand. I'm sorry to say I am here on official business. It is my unfortunate duty to inform you that I am in possession of reliable evidence to the effect that your son Jacob is the leader of a seditious group committed to the overthrow of the lawful government of these islands. Quite irrefutable evidence I am afraid. I need hardly remind you that treason is a hanging offence."

Mme Beck gasped. Then, abruptly, the colonel did sit down.

"Actually, Giselle, it doesn't have to be official. I am hopeful that we can work it out."

After the colonel left Mme Beck hurried to the laundry.

CHAPTER 16

Do What Thou Wilt

Mike and Sharon
2020

Fuck those bishops went on. Case study St Edward alone runs over 3 vols. Seems local bishop 20s to 40s later fretted about tampering with local customs, plus wot they made him put in freshly consecrated ground which was in fact a compost heap

Get to the fucking point

Geoffrey Fisher told him to get a bloody grip.

I would too. What a wimp

Yes we know you would Mike.

Fuck off Sharon

And all thats on top of Hush Hush by Cynthia Gribble.

Deirdre says its worth a read.
Trouble with French.

Dierdre have a life?

Dierdre can find anything.
Dirty book, Do What Thou
Wilt, modernist classic by
Gwladys Baring, published
Shakespeare and co 1931.

*　　*　　*

1926

In her studio Mrs Hodgkinson's typewriter beat its furious tattoo.

arrr she your daughter master daughter the sting
of the whip nay nay sir first time she come to me
sir sire i swear nay nay the whip it sting it hurt
master it were harvest time nay they tied him up
poor boy sowing in the noontide and the dewy
eve the rope cut deep sire aye she be wearin that
white shift lord *she comin she comin* to my crib
harvest time master hair loose *lips wet eyes wet*
sweet thing pretty little harvest time full ripe it
were sire aye the heat oh to meet all hopes and
desires *she breathe she breathe she breathin the cold
cold air* in remembrance of me the white shift on
the floor the sheaves the sheaves bringing in the

sheaves on the threshing floor so warm the earth
she said *on the ground* she said time is dead time is
eager eager heat the heat sweat nay master nay the
whip is your friend lad *she say she say* time is dead

Three hundred nautical miles from St Edward the rusty tramp *Marianne* was steaming slowly through a glassy sea, heading towards the islands. Her passage from Marseilles through the Mediterranean had been uneventful, but since she had passed through the Strait of Gibraltar the barometer had been falling, and now black clouds were piling up on the horizon ahead of the little vessel. The captain tapped the barometer, spat, and despatched the cabin boy for a fresh bottle of absinthe.

"Merde."

In the hold the cargo rocked gently from side to side, watched over patiently by a small Frenchman in a neat overcoat and bowler hat.

That evening wind whispered in the great Norfolk pines on the foreshore, the waxing moon was rising over the harbour— peaceful, although the gulls were acting strangely. At the Dreamland Ballroom Yvette the Venus Butterfly danced gaily through the crowd of farm workers, shop girls, sailors and slumming equities traders, politely deflecting the sons of French notables.

"*Mais non, messieurs*, I am here for my pleasure, not yours. If you wish you will find me upstairs at the Café des Artistes most of the time, but not *ce soir*."

Yvette continued her progress through the crowd, and stopped next at the young man in evening dress, leaning against the wall next to the bar.

"Ah, lieutenant. You come again?"

"As always."

"You must be patient."

"She will not come?"

"I ask. She refuses always."

"Tell her."

"Monsieur, you broke her heart."

"Engagement is off."

"Oui. But once it was on."

"It was never on, it was … was a mistake."

"You must be patient."

"Tell her, please Yvette."

Yvette laughed, and swirled off into the crowd, dancing with a group of farm girls from The Thimbles.

Orlando was in the confession box. "Forgive me father, for I have sinned."

"Oh, indeed, my son, you have. The sisters have informed me of the fate of our brother, the hero of the Mandingo Wars. The sisters hear everything eventually, and those revolutionaries you recruited do talk, as all young men will, particularly to a pretty nun. Left in the rear of the Governor's monstrous automobile." The Monsiegneur sighed. "Paris is not happy."

"Ah, Monsignieur Lebecq, it was through no fault of mine."

"Forgive me my son, but was not the agent Beck under your

supervision? Does not, as our American friends say, the buck stop with you?"

"Monsignieur ... I ..."

"The next shipment arrives tomorrow night with a new escort. You must pass a message through the usual channels to Jacob Beck telling him to make the necessary arrangements. And you must be there to make sure nothing goes wrong."

"Oh, monseigneur, I am a simple businessman."

"Not so simple, I think."

"But not a revolutionary general."

"This is your operation, Monsieur Orlando, you are in charge and you must be there to make sure nothing goes wrong this time. France has no more heroes to spare."

"*Ça va*. In that case it shall be done monseignieur."

"Make sure it is."

"*Putain de merde*," thought Orlando, as he rose to leave.

"One more thing, Monsieur Orlando. The Englishwoman ..."

"Ah, Monsignieur Lebecq, the flesh is weak."

"Yours perhaps, but from what I am told hers is remarkably robust. You must not see her again, it is too dangerous."

"I have arranged to see her this evening, I will break it off then."

"Be sure you do. Ten hail Marys."

Mme Beck was in the laundry with Nathalie.

"I have here a message from Monsieur Orlando for your brother. You are to take it to him. In addition, you must deliver this copy of the message to Lieutenant Threlfall."

"Maman, no."

"Yvette tells me that he has been mooning about The Dreamland Ballroom looking for you. You must go this evening."

"But maman ..."

Mme Beck gripped her daughter's arms firmly. "Nathalie, *cheri*, Jacob's life depends on it. The English will hang him if you do not take this message. And besides, this way we can be free of this *cochon* Orlando."

Slow Slow Quick Quick

Mike and Sharon
2020

Dierdre can find anything. Dirty book, Do What Thou Wilt, modernist classic by Gwladys Baring, published Shakespeare and co 1931. Rave review by James Joyce. Hysterical. Point is, you only have to sit in the London Library for half a day and you get most of it

God Sharon *half a day *?
Youre a fucking civil servant.
You haven't got half a day

Deirdre can find anything.
Meeting her for a drink L8R

I was thinking maybe quick
fuck at mine

Piss off. Bottom line French war hero killed in OH&S accident. Incompetence.

We gave him decent burial.
And the piece de resistance.
War hero liked to wear
sexy knickers

Not funny

Next to the skin. Im serious.
Even better the offending
briefs are with the rest of
the Craddock papers in
the Bodleian

So?

You really are being more
than usually thick today
Mike. Ever heard of DNA?

*　　*　　*

1926

At the Dreamland Ballroom, Norman was in his usual spot leaning against a wall near the bar. One more night, he thought. If she doesn't come tonight, that's it, enough is enough, I will give up. Unrequited love can remain unrequited only so long.

"Excuse me Lieutenant. May I have this dance?"

"Is it you?"

"It is."

"I had almost given up."

"So easily?"

"It hasn't been easy. I have missed you."

"And your fiancée?"

"She was never my fiancée."

"That is not my understanding. Nor that of the Port Charlotte *Truth*."

"You can't believe everything you read."

Norman put his arm around Nathalie's waist and together they swung smoothly onto the dance floor.

"Oh, you are too cruel. How can I resist when you dance as you do?"

"No more than I can resist you."

"But Lieutenant, you must. What would the governor say? His wife? What would your king think?"

"Marry me."

Nathalie stops abruptly.

"Silly boy."

"Think about it."

"There is nothing to think about."

Again they danced.

"Please, think about it."

"Meet me here next week. It will be the eve of the summer solstice. A very special night." Nathalie tucked a tightly folded scrap of paper into Norman's pocket. "You will need a costume."

CHAPTER 18

Hurricane

Mike and Sharon
2020

You really are being more
than usually thick today
Mike. Ever heard of DNA?

How would that help

Not the blood. Microscopic
traces of semen. Or as
Craddock puts it on p 147
of Sex and Seduction in the
Sultry Tropics "unsightly
stains". Had a thing about
them pathetic sod. Bottom
line corpse was French, and
corpses dont cum. Et voila.
Shove that up Elysee Palace.
No reason not to leak it either

Fucking brilliant

*   *   *

1926

The climate of the Bailiwick of St Edward was generally mild, winter slightly cooler and wetter, summer somewhat warmer and drier. Occasional thunderstorms brought the rain that watered the estates, kept the slopes of Mount Raglan lush and green, and the gardens of Port Charlotte a blaze of colour all year round. In fact the climate was so mild that for most of the inhabitants one season shifted to another almost imperceptibly.

One exception, of course, was Old Sock. He kept a watchful eye on the calendar, for in his monumental work, *Steinpilz On Compost*, Professor Steinpilz stresses the importance of the seasons, and outlines the tasks to be performed on certain dates. At the start of the northern summer, on the twentieth or twenty-first of July—the summer solstice—the compost must be dismantled, spread, turned, carefully repacked, layered, wet down and covered. "Feeding the worms," as the Professor puts it.

The progress of spring into summer was also noted by others among the island's old hands, particularly those who put to sea. The captain of the *Dormouse* paid closer than usual attention to the forecasts from Pendennis Point. Fishermen watched the sky, noted the behaviour of birds. For, although there were only modest variations between the seasons in the St Edward group, there was one aspect of the Bailiwick's weather that occasionally threw the islands into violent disarray.

Summer was Atlantic hurricane season.

While Old Sock tended his compost, hundreds of miles to the west of the Azores the surface of the water had become unusually warm. Over the next few days a small group of thunderstorms formed over those warm tropical waters. Meteorologists call this a "tropical disturbance". Winds flowed into the disturbance, gently at first, causing water to evaporate, transferring energy from the ocean into the atmosphere. This warmed the air, causing it to rise, drawing more warm moist air in from the outside, accelerating the process, which rapidly became self-sustaining. As the air pressure in the centre continued to fall more and more warm air was sucked in toward the centre of the disturbance, the rotation of the earth caused it to spiral, and a serious depression was developing, moving slowly at first, gathering power and speed, building until it was raging like a wild beast, gaining strength, spinning, snarling, roaring and hungry.

St Edward was in its path.

Black clouds had spread across the ocean as the wind strengthened through the afternoon. The temperature rose dramatically as the storm's warm front passed over the Marianne, which creaked and groaned as she struggled through the rising wind. The captain wiped sweat from his face on the filthy rag he wore tied around his neck.

"We cannot continue monsieur, the storm will be too strong," he said to the silent Frenchman in neat overcoat and bowler hat who stood beside him on the bridge, gazing placidly out into the swirling inferno of wind, rain and spray. "It is too dangerous. We must run for shelter."

"*Mais non*," Baiser said quietly, pulling out a small revolver and pointing it at the captain. "*Continuez.*"

CHAPTER 19

La Petite Citron

Mike and Sharon
2020

Fucking brilliant

> Youre welcome. Mike we need to talk

Were talking now

> No were not. Were exchanging SMS txt messages

Whats your problem

> ISO talk IRT. Does that make better sense?

Fuck off Sharon. What U doing tomorrow night. Katie and the kids are with her Mum

> Was it the mention of sexy knickers or the semen? Fuck off Mike. And no. Meeting Deirdre for a curry then play reading in Hampstead

*　　*　　*

1926

Sir George, Bracegirdle, Campbell and Norman were pacing together on the cliff top. Sir George looked around carefully, to be sure they could talk freely without fear of being overheard. Old Sock was staking tomatoes, his beard flowing biblically in the rising wind. Foster, as usual, was polishing the Rolls Royce. Neither was within earshot. Wind whipped leaves from the horse chestnut trees, sent fruit from the cannonball tree bowling across the lawn, stripped blossom from the frangipani.

"Good work Threlfall."

"I did no more than receive the message sir."

"Bracegirdle, you'll call out the St Edward Rifles. There's only one path to the cove. Once their devilish cargo is unloaded you'll have them trapped."

"Catch the blighters red-handed Sir George."

"This fellow Beck must on no account be aware that we know of the rebels' plans until we pick him up. Threlfall, you'll take part. Not a word to anyone, including your contact. Beck must under no circumstances learn that we're onto him."

"But Sir …"

"Not another word lad. Orders."

In the clearing on Mount Raglan, Jacob Beck was briefing Mimo,

"Now Mimo, do you understand what you have to do tonight?"

"Yes boss."

"What do you have to do?"

"Go to the cove, meet the next great French hero, load the cargo onto the donkeys and hide it in the usual place."

"And?"

"And, um …"

"And this time no passa, no mastise, and whatever happens, keep away from the big house of the British governor."

"Yes boss."

"Yes what?"

"What?"

"Yes boss, no passa, no mastise."

"Yes boss."

"And?"

"And?"

"And keep away from the big house."

"Yes boss."

"And be very careful unloading the dynamite."

"Yes boss."

"Good luck Mimo. I will meet you at the stone circle."

As Mimo wandered off with his donkey Jacob gazed after him thoughtfully, then unpacked his binoculars. He had spotted a lesser Black-legged Kittiwake. "Interesting," he thought. "A long way from Morocco. I shall have to tell Lady Sutherland," then reflected that if this evening's mission was successful St Edward would soon be rid of the Sutherlands and others of their tribe. He packed the binoculars away again, and set off down the narrow path back towards Port Charlotte, his pack over his shoulder, the service revolver a comforting weight against his back.

He had reached the outskirts of Port Charlotte when Colonel Pole fell in beside him.

"Jacob Beck, a moment if you please."

Jacob shrugged off his pack and reached into it. Pole using his one good arm grabbed Jacob's wrist, as they were joined by a couple of solidly built soldiers from the St Edward Rifles who removed the revolver.

"No need for that lad. Better come with me."

It was the eve of the Summer solstice. Orlando, dressed in sturdy plus fours, with an Inverness cape, and a fore and aft cap in colourful tweed on his head, opened the loading bay at the rear of his warehouse. His new Citroën was parked neatly between towering crates of guano, covered with a silk cloth. With a flick of the wrist Orlando pulled the cover off the little car, recently acquired direct from the Quai de Javel Citroën factory in Paris—a favour from Colonel Truffe. Orlando was extremely proud of the 5CV, the cabriolet, in Grapefruit Yellow—*La petite citron*—practical, yet stylish. He loaded a folding stool, a thermos of coffee, a wicker hamper containing several baguettes, a pungent *Roquefort*, a charmingly decorated porcelain pot filled with *pâté de foie gras*, a selection of *petit fours*, and a rare work of Eighteenth Century French pornography. He added a telescope, and a lantern with which to signal the *Marianne*, squeezed into the driver's seat, started the car and set course for the narrow road that would carry him to the west of the island.

As he drove, Orlando reflected bitterly on the injustice of his situation. "*Putain*," Orlando thought. "*Putain! Putain! Putain!*" He had not sought the role of revolutionary ring-leader, he had been conscripted, no, press-ganged. He was a man of business, a simple trader in guano and negotiable instruments. Not a bold freedom fighter like the absurd Di Bortolo. It was the nuns, of course, the sisters, *les putains de soeurs. Les chattes.* They had obtained certain documents, God knew how, relating to some rather serious—frankly treasonous—financial irregularities, specifically trade with the Germans during the recent hostilities, the release of which would not merely embarrass him, but would also see him thrown into the awful British gaol on The Thimbles, probably to be hanged. The Monseigneur had given him no choice in the matter.

Orlando hoped everything would go according to plan so he could get back to Harriet, and put this wretched business behind him once and for all. He hoped his English *épouse* would be patient enough to await his return. He was feeling sorry for himself.

The sun was setting as Orlando arrived above the cove where the rendezvous was to take place. He parked some distance from the cliff top behind some bushy undergrowth. The wind was howling, towering black clouds were roiling, although the setting sun shone briefly below them, shining red on the cliff above the little cove. He could see the *Marianne* manoeuvring slowly towards her anchorage. Seabirds flew across the sky, like rags caught in the wind. Orlando settled his stool against the trunk of a camphor tree, sat down, and watched as the *Marianne* found some slight shelter behind a small headland, and dropped anchor. "*Merde*, they are early." He shifted his weight, he was hellishly uncomfortable. He thought of Harriet, the solidly built *Anglaise dodue*, reclining on his chaise longue. He lit one of his cigarillos, drew deeply, then extinguished it as he heard voices approaching. He stood and watched as the rebels quietly made their way down the narrow path towards the little beach. Wind whipped the trees. The donkeys bellowed restlessly. There was muted laughter.

"Come on Mimo, just one taste."

"No, the boss said, no, no Mastise, no passa."

"Where is the boss Mimo?"

"He will meet us at the stone circle."

"Yes, Mimo, where's your boyfriend?" Laughter, somewhat louder.

"Come on boys, no more Mastise. Remember what Jacob said."

"Ooooh, Jacob."

More laughter.

The setting sun's furious display of red and gold was rapidly extinguished behind the inky storm clouds, and night fell quickly. Wind howled and it had started to rain. Orlando was by now thoroughly miserable. The *Marianne* sat tossing on the stormy sea a mile off the cove, no running lights, a dark shape against the white surf. Orlando worked the signals, and saw a light flashing from the old tramp in response. He heard a murmur of voices from the rebels gathered on the beach, quiet though, good, he thought, at least they are more disciplined than last time. Through his telescope he could just make out the longboat being loaded and launched into the wildly heaving sea. The Lascar crew rowed steadily, and a neatly dressed Frenchman stood in the bow, apparently unperturbed by the violent pitching of the small craft.

And then, from his vantage point on the cliff top, Orlando watched in horror as a heavily armed detachment of St Edward Rifles, led by Commander Bracegirdle, emerged silently from their position higher up the hill and moved down the track in single file towards the beach, effectively blocking the rebels' path of retreat. *Merde merde merde!* Seeing what was about to happen, and with no way of alerting the rebels on the beach, Orlando waited quietly for the soldiers to pass, then tiptoed quietly back to his car and drove back towards Port Charlotte as swiftly as *La petite citron* could carry him.

The longboat rode in on a wave, tipped precariously, righted itself, and ran up the beach. Waves continued to pound it from behind. The Lascar crew leapt out and steadied the boat. Mimo and his companions started unloading the French arms. The little Frenchman had disappeared from view.

Commander Bracegirdle marched unsteadily across the soft sand at the head of his contingent of St Edward Rifles, sword drawn. "You men! Stop what you are doing and raise your hands in the air." Pandemonium ensued. There was yelling. As Norman ran across the beach ahead of the men there was a brief exchange of gunfire.

The rebels and the unfortunate Lascars were quickly subdued. Only Mimo managed to run into the dense brush that bordered the beach. He began to clamber up the rock.

Norman could see the longboat, caught by a savage undertow, drifting out to sea, tossed about in the surf. He saw the small man in overcoat and bowler hat rise from the bottom of the boat and calmly take the oars, piloting the small craft unsteadily through the thrashing sea.

As he continued to clamber up the rocky cliff, Mimo was also watching the departing Frenchman as the boat disappeared into a swirling cauldron of mist, spray and spindrift. Not as imposing, he thought, the little Frenchman, not the heroic presence of the great hero of the Mandingo Wars, but clearly nonetheless another French hero. Mimo sobbed. What had gone wrong? What had led to this? Who had betrayed them? How had another noble *combattant* come to be lost on the treacherous shore of St Edward? What would Jacob say?

Mimo kept climbing.

At the Dreamland Ballroom the Summer Solstice Gala Ball was well underway. Music was playing. Claudette Moreau and the Café Orchestra, dressed in sequinned tunics, embroidered with images of sun, moon and stars. The dance floor was packed, dancers in carnival costume, embroidered skulls wreathed with roses, honeybees, sunflowers.

Claudette Moreau sang:

> *À l'homme que j'ai dans la peau!*
> *À l'homme que j'ai dans la peau!*
> *C'est mon homme!*
> *C'est mon homme, c'est mon homme, c'est mon homme ..."*

At the stone circle on Mount Raglan another solstice festival was also underway. Fires had been lit. Drummers were warming up. White robes, red sashes, headdresses of fresh picked wildflowers—pimpernels, wild orchids, bluebells, sand crocuses, black spleenwort, chamomile—as well as flasks of Mastise and pouches well filled with passamanana. A huge trumpeter—the ba'al tekiah—blew into his huge ram's horn trumpet, a sonorous boom that was answered by a rolling boom of thunder. The dancers slowly started moving around and between the fires and the central altar stone.

Nathalie arrived at the ballroom with Yvette, both dressed for the occasion as harvest maidens, gauzy white muslin, wreathes of wildflowers. From Nathalie's headdress two little baby goat's horns protruded prettily. The two women danced together, one tall and dark, the other short and blond. Nathalie looked around, but could see no sign of Norman.

"Where is he?"

"I can't see him."

"Oh Yvette. He is not here."

"He will come."

"No, it is like before."

"Men, you know what they are like. Or perhaps you do not, not as I do."

"He said he loves me."

"They all say that."

"He asked me to marry him."

"They sometimes say that as well."

"Where can he be? Has he used me?"

"Keep dancing with me then."

"No, I think I shall go home."

Outside the ballroom the wind had stopped, the rain had ceased, the sky was clear, the moon shone brightly, the island was in the eye of the storm. The great Norfolk Pines on the harbour foreshore loomed, silent and still, inky shadows beneath them. Nathalie tugged her cloak tighter around her shoulders, and hurried through the deserted streets of the old quarter. She sensed movement behind her, and quickened her pace, walking rapidly through the darkened streets. She passed darkened doorways, empty windows, deserted alleys, dark like tombs. A black cat raced across her path. She spat for luck and breathed a sigh of relief as she turned a corner and saw the lights of the Café des Artistes ahead of her. Then she heard a movement behind her, a blow to her head, the sky exploded and she plunged into darkness.

Later, as the wind lashed the palms and the monkey puzzle trees of Government House, Orlando was in his elegant little Citroën with Nathalie, still unconscious and firmly bound in the passenger seat, driving towards the Mount Raglan standing stones and the hypnotic pounding of the drums and the brilliant flare of firelight.

Clouds blotted out the full moon. The eye of the storm had passed.

CHAPTER 20

The Horned Man

Mike and Sharon
2020

Was it the mention of sexy
knickers or the semen? Fuck
off Mike. And no. Meeting
Deirdre for a curry then play
reading in Hampstead

Seriously

Yes

Why. And since when are
you going to play readings?
LOL

Because I want to

Why

Why do I want to? Because
Deirdre invited me.
Remember the concept?
Goes something like this.
Hi Sharon would you like to
come with me to play reading.

Yes Deirdre I would like
that very much indeed. As
Against: Shag?

Whats going on with
you Sharon

?

Hanging out with London
Library lesbian. Its out
of character

I never said shes a lesbian you
bigot, but as a matter of fact
yes she is.

*   *   *

1926

As the wind rose and the rain came down and the palms, monkey puzzle trees and the great beech thrashed from side to side, the household was assembled in the morning room with Professor and Mrs Hodgkinson. Through the storm, the sound of drums could be heard coming faintly yet insistently from the hills.

In a corner of the room Sir George, Bracegirdle, Pole, Campbell and Norman were conducting a quiet analysis of the previous night's events, the successful interception of guns, explosives and gold, the roundup of most of the rebels, although Orlando was still at large.

Sir George: "Damn the blighter. Gone to ground like a fox."

Bracegirdle: "Hounds will flush him out sir."

Sir George: "Jolly good. And the French agent?"

Norman: "Presumed lost in the wild surf, sir."

Bracegirdle: "I saw the boat vanish into the maelstrom Sir George, no one could have survived."

Sir George: And the … fellow from the Rolls Royce?"

Norman: "Christian burial, sir. Seems to be the end of the matter."

Sir George: "And this chap Beck. What are we to do with him?"

Pole: "We have him in custody."

Norman: "Sir George, if I may, together with his sister and his mother, he has done us a great service. Without them we could not have brought this rebellion to an end."

Lady Sutherland—whose ability to listen to several conversations at once, and from the other side of the room has already been remarked upon: "And Jacob has been so kind to me."

Sir George: "Talk to him, would you Pole? And congratulations everybody, I'd say mission accomplished."

All: "Hear hear."

Sir George: "Another round of Mastise I think, please Craddock."

Craddock: "Certainly sir."

Mme Beck, as always, was working on her accounts. Her door burst open. Mimo staggered into the room.

"What is the meaning of this?" Mme Beck demanded.

Mimo spoke between sobs. "Madame, *c'est terrible* … Monsieur

Orlando has your daughter ... he says he will kill her unless ... unless you can guarantee safe passage for him ... Monsieur Orlando is at the stone circle on Mount Raglan ... he says tell the English lieutenant ... we were betrayed ... I don't know where Jacob is ... I managed to escape ... your daughter ... I don't know what to do ... he will kill her ... madame ..."

Mme Beck locked her bureau firmly and put on her coat.

The pastimes of those who lived before the Age of Television seem incomprehensible to modern generations. How did people amuse themselves in the evening before they were able to settle down in front of the TV? As we know, charades was one popular diversion enjoyed by the vice-regal household at St Edward; also bridge—which of course remains an obsession for many to this day, and has easily adapted to the online world. In spite of—or perhaps because of—the absence of television and streaming services, the evening hours passed happily at Government House, with parlour games such as Are You There Moriarty?, Hunt the Thimble, Beggar my Neighbour, Consequences, Memory and The Minister's Cat, as well as musical evenings with Lettice playing her signature piece, the slow movement from Moonlight Sonata, or accompanying Commander Bracegirdle's stirring renditions of Rule Britannia and Champagne Charlie.

One particularly elaborate amusement, and a great favourite of Sir George, was the *tableau vivant*. A popular work of art was nominated—usually by Sir George himself—such as The Night Watch or—on one occasion when he was in a playful mood—The Raft of the Medusa. And dressed in the contents of the dressing up box the members of the assembled household would recreate the scene as accurately as possible in the informal setting of parlour or sitting room. Indeed, the dressing up box was an important resource in any well-run middle or upper class household, an amusement for bored children, a source of costumes for amateur theatricals, props for charades.

And on very special occasions Sir George would call for the dressing up box and, suitably attired, would deliver a stirring speech, relevant to the moment, from one of the great orators of classic antiquity.

Tonight was such an occasion.

To acknowledge the resounding victory earlier in the day over the rebel forces, and to do so with the required level of gravitas, Sir George proposed to deliver some apposite remarks from Pericles' Funeral Speech, as recorded by Thucydides, in Book II of his History of the Peloponnesian War. In fact he proposed to recite the whole thing, for he knew it well.

Hearts sank, for while Sir George was universally loved, admired and respected by family, colleagues and vice-regal support staff respectively, there was one chink in his otherwise shining armour. He did love to demonstrate his knowledge of the great orators of antiquity.

"Where's Craddock? I need my robe." But Craddock was with Cook, fetching another flask of Mastise.

The door opened, Mrs Huntingfield entered and strode urgently to Colonel Pole. "Mme Beck is here."

"What, Giselle, here?"

The Colonel quietly left the room.

By the time Colonel Pole had returned the room was thick with pipe smoke. Mastise was flowing liberally. The mood had shifted from self-congratulation to hilarity. An impromptu game of Are You There Moriarty? had begun. Pole took Norman aside and spoke quietly. "Orlando has Mme Beck's daughter. You must save her, they're in no state." He nodded towards Bracegirdle who was chasing Lettice around the room with a rolled up newspaper, both blindfolded, both shrieking with laughter. "To Mount Raglan. Hurry lad. There's no time to lose."

Norman slipped from the room.

Finally Craddock returned with replenishments. "Ah, Craddock," said Sir George. "There you are. Be a good chap and bring my chiton, my cloak and my laurel wreath from the dressing up box."

"Certainly Sir." Craddock filled Lady Sutherlands glass, then left the room to fetch Sir George's costume. A few minutes later he returned, empty handed. "I'm so sorry sir. So strange. The items you requested seem to be missing."

"Damned peculiar. Do you know anything about this Campbell?"

"No sir."

At that point Surgeon Commander Clark joined the group.

"I say, has anyone seen my monkey skull?"

The little Austin was struggling through the wind and rain on its way to Mount Raglan. Lightning briefly illuminated the road, silhouetting the driver, white face, black robe, and strangest of all, a dramatically horned Viking helmet. Rain was pelting down, the little car slipped from side to side on the muddy track.

Faintly through the trees ahead the driver could see fire. The drumming got louder, audible now through the tortured whine of the Austin's engine and the roar of wind and rain. The road, now little more than a goat track, ran out. The driver parked the car next to a small yellow Citroën and continued on foot. The drumming got louder and louder. He could hear the chanting now. The scream of a baby goat. The panicked bellow of a mule.

Back at Government House, Sir George, now draped in a clean bedsheet, began slowly:

> "I will speak first of our ancestors, for it is right
> and seemly that now a tribute should be paid to
> their memory ..."

Lettice studied her two engagement rings and sighed. Colin was solid, dependable, a war hero certainly. Yes, a catch, decidedly a catch—although she did wonder what lay under his eye patch. And yet, and yet ... She pictured Norman dancing the foxtrot, his sinuous moves, smooth, sensual, the way he had moved instinctively against Mrs Hodgkinson—moulded his body to hers—brought to mind certain passages from Marie Stopes, and Lettice drifted off in happy anticipation of married love.

> "... of the military exploits by which our various
> possessions were acquired, or of the energy with
> which we or our fathers drove back the tide of
> war, Hellenic or Barbarian, I will not speak; for
> the tale would be long and is familiar to you ..."

Gene Hodgkinson yawned. His eyes closed. His head became intolerably heavy and he lowered it to his chest. As he began, gently at first, to snore, Mrs Hodgkinson dug him sharply in the ribs.

> "... our form of government does not enter into rivalry with the institutions of others. Our government does not copy our neighbours', but is an example to them. It is true that we are called a democracy, for the administration is in the hands of the many and not of the few ..."

Craddock stood patiently by the chiffonier, on which sat several decanters of mastise, resting his hand comfortably on its chamfered edge. "Christ," he thought. "How these people go on. The benefits of a classical education? Fuck me." Then his thoughts drifted, as they habitually did, to his little fancy, him and Foster, a pretty little farm in the west country, a small cottage, some hens, one or two cows for the milk ...

> "... and we have not forgotten to provide for our weary spirits many relaxations from toil; we have regular games and sacrifices throughout the year; our homes are beautiful and elegant; and the delight which we daily feel in all these things helps to banish sorrow ..."

Miss Davies, dozing silently next to Mrs Hodgkinson, had slipped into a reverie of her own, centred around the Palace of

Huffuff. She woke, and with a small start and a tiny cry of fright, realised that Mrs Hodgkinson was watching her with a look of such penetrating intensity that immediately blood rushed to her cheeks.

> "… we rely not upon management or trickery, but upon our own hearts and hands. And in the matter of education, whereas they from early youth are always undergoing laborious exercises which are to make them brave …"

Surgeon Commander Clark was cataloguing in his mind the contents of his cabinet of curiosities, and also a more secret cabinet, locked in the innermost recesses of his heart: a register of the many insults and slights—indeed wholescale conspiracies— that had derailed his career and had consigned him to this wretched island and, furthermore, those acts of revenge with which one day he would settle old scores.

> "… such is the city for whose sake these men nobly fought … they could not bear the thought that she might be taken from them; and every one of us who survive should gladly toil on her behalf …"

Mrs Hodgkinson occupied herself with not entirely pleasant memories of Little Mainwaring, her childhood home. There was something, she felt, in Sir George's rhetorical style or perhaps— more generously—it was that of Pericles, which reminded her of her father: that combination of smug self-satisfaction, with an aggrandising air of superiority and bullying swagger.

> "... make them your examples, and, esteeming courage to be freedom and freedom to be happiness, do not weigh too nicely the perils of war ..."

Lady Sutherland, with the experience of decades of loyal support to Sir George in his various postings, had put her mind in a holding pattern, ready at a moment's notice to spring into action, but for now not thinking about anything much at all. Although really, George, she reflected, was trying the patience of his audience as Pericles must have tried that of the Athenian demos.

> "... we live at ease, and yet are equally ready to face the perils which they face. And here is the proof: The Lacedaemonians come into Athenian territory not by themselves, but with their whole confederacy following ..."

Harriet was shifting restlessly, longing for a cigarette.

> "... if then we prefer to meet danger with a light heart but without laborious training, and with a courage which is gained by habit and not enforced by law, are we not greatly the better for it? ..."

Afterwards neither Norman nor Nathalie had a clear recollection of what had happened. Norman remembered walking towards the fire, the drumming and chanting becoming louder, more insistent, ringing inside his head. At the same time the fire became brighter, fiercer, even the driving rain seemed to be burning. There was a blast from the ram's horn, and as he entered the stone circle he raised his arms dramatically, silhouetted against the fire, white chalk and burnt cork running down his face, black robe flying in the tempest, the great stag's antlers rising from his head. The drumming stopped. Hands grasped him. Bitter drink was forced into his mouth. He could no longer feel his arms and legs. His head floated. The drumming resumed and he was pulled into the swirling vortex around the stone altar. More drink was forced on him. He called to Nathalie and she was torn from Orlando's grasp. Light pulsing around them both, he reached out to her, their hands were joined, he thought he heard someone whisper you may kiss the bride, and the world went spinning away.

With a final rhetorical flourish, Sir George was winding up.

> "... This is the crown and prize which she offers,
> both to the dead and to their children, for the
> ordeals which they have faced. Where the rewards
> of valour are the greatest, there you will find also
> the best and bravest spirits among the people."

There was an expectant pause, to make sure he had finished, followed by a rousing chorus of appreciation, to which the

Sir George, removing his laurel wreath, responded with smiles and modest, self-deprecating gestures.

"Huzzah."

"Jolly good Sir!"

"Bravo."

"Helluva speech, Sir George."

"Outstanding."

"Well said, sir."

"Brilliant, daddy."

"Hurrah."

"Very good dear, we must do it again some time."

"One more glass thank you Craddock, then bed I think."

"Goodnight."

"Goodnight."

"Goodnight sir."

"Goodnight all."

At 3 am Government House was in darkness. An alert observer with unusually keen eyesight might have noticed a match flare in a first-floor window, and the glow of a small cheroot. Colonel Pole peered anxiously out at the looming bulk of Mount Raglan, illuminated from time to time by a brilliant flash of lightning, and watched apprehensively as a single headlight moved slowly and erratically down the hillside.

Half an hour later the Austin drove unsteadily through the gates of Government House. The little car progressed jerkily up the drive, across Old Sock's neatly planted formal garden bed, onto the veranda, and lurched towards the front door. There was a loud crash, followed by a tinkling of broken glass.

Steam was still hissing as, with firm yet cautious steps, Sir George Sutherland, Governor of the Bailiwick of St Edward, descended the darkened staircase, a shabby flannel dressing gown over his nightshirt, armed with his old Wright and Ditson tennis racquet. He was closely followed by Lady Sutherland, similarly garbed, carrying a croquet mallet. At the bottom of the staircase Sir George reached carefully for the new electric light switch.

As the light came on the door was flung open and Cernunnos, the Great Hornéd Beast, Lord of all Creation, the forests and the streams, Sovereign of earth, sea and sky, Master of the beasts of the fields and the fishes of the deep, supporting his barely conscious consort, The Lady Hecate, staggered into the hall.

There was, unsurprisingly, a stunned silence.

Then Sir George roared with laughter.

"Oh, I say, marvellous!"

Lady Sutherland clapped her hands together. "Priceless, oh dear Norman, you are so clever!"

Sir George pulled his pipe from the pocket of his dressing gown, lit it, inhaled deeply and chuckled. "And my cape! Marvellous! Splendid!"

One by one the rest of the household arrived.

"Oh Norman," Lettice cried, her two engagement rings twinkling in the electric light. "Honestly!" Colin Campbell put his arm around her shoulder. "Buck up old thing."

Surgeon Commander Clark snorted angrily. "My skull!" He snatched it from Norman.

"I'm sorry Surgeon Commander," said Norman, removing his great horned helmet and swaying unsteadily. "Sir George, Lady Sutherland, Colonel Pole, Harriet, Lettice, Campbell, Miss Davies, please ... let me introduce my wife." At which point he lowered Nathalie gently to the floor, and then collapsed beside her.

In his despatch to Jenkins, Colonel Pole described the rescue:

> FRENCH CONSUL ORLANDO ABDUCTED
> CIVILIAN WITH VIOLENCE STOP DAUGHTER
> OF MME BECK STOP TRUE PATRIOT STOP
> INSTRUMENTAL IN ENDING INSURRECTION
> STOP HELD TO RANSOM STOP COURAGEOUS
> RESCUE BY LIEUTENANT THRELFALL STOP
> ORLANDO STILL AT LARGE PRESUME NO
> LONGER IN THE BAILIWICK STOP POLE

"I think it's really for the best, Let. He was really rather vulgar. Although he did have flashing eyes. And he was very generous. Cigarette? No?" Harriet lit one for herself.

CHAPTER 21

Moondance

Mike and Sharon
2020

I never said shes a lesbian you
bigot, but as a matter of fact
yes she is.

Three bloody cheers. Next
youll be putting her up for
an OBE.

Far better candidate
than most of those flashy
corporate/banking types
whose bottoms you like to
lick over cosy lunches for two
at Orrery.

Its called mentoring Sharon
like what I used to do
for you

ROTFLMAO. Somehow
dont remember the Confit
duck leg or the glasses of
Bourgogne Cotes dAuxerre
2012. £380 bill.

Did you look in my wallet

> Of course I bloody did. Oh
> and afterwards there they are
> in the Queens birthday list,
> your mates. Wonder how
> that happened?

Jesus Sharon. TTOTM?

> Piss off Mike.

> BTW message from nob PMs
> office confirming dna match
> with sexy undergarment and
> hero Mandingo wars. Macron
> back in *Elysee Palace* tail
> between legs LOL

gr8

Sharon?

*   *   *

1926

CONFIDENTIAL MEMORANDUM

Permanent Secretary to Permanent Under-Secretary, Colonial Office, Whitehall

Jenkins has confirmed that the rebellion at St Edward, The Thimbles and Gwern (the Bailiwick of St Edward) has been suppressed through the efforts of Sir George Sutherland, Commander Bracegirdle and Colonel Pole. It appears that young Threlfall played a key role, and I have spoken to his father about a possible return to his former duties at the Admiralty. However I am reliably informed that he wishes to remain en poste at St Edward.

Strangely, so too does Sir George, even though, as you suggested, we have offered him the far more distinguished post of Governor General of Canada. He has certainly earned recognition for his work during his tenure on the islands. Under his administration economic reforms introduced by his predecessor have been consolidated and have transformed what was a sleepy group of islands into a thriving financial hub. The French agent Orlando is missing, and we believe that the Deuxieme Bureau is, at least for now, out of the picture.

On the other hand, Jenkins has confirmed those rumours that were first reported to him by Miss Davies through her cousin Miss Gribble, one of Fitzroy Bancroft's people. It is now quite clear that there have indeed been serious lapses of protocol in the vice-regal establishment of St Edward, The Thimbles and Gwern. The temptations facing our colonial administrators are well known, and Government House at St Edward is not the first such household to be undone by perfumed tropic nights, the leaves of palm and banyan tree swaying in the gentle breeze, the murmur of the surf upon the shingle, the enormous full moon rising over a tropic sea, the gorgeous lotus, the perfumed moonflower, the seductive sloe-eyed native maidens and—let us be frank— the no less seductive native youths. Nor are the temptations afforded by drink and narcotic substances such as Mastise and passamana consumed by the descendants of the original French inhabitants of St Edward in their lascivious ritual dances any less seductive; such substances, I need hardly remind you, that inflame the passions and corrupt the soul. (I have sent samples of both to Sir Crawshore Gladman at the Board of Trade, and asked him to investigate the possibility of a health-giving tonic based on passamana and Mastise as an export initiative, a sort of Tono-Bungay for our colonial markets, now that trade in laudanum has sadly been curtailed through legislation introduced by our masters at Whitehall, no doubt well-intentioned, but nonetheless short-sighted and repressive.)

Furthermore, it appears that, just as Miss Davies reported, the vice-regal household at St Edward, the Thimbles and Gwern has welcomed into its circle the notorious pornographer Gwladys Baring.

Finally, and again as the indomitable Miss Davies has disclosed, young Threlfall has made a wholly inappropriate match in a pagan ceremony, lately solemnised by Bishop Stanley—a laundry maid, for Heaven's sake; it is positively Gwladys Baring!—the details of that union I have for reasons of delicacy decided not to pass on to his father.

You will, of course, recall those scandals narrowly averted in colonies as far-flung as Rhodesia, Ceylon, and Burma, and your own experience in Kenya; scandals that reverberated around the Empire, and which in some cases were seized upon by opposition parties to embarrass the Prime Minister, and indeed the Crown. Thus I am of the view that under the circumstances it would be most prudent to allow them all to remain in their present duties and close the book on these sordid affairs. Out of sight, out of mind, as the saying goes.

This fellow Beck does seem to have been useful. Without his intercession we may very well have lost the Bailiwick, and, of course, the handsome revenue generated by the British and American Phosphate Company, and of course the successful compulsory acquisition of the trading house Orlando *et Cie*. We should give him something minor in the honours list next year. Companion of the Imperial Service Order. Should make him happy.

A. C.

Old Sock was standing on the cliff top. The brilliant full moon was rising, its reflection stretching away from him out to the horizon. "Aye, the moon travels with you," he said quietly. He looked across his vegetable garden, at the orderly rows of carrots, celery, onions, potatoes, at the mounds of compost. The wind gently stirred the leaves of the Mimosa, the Silver Fir and the West Indian Cedar, and it seemed to Sock that it carried music faintly with it, the music he fancied he had once heard as a child in the Scottish highlands, the music of the Sidhe faeries. He looked down to the sheltered beach below Bishopscourt, where the moon cast shadows across the sand. Nathalie and Norman were dancing barefoot, to the music playing softly on the wind up gramophone.

> *When the moon hangs low I begin to glow*
> *And my day has just begun*
> *I'll get a moonburn when I'm with you tonight*
> *So very soon, I'll moonburn when you hold me tight*

The song ended, although the disc kept revolving, a gentle whisper as the needle travelled around and around, gradually slowing as the clockwork mechanism ran down, until finally it stopped and only the sound of waves lapping on the beach remained. Yet Norman and Nathalie continued to dance, dancing together in the moonlight, dancing with their shadows as the moon continued to rise over the Atlantic, and the earth continued quietly to rotate.

Sock nodded, and turned towards his simple accommodation, murmuring to himself. "Aye, this is the day which the Lord hath made; we will rejoice and be glad in it."

The Marriage Plot

Mike and Sharon
2020

Sharon?

      Sorry - was that a thank you?

Fuck off

      You're so welcome.

      Hello?

      Anyway remains of French hero have been repatriated, buried full honneurs militaires. Closed coffin obv. Nob says PM offered to send sexy camiknickers for Colonel di Bartolos burial shroud - no response from Macron's people LOL

      Hey, NBD

      Actually St Edward looks rather beautiful, D and I are going for a Short Break

It's D now? Jesus Sharon

> No Mike srsly. Two weeks
> little airbnb Les Humeurs,
> looks lovely check it out
> hang on Ill email link

Oh for fucks sake

Sharon?

*   *   *

1926

Mrs Hodgkinson sat in front of her typewriter, pondering. The endings, always the hardest part; the sex was easy, the harmonious resolution much harder. Her readers demanded both. Pages of passionate, often brutal fornication—coupling, coitus, mating, copulation, ravishing, intercourse, congress, coition, and, frankly, rape—followed by domestic harmony, with no loss of sexual tension. That was her art. She recalled Sir Stephen, the brooding highwayman, tamed by the love of Amelia, the gentle convent girl, in *Stand and Deliver!* Pyotr Ivanovich, the proud Cossack ataman, brought firmly to heel by Arabella, the lovely but somewhat austere Scottish nurse in *The Fourth Horseman*. And, of course, Cynthia, the captured governess, bought into sex slavery for 10,000 pieces of silver, at first ravished, finally châtelaine of the Palace of Huffuf in *Seraglio Governess*. Indeed, Mrs Hodginson's flirtation with the modern extended no further than style. Her storylines were traditional: the marriage plot, as reliable for Gwladys Baring in the early Jazz Age as it had been for Jane Austen in Regency England. Just spiced up a bit.

Do What Thou Wilt was nearing completion. The varied strands were coming together nicely: the reformed pleasure seeker Sir Ephriam was planning the rescue of the lovely young shepherdess Cecilia from the revolting clutches of the drooling farmer Barric Fallows of Fallows Fallow Farm, whose wayward daughter Missy, seducer of Sir Ephriam's deranged brother Winsted, was now in thrall to the handsome landscape painter Phineas Kneebone. Yes, all coming together nicely. Now all she had to do was write it up.

And so she started typing. Fang lay in the corner and slept restlessly, dreaming of the hunt, the rabbits, hares, the pretty little gazelles of his native Afghanistan.

Hours later Mrs Hodgkinson lit a Sobranie, and finally typed the magic words:

THE END

A NOTE TO THE READER

Although some of the locations and incidents portrayed in this novel, past and present, bear a certain resemblance to actual places, events and institutions, the Bailiwick of St Edward, Gwern and The Thimble Isles is a place on the map of a comical world which closely resembles the one on which our grandparents stood, without corresponding exactly with it. Instead, it is populated by figments of our imagination.

Purists will, of course, note some historical anomalies. We were well aware, for example, that the first crossword puzzle was not published in *The Times* until 1 February 1930, but a backward adjustment of some years suited our purpose. Nor did Bing Crosby record *Moonburn* until 1935. Such are the small liberties novelists feel entitled to take in pursuit of larger truths. Finally, apologies to Virginia Woolf, from whom we have stolen a couple of lines.

*   *   *

Nearly ten years ago my brother Angus sent me an amusing piece he'd written about a young British naval lieutenant, aide to the governor of an imagined crown dependency in 1926, explaining to the governor's wife that a headless torso (male) had been found in the back seat of the vice-regal Rolls Royce wearing nothing except very expensive French cami-knickers in *mousseline soie*. It appears in the opening chapter of this book almost unchanged.

Angus wondered how had this curious episode come about? Where could it go? Could it form the basis of a comic novel? Together we worked out a plot and started writing. We were going strong when Angus got side-tracked on his remarkable book about Helena Rubinstein's early years in Australia. Shortly after that work was accepted for publication, he died (too young, only 58), leaving our novel incomplete. I finished it last year. I felt I should. For Angus, of course, but also for me—I had become attached to these characters, and I wanted to know how it all turned out. Doing so was a strange experience, filling in the gaps without Angus as a sounding board, or me as a sounding board for Angus for that matter, although sometimes feeling a spooky connection with my dead brother.

Angus and I never really discussed publishing the work, we simply had fun writing it. However once it was finished I felt it should appear in print, Angus had put so much of himself in it, and it's a side of his personality that many of his friends and colleagues would recognise and enjoy. So I went through the dispiriting exercise of looking for a publisher or a literary agent. Most, of course, don't respond. Those who did were kind, but politely passed. Clearly Lieutenant Norman Threlfall isn't going to be the next Harry Potter. So we're self-publishing. Angus would have probably preferred a proper publisher, and I'm sure he would have liked some royalties, but he doesn't need them now. Nonetheless, if we can cover production costs that would be nice.

I hope you like it, at least good bits. Anything you don't like, blame me. And if Angus is perhaps somewhere in The Cloud, and is able to read it, I hope he approves.

Thanks to Angus's former agent, Mary Cunnane, who was very encouraging, but has retired; to Fiona Wood, who steered us (me) away from at least some of the potentially disastrous waters of post-colonial and #MeToo sensitivities into which Angus and I had drifted; to Sylvie Blair of BookPOD not only for elegant typography, but also for her considerable patience and thoughtfulness; to my brothers Hamish and Simon for proofreading, support, encouragement and legal advice; to Ned, Annie and Molly Trumble, who offered valuable insights; to our father Peter for the title, a Bing Crosby tune he would hum when searching for the elusive ideal picnic spot in the black Citroen Light 15; and to Lesley, as always, for love, guidance and moral support.

www.ingramcontent.com/pod-product-compliance
Lightning Source LLC
Chambersburg PA
CBHW021752190726
48290CB00008B/2588